BETWEEN MACKEREL SKY AND STARRY SEA

RUTH VENN

This book is dedicated to my family.

Highlands of Scotland Map

Chapter 1

Mackerel sky, mackerel sky
Never long wet
Never long dry
    Weather lore

1987

The man leaned over the rusty ship's handrail and watched the spectacle that unfolded before him. The setting sun turned the rippling clouds in the pale winter sky, crimson, orange, gold and purple. Hues that flooded the water below and surrounded him in a transient beauty. The colours reminded him of home – of heat, loud music and fun – and in that moment he forgot his worries, the cold biting into his face and fingers, and was mesmerised.

Being a mariner, he understood that the clouds foretold change, and he could only pray that this would be for the better. As the day faded, the lights twinkled in the near distance. They were not so far away, yet were completely inaccessible to him, marooned as he was at sea. Not even an island to stand on. And in the last of the fading light, a single tear made its lonely passage down his cheek and disappeared into the black of the night.

Chapter 2

Late lies the wintry sun a-bed
A frosty, fiery sleepy head;
Blinks but, an hour or two; and then,
A blood red orange sets again
    Winter Time
    Robert Louis Stevenson

The boy wandered down Quay Street taking in the Christmas lights as he went. I ought to go straight home thought Alex, but it was nearly the end of term – almost Christmas – and he fancied checking out any activity at the pier. His last year at primary school. He was unsure about moving to high school, it was much bigger and none of the teachers would know him – Come to think about it, that might not be a bad thing! Alex looked around and shook his head. How could I have been so silly? The sun was almost down; any crowds – ships' captains and mariners, or just passers-by would be gone by now. Oh well, he thought, and carried on down the hill.

The clouds were drifting across the sky, and as he approached Shore Street, Alex caught his breath – Loch Broom was gradually turning red, orange and yellow as the mackerel scales of the sky merged with the ripples on the water. Even the white buildings that faced the sea were turning pink and apricot, just as if someone had turned on a fantastical floodlight. Then, in an instant, it was gone. Darkness comes rapidly in the Scottish Highlands.

Alex looked out over the loch at the lights that were now twinkling on the fishing boats and factory ships moored up as far as the eye could see. He scanned towards the horizon, and there – over to the left, all alone – was a single light. He wondered who, or what was there.

Chapter 3

The birds sit chittering in the thorn,
A'day they fare but sparely;
And lang's the night frae e'en to morn,
I'm sure its winter fairly.
Up in the morning early
Robbie Burn

'What are you doing here?' Moira asked Alex, as he stumbled through the narrow door of the shop, ushering in a blast of cold winter air.

'Sorry, Mum,' he said. 'I went down to the pier and forgot about the time. I saw this amazing sunset, did you see it too? It was like the sky was burning.'

His mother's face softened. 'Yes, I did. The sun going down in a mackerel sky is always spectacular. There's nothing like such a sky to lift the spirits, especially one that was cooked to scarlet perfection like that one.'

'Why is it called a mackerel sky, Mum?'

'I guess because the clouds make patterns a bit like fish scales. Long ago, people used to think it was because mackerel jumped so high to get out of the nets, that they jumped right into the sky.'

'Don't be silly Mum, that's impossible,' Alex said.

She laughed: 'Don't you know when I'm pulling your leg! Now sit on that stool while I finish up here and then we can walk home.'

Moira had worked at the grocery store for several years and had become integral to its smooth running. From the exterior, it was completely nondescript. The white-washed building stood alone, as if the nearby buildings had foreseen a possible expansion. An iron staircase led down the outside of the building to the basement storage area, whilst a large picture window for displays took up nearly all of the front wall. But it was the adjacent door which was odd. For some reason, it had long ago been divided vertically and each half opened independently, as if it were a narrow child's wardrobe. But these doors opened into a community hub, where alongside provisions, customers could chat and pass on gossip.

Angus, the owner, had left Moira to lock up today, but first she needed to cash up and put the takings in the large safe housed in the rear office. They must be ready for the Christmas onslaught of the next days. All the extra stock was to be delivered, orders made up, people popping in for last-minute forgottens. The store could just about cope with all of this, but on top of that there were the seafarers requests to be sorted. The shop was like an Aladdin's cave at this time of year – full to bursting with products to suit all nationalities. It became a ship's chandlers, supplying the needs of the numerous trawlers and factory ships moored all around the loch.

With no more customers in sight and nothing more to be done, Moira grabbed her coat and hat, and the pair made their way out. She checked that the closed half-door was fully bolted top and bottom and they squeezed through the half-open side, and she finally locked the door.

Alex often complained that the narrow door was silly, and she was inclined to agree. Huge sailors, men with shoulders as wide as barn doors had to turn their bodies to squeeze through. It could make for bedlam and often cursing, uttered in many languages – something her son had picked up with ease. It made her smile. Still, in the depths of winter, when the cold wind came in from the sea, over the loch and hit the village of Ullapool it did make sense; why the door still stayed closed in summer was one of life's mysteries.

They walked home, her arm round his shoulder, their bodies close. He won't want to walk like this for much longer, she thought. He was already growing into the man he would become, and she was grateful for the moment: mother and son, as one. She unlocked the door and the closeness was gone. Alex slung his coat on the peg, threw his shoes by the door and rushed up the stairs to his beloved Meccano that lay waiting for him in his bedroom. The terraced house was snug – electric heating was a blessing – a huge improvement on the open fires of old, but they were both pleased to have the real fire in the sitting room. As the young master of the house, Alex had recently taken over all fire lighting duties – he enjoyed the responsibility – and loved the resulting praise.

Moira didn't have a lot of money, but there was sufficient to pay the council rent and utility bills, and they were never short of food, courtesy of Angus, who made sure that they always had sufficient. He was a good man.

Moira popped the leftover stew from the night before on the hob and with the addition of a few potatoes and some cabbage, dinner was plated and on the table in no time. The call up the stairs of, 'Dinner's ready,' met with total disregard; it was only on her third attempt, with her foot on the bottom step that his cheeky face peered over the banister. He rushed down the stairs, two at a time, plonked himself down and was off! Some days he was constantly ravenous, and today was one of those. Luckily, after two helpings of stew, but definitely no more cabbage, he found himself the lucky recipient of apple pie: courtesy of Mr Kipling and Angus.

Moira could see that he was desperate to get back to his Meccano, but she had trained him well, he had to help with the washing up first, so took his dirty plates to the sink and stood waiting, tea-towel in hand as she did the dishes.

'How was school today?' she asked, passing him a plate. 'Anything special happen?'

'No,' he said, then remembered the single light he'd noticed. 'I saw a single light, way out in the loch, all on its own. Do you know what ship it's on?'

'There's a long story about that ship,' she said, 'give me a hand putting these away and I'll tell you about it when I've made us both a drink. What would you like?'

'Hot chocolate,' Alex grinned. It was his favourite.

Moira knew that he already had a lot of knowledge about the local inshore fishermen, the prawners, the scallopers, the local men who caught herring and mackerel, so there was little need to tell him about them. In fact, he could probably teach her a lot: he spent so long listening to weathered fishermen by the pier. She often wondered if, like so many of the men, that would be his future. There was little more than fishing and tourism to feed the families here.

'Why don't you tell me what you already know about the boats in the harbour.' Moira said as she sat down beside him.

'Oh mum, must I?' he groaned before carrying on. 'Well, the huge trawlers that catch the fish, and the factory ships that process them, arrive in the autumn when the mackerel do. They stay for a few months, then they go again, in dribs and drabs, when their holds are full and the fish have moved on.'

Moira nodded, 'Yes that's right. Those catches are valuable, and that is why the factory ships are called Klondykers.'

'Like the gold miners?'

'Exactly, that's how they got the name.'

'Oh, I didn't know that, Mum, but no more boring stuff; just tell me about that ship with the single light. Why is it alone, and why only one light?'

'That old wreck's been coming for years now and each time it's got more run-down. I've heard it's from Nigeria, but I'm not sure about the crew, wherever they're from, they're stuck here now poor souls. The ship's not seaworthy and they've been ordered to stay put.'

'What's wrong with it?'

'I don't know all the details, but I've heard that its very rusty in places, and some handrails are ready to drop off and there's a danger that they could fall through the decks. There's something wrong with the engine as well.'

'That's awful, how long have they been there?'

Moira swallowed her tea and sighed. 'It was the end of September or the beginning of October when they arrived. The coast guards were so concerned to see it here again that they reported it to port control and it hasn't been allowed to move since.'

'How many men are on board?' Alex asked, leaning in for the answer.

'About twenty-five or thirty I think, certainly not hundreds like the big

ones.'

'Can't they go home for Christmas?' asked Alex. 'I bet they want to be home then.'

'I don't know all the ins and outs of their situation, but they must be running low on provisions, and I've heard they haven't been paid. Angus is asking around to see what can be done, so we could know more soon. But for now it's your bath time – you don't want to be a dirty shepherd in the Nativity tomorrow.

With a degree of reluctance, Alex left the cosy kitchen and climbed the stairs to cleanliness, another day drawing to an end and just one-and-a-half days to the end of term. As he stripped off and slipped into the bath, his thoughts turned to Meccano. Would he get some more for Christmas, and perhaps some chocolate too? Alex loved chocolate in all its forms; there was no such thing as bad chocolate, it was all yummy. Not like cabbage which wasn't yummy at all.

I wonder if the men on that ship have got chocolate, he thought, but expected probably not. Could their mums send them some? My mum would if I were in their position. Clean and pyjama-clad, he ran downstairs to watch a bit of television. He liked the lounge, it was spacious with windows at both ends, but with the thick green curtains tightly drawn he could neither see the rear garden out of one, nor the little cul-de-sac with its row of five terraced homes out the other. That didn't matter though, the Christmas tree was stood proudly in the corner, lit up with fairy lights and adorned with baubles and tinsel, exactly the same each year. He eyed up the space beneath; nothing there yet, but he crossed his fingers in anticipation. In the other corner, nearest the garden, the TV was coming to life, it was time for the A Team, one of his favourites. Not one of his mum's, but she would sit on the sofa opposite the fire and knit or sew; she liked these pastimes and was good at them. He lay on the floor and stretched out, with his elbows beneath his shoulders and his forearms and hands supporting his head: a perfect way to watch TV he thought, even if Mum didn't exactly agree.

As the programme ended, Moira bent over and whispered in his ear, 'Time for bed Alex.' And on this occasion, he was remarkably obedient, and did exactly that. Safely tucked in his bed, with strict warnings not to play any more with the Meccano, he hunkered down under the blankets and was instantly asleep, dreaming of shepherds and presents, and still wondering if there was chocolate on that ship.

Chapter 4

Abandon'd, forsaken,
To grief and to care,
Will the sea ever waken
Relief from despair?
> My Grief on the Sea
> Douglas Hyde

The lone man pushed his misery to the far reaches of his mind, wiped away the vestiges of moisture from his cheek and slowly, carefully, made his way through the rusting door and down the rickety metal steps, towards the noise of people below. He shivered, trying to cast the cold from his body. Everywhere was cold, except of course the crew mess, which was heated by a tiny oil stove and the bodies of twenty-six men. He wanted solitude, time to clear his head, before joining the melee of steaming bodies and the loud voices of his shipmates.

A shudder ran down his body at the thought, but Jim knew that he must return. He found his way to one of the hatches of the below deck's factory; climbed down in the dark, fumbled for the light switch and looked at his workplace. It was eerily quiet. The smell of stale fish permeated the body of the ship and now filled his nostrils. He had never even got to work down here.

They had not been allowed to take even a single fish on board. The chutes down which the fish should cascade descended from another hatch to the conveyor, much like a luggage system at the airport. The filleting-benches, skin-peeler, the packaging-conveyor, all idle – just cold metal and rust. A mobile slaughterhouse brought to a conclusive shutdown by maritime rules of safety. Strange, he thought, my own country has scant regard for such matters. He sat on the cold conveyor and looked around, willing the machinery to jump into action to give them work to do – that would at least make the days pass faster. The enforced idleness was almost worse than the near squalid accommodation and the deteriorating diet. They were all big men, west Africans, used to hearty meals, and hunger was making them irritable. Would this hell never end?

Some of the crew had made this journey many times before, but not him. He had only joined out of desperation. His life, which not so long ago had been good, had taken a sudden downwards spiral – his best efforts to pull himself back up, were now being thwarted by strangers. None of the crew, not even the Bulgarian captain and his six officers had been paid: not a Lev, a Pound, a Nigerian Naira or a Dollar had been placed in their hands. The bank account that should by now have been the recipient of nearly four months wages, lay empty, not even a few Naira with which to buy anything. It had taken twenty days for the ship to travel from Port Harcourt and he certainly couldn't swim back. The misery washed over him, like the waves that rocked the ship, and he realised that he must snap out of it. He couldn't pray to the God he used to believe in; He had deserted him along with the ship owners – faceless people – and he hated them. He urged himself to think positively. Surely, however improbable, matters would improve before long. He slid off the conveyor, returned to the hatch, turned off the light, and in absolute blackness made his way out.

Leaden feet carried him along the metal passageway and through a heavy door that led to their sleeping quarters. The bunks were narrow; there were six men to a cabin, squashed in like rebellious sardines – no ordered head to toe here. The single dangling bulb illuminated the scantily dressed women on the walls and cast shadows on the flimsy mattresses – which had, like everything else seen better days. Threadbare blankets had been adequate in the summer, but were now as inadequate as their situation. He consigned his rubber boots and coat – multipurpose wear for factory and deck – to the designated area, before using the men's only fully functioning toilet. There were two toilets, but the other had never worked properly. He wondered if it would have been better maintained if the Bulgarian captain and officers had to use it, but they had their own. The officers had larger cabins and eating areas, not luxurious for sure, but a bit more tolerable. Once again there was no soap for the sink, and the towel was much too dirty to use, so he wafted his hands under the tap, then flapped them around in the air, before finally drying them fully on the seat of his pants. His clothing was inadequate, and anyway there was little room for more in his tiny locker and single drawer. Still he would wash some bits in the morning, that would give him something to do.

The crew had rigged up a rope in the factory to use as a washing line, at least there it wasn't raining; not like outside where rain fell as if it was the norm. Sunshine was a fleeting reward for enduring all the previous days of wet, wind and cold. A poor consolation for a man used to around seven hours of sunshine in December and a temperature that rarely fell much below 80F.

The smell of something cooking wafted around, and with heavy feet he made his way along the grey-metal corridor and into the crew room. Three long Formica covered tables occupied most of the scruffy room, where peeling paint just about managed to hang on to the metal walls. President Babangida, in smart military uniform, surveyed the room from the safety of his picture frame; the grease smeared glass shielding his view of the men's misery. He wouldn't have wanted to be there in real life. The room was packed. It was meant to house the men in shifts: fish processing was carried out twenty-four hours a day. Jim squeezed through to join two compatriots, slapping hands with mates as he went. The slop of the day was just being served from the galley – it had never been good, and it was getting worse. Still, cook did his best with the ever-diminishing supplies; the meal might not fully fill them up, but they weren't starving yet. The brown sludge was mopped up with hunks of dry bread, silence prevailed, talk could come later when their bellies were fuller.

Mugs of hot drinks were passed around, dinner was cleared away and the playing cards and Oware boards were pulled out. This was the best time of the day. They played games that united the different ethnic Nigerian crew, and the room would ring out with shouts of: 'Cheat' 'Mine', banter and general good humour. But the distress of their circumstances was never far from the surface and fractious arguments could develop in a flash. Before any violence could escalate, potential combatants would be pulled apart and calmed down by their shipmates. But as the weeks had passed, these occasions had increased, and Jim didn't like that; he was a peace lover at heart and wanted no part of any fighting. Still it was reasonably calm tonight and his previous cloud of depression lifted.

All heads turned in surprise as Captain Ivan Lyudmil walked through the door. His wiry frame and sallow skin was in marked contrast to his men who were all about twice his size, but when it came to voices, his resonated with all the vigour of a regimental sergeant major. A mere clearing of his throat stunned them all into silence ready for today's pronouncement, which was delivered in his usual formal language:

'Men, the representative of the owners visited us today and promised that wages will be paid. He apologised that his previous pledge of payment had not resulted in a positive result, but was confident that the former obstacles, had now been overcome. I believe that this is true, but we must, in the meantime carry on as we are. We are allowed to move the ship in the morning, to the pier, so that we can take on some fuel. I do not, as yet, know if you will be allowed to disembark for exercise, but I am in discussion with the authorities about this, and will update you in the morning. Good night gentlemen.'

He left immediately – there was to be no opportunity for questions. As the door closed behind him the noise was elevated to a deafening roar. Words of joy, and the uncommon sound of laughter, bounced off the walls. Once translated for him, Jim smiled; he would sleep better tonight than he had for days.

Chapter 5

In the bleak mid-winter, frosty wind made moan,
Earth stood hard as iron, water like a stone,
    Christina Rossetti

The porridge was gently bubbling in the pan, one more stir and its bloop, bloop, bloop, told Moira that it was ready. Another shout up the stairs:

'Breakfast's ready,' resulted in Alex jumping down the stairs two at a time.

'My you're keen this morning, what brought that on?'

'Don't know, just wanted to, get that stupid Nativity done and then just half-a-day to the holidays.'

'Well get that porridge down you,' instructed Moira as she cleared her dishes away.

'How many times have I told you, not soooo much sugar and make sure you clean your teeth, or you'll have a gummy smile like the old sailors at the port.' And for once, he complied. Moira retrieved an ageing canvas bag from the understairs cupboard. It contained a tea-towel, a length of cord and a robe made from an old sheet – the last nativity outfit she would have to provide.

The pair huddled inside their coats, kept their heads down against the biting wind and made their way to school. The darkness was lifting, and the mountains surrounding the loch came into view. They were covered with a heavy fall of snow, and for a brief moment they both stood still and looked at the magnificent backdrop to their lovely village. Parents and children were already gathered at the school gate; events were being discussed and gossip spread, as children ran amok in the playground. Mothers ran after some waving bags of costume they had forgotten to take, and at precisely eight-fifty-five, the piercing sound of the whistle restored order and the children lined up and marched into school.

Moira wended her way down Quay street, glancing at Christmas lights that twinkled in shop windows and houses, but none were as striking as those that festooned the Caledonian Hotel, where she turned left past the towering Ullapool clock, into Argyle Street and work. Angus had been there for some time; Moira could hear him on the ship-to-shore radio in the back, taking yet more orders. Angus's positive nature and jovial personality made him popular with locals and visitors: everyone's favourite uncle, and as a result they were always busy. Supplies would be arriving from the wholesalers in Inverness today and some of the captains might be making last minute adjustments to their requirements. Between calls he popped his head round the door greeting Moira with a cheery,

'Morning. You'd better be feeling rested, it's going to be another tiring one.'

She turned to him, nodded her head, 'I'll get on with the new orders straight away.'

Moira carried as much as she could lift into the van parked outside, as Angus loaded the heavy sacks of rice, dried beans, and flour. Just as they had finished the wholesaler's lorry turned up, and disgorged its load onto the pavement. There were yet more sacks of dried beans and rice, bags of potatoes, nets of cabbages, onions, carrots, swedes, pallets of this and cases of beer, and finally, a carefully handled mountain of eggs. All to be left stacked on the pavement – there was no room for all this in the shop, and yet it would be safe, no one would steal it – this was a close law-abiding community.

A launch was waiting for the van and would take its contents to the furthest ship – Angus liked to get them delivered first – just in case there was a change in the weather. Launches from other ships arrived to pick up their goods, and some brought men with trolleys to convey everything carefully back to the pier. People and goods travelled up and down like scurrying ants carrying loads back to their nests. Crew men collected rations from the shop and hung around waiting to meet old friends and new. Stores were transferred from shelf and pavement to van and trolley; wads of notes were handed over and receipts passed back with much jollity and slapping of backs. Locals steered themselves along the narrow walkway left in the middle of the sacks and crates – like walking a land-based gangplank – to buy milk, bread, daily essentials. They could see that today was not one for long discussions about neighbours, or the health of old Mr McKay; that could all wait until it could be given all the attention they believed it merited. A quick chat was all that could be managed today.

The locals were ambivalent about all of the activity. They welcomed the income, especially in the winter months when there was little tourism, but they treasured their tranquillity and their fish, both of which were being taken from them in the foreign race for wealth. Still, neither of the village's two main shopkeepers were ever heard to complain; they made a decent living and there was friendly rivalry between them – each trying to lure skippers into their nets of goodies.

There was a lull around noon and Moira made coffee. The sit down, however brief, was most welcome, but they kept a constant eye on the front door – always on the lookout for a customer. There was no time for lunch at home today, just a pre-prepared sandwich, and for Moira, a rush up the hill to see the nativity.

With only moments to spare, Moira weaved herself past knees and handbags, to a seat fairly near the front of the school hall – just in time for her son's last incarnation as a shepherd. It had been fun when he was little. Parents had given proud smiles, and little giggles when halos slipped, or wise men dropped precious gifts, and much mirth when Joseph or Mary tried to assert themselves over the proceedings. Alex had never risen to the lofty heights of a main player and was content to play a shepherd, a third onlooker, the back end of a donkey – any part that involved minimal lines and acting was fine by him. They would both be relieved when this final production was over. It all passed fairly smoothly, only one angel nearly fainted and had to be removed from the stage, whilst Mary had niftily avoided tripping over the shepherd's crook laid as a trap by shepherd four – which fortunately was not Alex, he had been elevated to shepherd one – his primary school thespian highlight.

'Go straight home, as I'm not sure when I will finish work,' instructed Moira. 'There's biscuits and squash in the cupboard, that should keep you going until dinner.' He would be fine with that, home half-an-hour early, biscuits and Meccano, what more could he wish for? She watched him dash away grinning with anticipation, and turned back to work.

Moira busied herself, restocking shelves, bringing order to chaos. Snow was beginning to fall, and much to her relief kept last-minute customers away. Angus dashed to the office when the phone rang.

'Is that another call about that stranded ship?' Moira asked, as Angus joined her restocking shelves.

'Yep, the Seaman's Mission has got involved. Hamish has been contacting the authorities in Inverness, the MP and any local charities that might be able to help those poor men. Ironically, their floating prison is called The Harmony, but I don't think there's much peace on board. The men's clothing isn't adequate and morale is understandably low, especially as supplies are running out. At least the owners have finally wired a little money for provisions'

'Thank goodness for that,' Moira said. 'It must be awful for them.'

'I'm sure it is,' Angus agreed. 'We need to get their order ready by Christmas Eve. Did you know that the Church has asked parishioners for contributions of winter clothing?' Moira shook her head.

Angus eased his aching shoulders and carried on, 'Well the message seems to be getting round the village at full tilt, so we could deliver any clothing along with their order on Thursday.'

'I didn't know that things were so bad. I'd heard some mutterings, but the details seem to have passed me by. I've not got any men's clothing at home; it was all thrown out years ago – along with their drunken wearer. But I bet Roddy has got some of his old gamekeeper's stuff. I'll ask him later, we should be able to make some sort of family contribution.' Moira passed more tins to Angus and continued. 'Alex could help collect contributions after his last half-day of term; it'll keep him occupied and take his mind off Meccano and the currently empty space under the Christmas tree!'

'Good idea.' Angus said as he placed the last tin on the shelf. 'Better get off home Moira, that snow is getting worse and we've got another full day ahead.'

Chapter 6

Clear, unscaleable ahead,
Rise the Mountains of Instead,
From whose cold cascading streams
None may drink except in dreams
    Autumn Song
    W H Auden

Jim, looked out from the deck and shivered; the cocoon of inadequate clothing could not keep the cold at bay. Yet he remained, mesmerised by the white mountains facing him – like a challenge he should scale. Peaks of white reached for the sky, then descended into smaller replicas of themselves, before levelling out into gentle slopes of fir trees, rocks and earth. In all his twenty-nine years Jim had never seen snow – he'd seen it in films and understood that it was cold like ice in a glass of cola, but until now, had no sense of how majestic it looked when it coated nature's finest. The rising sun tinted the vista with a misleading glow of warmth, and he watched as the day dawned and the high peaks came into focus. The village stood silent on its promontory, looking for all the world as if it were floating – like a tethered raft of little white cottages with grey roofs, whose colours matched the mountain backdrop – all offset by the pure gleaming blue of the water.

Despite the multi layers Jim shook with the cold, and jumped around to raise his body temperature – there was no attraction inside that could be better than this. He star-jumped, jogged and flapped his arms back and forth across his body, but eventually the cold won, and he retreated to the mess to hear the captain's ten am briefing.

The mess door opened at exactly the pre-arranged time, and the men, all squashed inside, waited with childlike anticipation of the good news they expected – their eyes peered forwards as they tried to read the captain's mind.

'Men, I am afraid that for today I must disappoint you, we will not be moving the ship to the pier, which is still busy with men and boats transferring stores to the outlying ships.' His raised hand quelled the vocal objections to this news, and he continued: 'However, we will be going tomorrow, not only to refuel, but also to take on some stores. The ship's owners have made funds available for the purchase of goods.'

He raised his hand again to stop any further interjections and carried on: 'I must inform you that most of the officers will be leaving the ship in the morning; their families have arranged train tickets to London and onward flights to Bulgaria. I of course, will be staying, along with the first engineer. There will be another briefing tomorrow at ten am.' Once again he turned and swiftly walked away.

The quiet was replaced with decibels of anger and displays of emotions too hard to bear. What was to become of them? Fed, but leaderless. Some like Jim, whose English was not good asked their compatriots to explain. They all had so many questions to be answered: WHEN would THEY be able to leave? HOW would they get the ship home without the officers? Were they to be abandoned, left to fester on the ailing ship? Utter confusion overwhelmed them, and they drifted back to cabins and quiet corners. Anywhere they could collect their thoughts.

Jim sat on his bunk, legs dangling over the edge, hands clasped on his knees and head forward, taking in everything his friend Samuel was telling him. They had no options. Without money there would be no tickets for trains or planes. The daybreak happiness was gone; replaced by gloom and a confused understanding of their position. Jim needed distraction. He banged his clenched hands against his chin, then his forehead, as if to knock inspiration into his head. Such was their impoverished state that all that came to mind was his washing – much of which he was still wearing. He removed layers and carted them to the large sink reserved for this purpose in the area entitled Laundry, thankfully there was still hot water available and a bar of laundry soap. Jim pummelled and pulled the laundry removing every vestige of dirt. His anger draining away with the grubby water, leaving him as limp as the washing which was now ready to be hung out to dry.

The crew had by now formed into two groups, conversing in their own dialects, the words spilled out of their mouths like waterfalls and resounded around the room. Raised voices bounced off walls and ceilings; the lunch time gruel was eaten under a canopy of noise. Leaders rose from the turmoil and started to take charge, telling their fellow kinsmen that they would demand to see the captain and return with more news. And so it was that one from each group, stood tall, shoulders back, heads held high and made their way to the inner sanctum of their only hope: their chief, their captain.

The men chatted, played games, drank cups of coffee eeked out from previous dregs, and waited, then waited and waited some more. Nothing. Time suspended until, at last, the mess room door opened and the two men, who now appeared a little shorter, their heads held not nearly so high, informed them that there would be no more news today. Another day that had started with some cheer and beauty had let Jim and all the others down, and all he had to anticipate was how to dry his laundry.

Jim descended with leaden feet into the silent ship's factory and draped half-dry garments on any tepid pipes that he could find. His thoughts turned to the God that had deserted him and he leant against the fish packing machine contemplating his predicament. Perhaps God had been on a celestial holiday, and was now back to console and comfort him – as His emissaries always promised. So, in a corner of the ship's bowels, where underpants took the place of frescos, a hanging shirt a cross, and a can of oil an altar, Jim fell to his knees and prayed. Silent prayers, speaking directly to God, passing his distress into the hands of a master, the ultimate saviour, who could cast aside this misery and lead them all into a better place. A tap on his shoulder by a ship mate brought Jim back to reality.

'Hey man, you all right down there?'

'Yeh, just looking for a button that came off this shirt,' was Jim's quick retort, and he was quietly pleased at the sudden agility of his brain. Maybe God was on his side after all.

Chapter 7

We shall walk in velvet shoes;
Wherever we go
Silence will fall like dews
On white silence below.
We shall walk in the snow
    Velvet shoes
    Elinor Wylie

At the shop, orders were completed and shelves restocked – Moira was finally finished for the day and made her way home, taking cautious steps through the now settling snow. An easy dinner, sausages and mash, could be prepared promptly. Alex would be pleased, it was one of his favourites, especially with no cabbage leaf in sight; he didn't consider onions as veg, so ate those without thought. He responded to her cheery, 'I'm home,' with a quick, 'OK,' and she heard no more from him until, 'Dinner's ready,' that once again resulted in a dash of Olympic speed down the stairs and a rapid seating of his bottom. He sat poised for attack, cutlery held ready, and immediately set about the meal as it was placed in front of him. Gobbled up as if he hadn't eaten for days.

Moira raised her eyebrows and gave him a sideways look, he understood what it meant, but he was unlikely to be slower next time. The pair chatted away until Moira had finished, then Alex remembered,

'Have you found out about that ship yet?'

'Yes I have.' Moira said and brought him up to date. 'Will you help collect some of the clothes after school?'

'Yep. Got to do my bit. But it won't take too long will it? He replied with less than full commitment to his role. 'You know mum, I feel sorry for those men, it can't be much fun for them can it?'

'It most certainly can't.' Moira said, as a glow of maternal pride coursed through her body. 'I expect you'll want to watch Grange Hill shortly, so help me sort the kitchen and I'll not even complain about that awful programme.'

'Oh Mum, you do go on; it's good education for High School. You need to keep up with the times!' Moira flicked a tea-towel round his ear and shushed him towards the lounge.

The last of her days allocation of energy was used on a few domestic chores before she made the obligatory mug of tea and sat herself by the phone. They are sure to have some spare things. Moira dialled and heard:

'Hello.'

'Hello Roddy, just the man I want.'

Her brother laughed. 'That makes a change, you usually ask for Aila. To what do I owe this pleasure?'

'Have you got any old winter clothes you could add to the collection for the men on that stranded ship?' Moira asked and heard him tut, inhale deeply then reply.

'I might have, but I've not got time to start looking. I'm sure they'll cope. Here, talk to Aila, I've not got all day to hang on the phone.'

Wow, what's got into him? A bad day? 'Yes that'll be it,' Moira voiced to the wall. Aila, her sister-in-law was much more forthcoming,

'Oh, I'll see what I can find, men aren't much good at this sort of thing.' whispered Aila down the line. 'Roddy hasn't had the best of days. The work in the ice factory gets him down. The extra money is always useful at this time of year, but we all know he'd rather be out on the moors and mountains, stalking, shooting and walking the estate.'

'Oh, I understand,' Moira said, 'neither of us would be keen on making ice in the middle of winter, but the trawlers need it and work is work after all.'

'Anyway, his stint in the factory is nearly over,'

'Oh good, he ought to be feeling more cheerful on Christmas day then,' Moira chuckled.

'He'd better be. Can't have him spoiling our fun.' Aila replied.

'As if we would let him! Anyway, I'm about done in, see if you can find some warm stuff, and we'll catch up in the morning,' Moira said, then made her way upstairs.

There was time for a quick shower – she much preferred a nice soak – but there was no time for lying around and being self-indulgent. A bit of cleanliness was all that was required, then she slipped between the sheets, curled up with her hot water bottle and drifted asleep.

As the alarm went off, Moira could tell by the eerie silence outside, that there had been heavy snow. It was still dark as she drew back the curtains, but the roadside light illuminated the whiteness: buildings, road, pavement, bushes and trees were all cloaked with snow – a picture book image of winter – with not, as yet, a single footprint to spoil the scene. Alex was quick to be ready and gobbled his porridge and rushed outside. The first proper fall of winter was welcome after all the rain of late. The walk to school was rich with giggling and merriment. Alex and his chums merged along the route, throwing snowballs as they went. Moira avoided a last-minute hit as she peeled off to work and yelled after him,

'Don't forget to come straight to the shop after lunch.'

Crewmen were already loading trollies and steering them through the snow, downhill to the port – slithering and balancing as they went. The east Europeans were used to snow and negotiated their routes with commendable skill, and only the occasional mishap. For other nationalities from hotter climates such as Spain and Africa, it was a different matter – this terra was distinctly not firm. They slipped, skidded, and moved around like drunks on the alien surface. It might be cold, but it was fun, and after initial hesitation they made snowballs and threw them at each other, acting just like the school boys and girls they had watched a few moments ago. They were brought to order by their senior crew, who shouted,

'Get on with the job in hand.' Their fun was over. Their stacked trolleys were manoeuvred through slush and snow, to the water's edge. A net of cabbages fell and split apart, cabbages rolling around like marbles, before coming to a halt, just feet away from the water's edge. That particular crew laughed until their eyes watered; it was worth all the effort to retrieve the recalcitrant cabbages, and they departed with whoops of glee and laughter.

Moira saw only a little of this, she was diligently loading the van with tin after tin and packet after packet. The laughter became louder and carried over the snow and made her smile. Even, Angus, weighed down with sacks, was uplifted by the contagious joy of the men and the pair looked at each other and simultaneously burst out laughing.

Alex walked through the door like an apparition; neither Angus nor Moira had realised the time. He sat in the corner while she finished serving Miss McKay, the former headmistress, but he was keen to get outside and play in the snow, totally forgetting his previous ardour for good works. The crate marked 'Ullapool Relief Effort' already held a significant number of hats, gloves, scarves, a few coats, and jumpers, and Alex realised the snow would have to wait. Thus, he set off with a list of addresses, from where he was to pick up additional items. The donors were mostly elderly people, eager to do their bit, but sensibly not going out in this weather. He rushed around, keen to get his good works, now labelled chores, done before anyone gave him yet more jobs to do.

Work continued on apace in the shop, and with just the final order waiting to be collected, Captain Lyudmil finally arrived. He all but fell into the shop, apologised for his late arrival, then, in one misplaced stride stumbled into the tinned fruit, which scattered like errant mice. More profuse apologies followed and his sallow complexion took on a red hue. Moira's giggles broke his embarrassment though and the tins were rounded up and returned to their rightful position. Outside, eight of the crew were expectantly waiting. They shivered as the produce was loaded onto their trollies and carefully steered them back to the port. Just in time, Moira remembered the crate and called the captain back:

'We've got some things for you,' she shouted. He looked confused, as she handed the crate of clothing to him.

'Clothes? Why? I have things to wear.'

'Not for you,' Moira said. 'We heard that your men might not have sufficient clothing and so the villagers have collected these. They aren't new, but they will help keep the men warm in this Scottish weather. Please take them, and we will try and find more.'

At first, he stood looking slightly vacant, as if he had not understood but eventually found his unusually hesitant voice,

'So, people that we have never met or seen, are giving us these, do I understand that correctly?'

'Yes, they are for The Harmony.'

'I don't know what to say, we can give nothing in return, such is our current situation, but from the bottom of my heart, and on behalf of all the men, I say, thank you ... thank you.'

The Captain looked so choked with emotion that it was all that Moira could do to hold back tears as he struggled back through the silly door, in much the same way as he had arrived, but now muttering something about, the kindness of strangers.

Moira dabbed her eyes, then put her hand to her mouth in astonishment as Alex, both hands full of carrier bags stumbled into the shop, muttering:

'Stupid door.' She had totally forgotten about him.

'Oh, they've just left. Run and you might catch them at the pier, but be careful, it's starting to freeze again.'

'Oh, Mum,' he sighed, and turned around and negotiated the way out. Fortunately, Angus was just coming in, so held the door ajar and

Alex was off, running and sliding on the ice, both arms out like a windmill, the bags bouncing around like sails. He slid to a halt at the pier and saw a ship that any self-respecting sailor would call a 'rust bucket,' and realized that was the one. He shouted out at the men walking towards the capstan and waved the bags even further in the air to gain their attention. As Alex got closer he garbled an explanation about the bags, but Jim just shrugged his shoulders, and carried on. 'Can you speak more slowly please?' Samuel said as he waved his hands up and down. 'It's difficult to understand when you talk so fast.'

Alex carefully explained again, and this time Jim nodded his head in understanding. But they looked confused, Samuel bent over,

'What is your name, and who gave us these?'

'Oh, I'm Alex,' he said cheerily, looking up at the two tall men. 'Lots of people gave them, there might even be some more. Here just take them,' he said thrusting the bags forward, 'they're all for you.' He turned to retrace his steps, then looked back, 'Where are you both from?' Samuel answered,

'Nigeria.' Alex's eyes lit up, ' Ooo, I don't know much about there.'

Only a signal from the captain stopped the conversation continuing, but as the men turned, Alex asked, 'Do you have chocolate on board?'

Jim and Samuel looked at each other and then at Alex; then at themselves again, shrugged their shoulders,

'No, we don't,' they replied. Alex pondered this for a brief moment before putting his hand in his pocket and pulling out a small bar of Cadburys Milk Chocolate, not huge, because it was an end of term gift from his teacher. Then, in possibly the most difficult and generous gesture of his life, he handed it to them and said,

'This is for you. You should have chocolate at Christmas,' and walked away before he changed his mind.

Chapter 8

My now is poor, my future worse
No hopes, just fears.
Are there options or prospects,
Or just never-ending despair?
     Anon

Meanwhile, on The Harmony, the same day looked different. Those crew men that didn't have a critical job were crammed into the mess watching the door. At precisely nine-thirty the door opened like a cuckoo clock to reveal Captain Lyudmil who was greeted by a wall of silence. He responded with his normal booming voice:

'Following on from yesterday, I am pleased to inform you that the immigration authorities have finally stamped all your passports allowing you to leave the ship but not the village. We will be refuelling and therefore moving to the pier.'

The men cheered and hugged each other as the captain raised his hand and continued. 'We will be picking up supplies from the village, and I will take eight of you to transport them. The remaining eighteen can disembark – in two groups – to exercise along the foreshore. But the foreshore only. Please abide by these rules, as I have been led to believe that more such trips will be allowed if all goes well. The departing officers say goodbye and they will do what they can to improve your situation and get you home. Indeed, we are all working to that end, and I am in frequent discussion with the Nigerian agents. We will move at 2pm. Thank you.'

Two o'clock saw the crew inadequately clothed for the mission ahead. Rubber boots and coats provided the outer layer – the original yellow and orange of these garments had long ago faded and lost their gloss. Only the men's eyes – full of anticipation – shone out. Anchors away, and they were off. The crew acted with all the enthusiasm of passengers on an inaugural world cruise. The shopping party rushed onto dry land and steered their trolleys behind the captain as he led the way to the chandlers. The houses and shops, that for nearly three months had looked like toys, were now proper size and their reflections in the sea duplicated their charm. The men were fascinated by this little place that nestled in the heart of both low hills and towering mountains. The land seemed unstable and made them sway. Balance, so used to the motion of the sea, was tricked into an unsteadiness that was worsened by their first walk on snow, but their spirits were raised by the sheer delight of walking on land, however wobbly.

The short walk was taken leisurely as they took in their surroundings. They turned the corner and saw sacks piled up along the pavement. Jim's eyes lit up a – a bit like the streets at home, just different colours, and he inclined his head and nodded. The shopkeeper introduced himself as Angus and helped them with the loading, ensuring that all was as secure as possible for these wobbly men and their precious loads. On the second trip, feet and mind were more balanced, and the crew peered into shop windows – at products they could not afford – but looking was free. Christmas lights twinkled, some blue and white like the surroundings and some, multicoloured, sparkling like those at home. They pushed their laden trolleys as carefully as possible; heads turning left and right, taking in the detail of the place that had, for so long, been like a distant photograph. Men were waiting to carry the loads on board, sacks lifted onto shoulders as if they were full of feathers and crates of tins held aloft and perched on heads as if they were little more than cushions. The captain joined them. He was huffing and puffing and handed over a large crate that overflowed with jumpers, trousers, jackets and other miscellaneous items. 'Strange,' said Jim and Samuel, but it was time to leave the pier, their jaunt was sadly over.

The pair were unwinding the ropes, just as a boy came running towards them. He was waving bags in the air and gabbling so fast that it was impossible to decipher the language, let alone the message. The bags contained more clothes, but neither Jim nor Samuel could understand why. The boy explained a little, and told them his name was Alex – he seemed keen to chat. As he left, he handed them a bar of chocolate, a Christmas present apparently, and ran on. They looked at each other, not knowing if they should return the present, but their benefactor was now running up the hill and they must get on with their work. In the end the decision was easy, it was a Christmas gift, and they would wait until Friday before sharing the bar between themselves.

The crew were happier for being on shore, although in reality their situation was little changed. At least they could look forward to a larger meal tonight – meat on their plates and, even better, a sweet course – rice pudding and jam!

The evening followed the normal pattern of cards and Oware or quiet corners for some, and physical exercise for others. Jim returned to his cabin, where he carefully opened his drawer and looked, once again, at the gift from Alex: but he wasn't tempted to eat it. No, it was the gesture that he was looking at, a gift that was obviously important to the boy and was, because of that, even more meaningful to him. With his eyes closed he tried to recall Alex's face; round, rosy cheeks, big blue eyes that looked straight at him from under a brown woollen hat, and in his head, Jim said, 'Thank you, thank you,' and made up his mind. If he were to see the boy called Alex again, he would want to thank him properly, and to do that he must improve his English and went off in search of Samuel.

Lessons started the next day – straight after breakfast – which for the first time in months included egg. 'Fodder for my brain,' Jim mumbled to himself . However, egg was not sufficient to make the lesson easy. Neither teacher nor pupil were exactly sure how to go about it, and after an hour Samuel was ready to walk out, and the pupil's brain was hurting: this was going to take some time. But they made it to the end of the lesson, just moments before it might have ended in a brawl. Jim was later to be found roaming around the deck with his new, well to him anyway, woolly hat pulled down to his eyes and the slightly too small gloves stretched over his fingers murmuring, 'Thank you very much, you are very kind,' over and over again.

Jim's language skills came to the fore at lunch the next day. The gruel was a different colour and the larger portions were welcome, but it was the addition of fresh bread that made all the difference. Jim took his portion and said, with relish, 'Thank you very much, you are very kind.' Heads turned, eyes widened and they all roared with laughter and even Jim managed a chuckle at himself. Underneath though, he was certain that he had taken the first step on an important journey; he would use this terrible time to improve himself, it wouldn't be easy, but it would be done.

The captain's two o'clock announcement had a mixed reception:

'Now that the officers have left I intend to assume control of their roles. We are all in this together and must support each other to keep morale up. I have made rotas for tasks to be carried out. We must maintain discipline and keep ourselves occupied.' He pinned two sheets to the notice board and continued, 'To ease the cramped conditions in the mess, I have made two lists, one is for nights and the other for days.' The crew responded with raised voices and their hands gesticulated annoyance. A piercing shout of, 'Silence!' met with exactly that. 'I sense some anger at this and will therefore allow swapping of shifts, let me know your decisions,' and he walked out. Somehow, they managed to sort the shifts and order was restored. Jim and Samuel breathed sighs of relief that they remained on the allocated day shift. The new regime would start on Saturday, the day after Christmas.

Jim's dusk time walk on the deck was, by now, becoming a habit, there had been little sun, so there was no dramatic sky to see tonight, just grey and white all around, hard to tell where sea, sky and the mountains started and ended. But, in the distance were the twinkling lights of the homes of the people he wanted to meet one day. As he focused, some of the lights shone brighter, colours of the rainbow twinkled, and then he heard singing, blown to him on the breeze, lights and voices in harmony. He wondered if it were real or imagined, but when the air became still the singing ceased; it must have been the breeze singing to him after all. My mind will be the undoing of me, and he wandered back inside, to anything but a special Christmas Eve.

Chapter 9

'Twas the night before Christmas, when all through the house,
Not a creature was stirring not even a mouse.'
    The Night before Christmas
    Clement Clarke Moore

Customers trickled into the store for their orders and took the opportunity to hand over cards and distribute season's best wishes.

'Will we be seeing you at the carols?' they all asked.

'Oh yes, we'll be there,' Moira replied to each of their departing backs.

But before then she would have to give Angus his present. It was always the same: a homemade Dundee cake. Some villagers said hers was the best for miles around – she was fairly sure that they exaggerated – but even if it was only half true it made her feel proud. Angus always reciprocated, and each year his gift became larger. This year a bag of delicacies and a bottle of single Malt. Moira always appreciated the gesture; he was such a generous man and had become a good friend. They wished each other season's greetings and after a brief hug she was off to continue the day's rituals.

Moira found Alex playing with friends and hurried him home. He pretty much turned feral in the holidays, but this was a safe community and the children were guarded by many hidden eyes. The annual routine kicked into gear straight after lunch. Alex refilled the coal scuttle and laid the fire: twists of paper first, then a wigwam of kindling followed by larger sticks – ready for the most important fire of the year.

Moira's mother, Iris, always joined them on Christmas Eve. She lived four houses away, at the end of their terrace, in the place where Moira had grown up. This was Iris's time to be fed before she reciprocated for the whole family the next day. Table setting had become another of

Alex's roles, and he stood back and appraised his work, then placed his Christmas stocking under the tree, where a few presents were already waiting. Probably for Mum from neighbours, he thought, but had a quick check, to make absolutely sure there wasn't a sneaky one for him.

Iris, appeared at the door, hugged her grandson. 'You'll soon be taller than me,' she said stretching herself to full height.

'I think he already is,' laughed Moira, as she handed Alex his coat and they made their way out.

The carols took place around the tree that stood prominently on Shore Street. It always had pretensions of grandeur – more Trafalgar Square than village – and all the residents were proud of it. The stately tree was adorned with ropes of tinsel tied on with sailors' knots. Hundreds of lights swayed around on their tethered strings and twinkled brightly in the long dark nights of mid-winter. As darkness fell, hundreds of people huddled round the tree and sang their hearts out. Old Mr McTavish could be counted on to bring volume, as he led the proceedings with all the gusto of Pavarotti, whilst his wife trilled away like a flock of canaries recently released from captivity. This made it easy to join in, something Moira was always grateful for; she was better at miming than singing. But on Christmas Eve, even she could join in, knowing full well that her less than adequate singing would be drowned out by loud renditions of Good King Wenceslas, Oh come all ye faithful, and the like. She had to be a little more careful during the hushed tones of Silent Night, lest Alex nudged her and shook his head in disapproval. Just a few words from the minister and the crowd dispersed: they peeled off into pubs or homes, shouting seasonal messages as they went. Moira and Iris linked arms with Alex, swinging him in the air, as they sang carols that they couldn't really remember and with all thoughts of inadequate singing gone from their minds, they carolled their way home.

The gammon had roasted in their absence and its mouth-watering sweet and salty aroma greeted them at the door. Moira carefully removed its case of foil and anointed it with a glaze of mustard and honey, then popped it back into the oven for its final transformation into a mouth-watering delicacy. Alex carried out his chores and had a blazing fire in the lounge in no time. Mum and Granny joined him, each carrying a small sherry, the same thing they had done for many years. Traditions die hard and this particular one predated Iris's widowhood five years previously, and Moira's divorce not long before that. Alex took a sip of his mum's drink.

'That's disgusting, can I have ginger beer?'

Moira laughed and nodded her head in the direction of the little side table in the corner, where unnoticed by him, it was already poured and waiting.

'So how's school been this last week?' Granny asked.

'Oh, the usual, nothing much.'

'Hardly seems worth going, you always tell me the same! We did a lot when I went to school you know,' laughed Granny, just as Moira indicated that dinner was ready. She could feel Alex's relief that a near inquisition by Granny would be interrupted, and especially by a meal.

It was a happy meal, convivial, full of the week's highs and lows.

'Do you think Mr McTavish's voice has got even louder ?' Iris asked. 'It seems to have grown at a similar rate as his moustache.'

'Just what I thought,' Moira said, 'that moustache lies across his face like a pair of sleeping hamsters – their tails to the side and curled like corkscrews.'

Iris started to giggle uncontrollably, 'Do you think that his poor wife's voice has been tickled into life by his night time kisses?'

This was much too good an opportunity for Alex to miss and he fetched the washing-up brush, held it to his lips and proceeded to pretend kiss the ladies who pushed him away with cries of, 'Get away,' as tears of laughter rolled down their cheeks.

There was time for a little TV in front of the fire before Alex could carry out the best job of the year – it was time to put out Santa's goodies. He poured whisky into a crystal glass and placed it on the hearth alongside the special Christmas plate on which he placed a mince pie and a carrot for the reindeers. The glass sparkled in the firelight, casting coloured rays over the pie and he was satisfied. Alex had long ago stopped believing in Father Christmas but still liked to hedge his bets; he was beyond such foolishness, but, and here lay his quandary – who drank the whisky? Mum didn't like it so where did it go?

The most welcome bedtime of the year arrived and despite the manic activity of his brain, sleep overtook his excited body and peace reigned in the house. Of course, Moira had parcels to remove from hidey-holes, many so secret that she sometimes had difficulty remembering where they were. On more than one occasion, Christmas Day had come and gone with no sight of the new slippers or T-shirt that, must be somewhere. Only to be discovered mid-summer, by which time they were too small for his growing body.

As Moira inspected the tree, which now looked as full underneath as on top, she whispered to herself, 'I think I've cracked it this year,' and with a contented look on her face she turned off the lights and made her way upstairs for a well-deserved long soak. Then, like her son, she climbed into bed and was almost instantly asleep.

Chapter 10

Always remember to forget
The things that make you sad,
But never forget to remember,
The things that make you glad.
     Remember to forget
     Anon

Jim lay in his bunk, his mind miles away in Nigeria, 'Christmas Day should be special,' he murmured into the wafer-thin pillow. His family was important to him and he recalled the many good memories – huge gatherings full of merriment – his mother, brothers and sisters, aunts and uncles, plates loaded with meat, cassava, yams and other delicacies; he could almost smell the food, hear the laughter and see his family, but his mind could not linger there. That would not help. He had to stay focused in the here and now. Get up, have a wash and greet the day with all the positivity he could muster.

The captain must be of a similar mind, he thought, as he went in for breakfast. A few pieces of tinsel had been draped over the Nigerian president's picture, and the two-year-old calendar was similarly adorned. Baubles hung on strings from the ceiling, and near the serving hatch was a Christmas tree that was plainly past its prime; on top of which was an angel of dubious origin. Jim was not sure whether it was a joke or a genuine attempt at the season's festivities, but whatever, it obviously encapsulated their current situation and made him smile. There were no presents to be handed out, no cards to give, just words to pass around. None of which gave much comfort or joy. Still they all tried – well nearly all – some preferred wallowing in the mire of the moment and were not easily removed from that place.

No one Intended to clean decks or do laundry today, and the congested room was getting hotter and hotter. Samuel opened the door to let cool air in and jumped backwards as the Captain all but fell into his arms.. I must stop entering like this, the Captain thought as he regained his composure and placed a large tin of sweets on the nearest surface and boomed:

'I would like to wish you all season's greeting. I do not think that for any of us this will be a happy day, but we must make the most of it. This tin contains sweets and is a gift for you to share. It was given by the seaman's mission which sends you greetings. Cook will try and give you a special dinner, well, if not exactly special, an improvement, and I am delighted to tell you that I have managed to obtain a bottle of beer for you all. The engineer and I would have joined you for this meal, but it is obvious that there is not a square inch into which we could squeeze, so we must eat on our own. Please divide the sweets fairly and I will see you all later.'

That tin of sweets was opened up and the contents handed out in a moment. Some grabbed handfuls like little children, rather than the huge men they were, only to be brought under control by compatriots, and by some sort of miracle they all finished up with roughly the same number. The bartering then started, some liked purple ones, others red, but the green ones were less desired. Never had one tin of Quality Street brought so much pleasure to so many people. Most ate theirs with such gusto that the flavours barely had chance to be tasted, but some, and that included Jim, ate just one and savoured each mouthful, moving the delicacy round their mouths, enjoying the flavours that trickled down their throats. The other sweets would be saved for later in the day – precious moments of pleasure.

Jim carefully placed his sweets in his drawer, there were three – purple, yellow, and red and they lay like jewels next to the bar from Alex. Presents from people I do not know, he thought, and felt both more, and yet less alone. He pulled on his newly acquired jumper and rubber boots and climbed into the great outdoors. The cold air bit into him as he focused on the mountains that soared over the Lilliputian village and he imagined its inhabitants. They are the only ones caring for us he thought, and glanced around the deck, where ship mates, each in their own space and deep in contemplation, rested their arms on rails and looked out at the great beyond. At that moment they were family, brought together by adversity. The best they were going to get today. They ambled back in silence, before joining the others below.

Christmas dinner proved to be a triumph. Cook was most undeniably the hero of the day. A stew of venison met all their demands for meat, and was devoured along with the accompanying rice, potatoes and veggies in near silence. The first proper meal they had eaten in weeks. The beer was so special that most of them savoured it drop by drop, and spirits lifted with each sip. Fullness was a feeling they had all but forgotten and it mellowed them all – conviviality took over. There was some chat of homes and families far away, but they managed to keep focused on good memories and those they could share with laughter. They spoke with fondness of the little community that was helping them, and of the sight of snow on mountains. Someone suggested that they could start fishing, not with great nets – they didn't have any after all – but they could keep some little bits of bread for bait and find some nylon for lines. They were to become anglers and attempt to boost their rations that way. It was good to feel this full and they intended to feel like it again.

As promised, the captain entered and moved around the room, chatting to each man individually. Jim did his best to string a good sentence together and haltingly explained that he was learning English.

'Good idea Jim. I'd like to help – it would pass the time for both of us. Maybe we could borrow some suitable books from the school.'

'Oh, thank you.' Jim was too surprised to say more.

The captain was told of their fishing plans, and he agreed to find materials for rods, lines, and hooks. 'Something positive to look forward to, that is what we all need,' he said and turned to the door, 'have a pleasant evening,' and left. 'A strange thing to say,' Samuel said, 'makes it sound as if we are having a night on the town.' Jim merely shook his head and left the room.

Gradually, they all drifted back to their cabins; this had been a better Christmas than they could have dared to imagine; semi-good memories had been made in their time of sadness and they would not be forgotten. Samuel remembered the bar of chocolate and the pair of them laughed at their forgetfulness; they had presents after all, and as they lay in their bunks, all thoughts drifted back to Africa before they finally fell asleep.

Chapter 11

It's the stick together family that wins the joy of earth,
That hears the sweetest music and that finds the first mirth.
    The Stick-Together Family
    Edgar Guest

Christmas in the village was a vastly different affair. A well-oiled machine sprang into life, as did Alex. He was up and at the tree in the blink of a sleepy eye, retrieved his overflowing stocking, and raced back upstairs where Moira was just wakening and bracing herself for the onslaught. He exploded through the bedroom door, dived onto her bed and was off – paper and sticky tape torn apart and cast aside. There were chocolate coins, nuts, satsumas, a Pez dispenser with tubes of sweets to put in it, some biscuits, underpants, and socks. It was pretty much the same each Christmas and as much fun was had in the opening as in the contents, which, as far as Alex was concerned, were great, or boring – little in between. The larger presents that still lay under the tree couldn't be opened until after breakfast. This was a rule that was never broken and all he could do was urge.

'Get up, Mum I'm starving. Oh, Mum, do get up. GET UP.'

Moira grinned, 'Happy Christmas to you too Alex,' she said, and shooed him out of the bedroom with clear instructions to get washed and dressed before coming downstairs.

Moira pulled on her dressing gown and set about breakfast. Not porridge on Christmas day, but Alex's favourite – pancakes – over which she poured syrup as he sat himself down. The first one was devoured in moments.

'I'm ready for the next one,' he yelled a little too loudly.

'Hold on there,' Moira said, 'I'm not a magician. You slow down and remember, no more than four.' He pulled a silly face, and fidgeted in his chair,

'Yes I know that, but hurry up Mum and get yours.' Moira slowly ate the last pancake, savouring every mouthful – much to Alex's annoyance. 'Oh do hurry up Mum, we've got to go into the lounge.'

Moira wrapped her hands around a fresh mug of tea as she watched him grab the largest present. He had discovered it on top of her wardrobe several days before and had pestered her endlessly about its contents. It had taken Moira a long time to save for the present, which was more than she could truly afford, so was overjoyed at the delight on his face as he pulled out the Premier Meccano set with six-speed motor. He jumped up and down and threw himself at her, flinging his arms around her neck saying:

'Oh thank you, thank you,' over and over again, before regaining his composure, and setting about the other parcels. Nothing could compare with that present, but he understood that pyjamas and a new dressing gown were needed, as was the jumper and trousers, so he was happy. He looked at Moira sitting there with no presents of her own and scrabbled under the tree and retrieved four presents. All for her. There was bubble bath from her friend Doreen next door, a pack of handkerchiefs from a mystery donor and in the last two, given to her with a real flourish, was a bottle of Yardley's lavender eau de toilette and a box of matching soap. He looked intently at her face as she opened the last two, it had taken him so long to save up the money. The presents had been carefully chosen by him and Granny and he wanted her to be delighted. The bear hug she gave him made his efforts all worthwhile, and they held each other tightly.

'I've still got a lot to do,' Moira said, to a Meccano focused Alex who was lost in a world of his own. She carefully stacked the presents back under the tree before getting washed and dressed. She slipped into her favourite outfit of black trousers and a red cashmere sweater. The feel of that jumper on her skin always made her feel special – like a film star – silky and smooth yet warm as toast. No one ever noticed the flaw under the arm that had made it affordable, and she had long ago forgotten about that.

The previously prepared foodstuffs were packed into her basket and Alex reluctantly tidied away his precious six-speed motor in its box, before walking the few yards to Granny's at number twelve. Roddy, Aila and their two girls – Fiona and Flora – pulled up in their car,

'Perfect timing,' Moira said as they all crammed into the hallway.

Season's greetings were passed around, but the children rushed off into the lounge to discuss presents and avoid the cheek kissing that was coming their way. The adults piled their contributions on all the kitchen surfaces and before long everything was under control. The children shouted to the adults:

'Come into the lounge, oh do come on. We want to open our presents.'

Round two of present giving could begin. Sweets and goodies appeared from shiny paper, books and miscellaneous articles from boxes, the always anticipated board game – Hungry Hippos this time – and then there was only one long package left under the tree.

'Who's the last present for?' Flora asked.

'Let's see,' Roddy said as he pulled the package out and handed it to Alex. 'Happy Christmas, young man. This is from me, Aunty and Granny, oh and the girls of course.'

'But I've got all I asked for,' Alex said with confused delight. 'What is it?' He pulled off the tightly wrapped paper with all the force he could muster and revealed his own fishing rod.

'We men have got to stick together, pass on those fly-fishing skills,' Roddy said with a wink.

'Oh, thank you,' Alex said, so overcome with gratitude and pride, that he nearly lost the power of speech. And, he even managed kisses for his aunt and uncle, but not for the girls, that would be too much.

The youngsters played with their presents whilst the adults had a drink: sherry for Moira and Aila, and whisky for Granny and Roddy. Then it was all systems go for lunch, pans heated up, turkey resting under a sheet of foil, oven turned up to roast the potatoes and then the feast could begin. Crackers were pulled. Too large paper hats were plonked on heads, and silly jokes were shared. The children sat at one end with their heads together in deep discussion of presents, hardly noticing how good the meal was; whereas at the other end they were short on conversation but long on appreciation of the Highland salmon which they all agreed, was better than ever. The meal continued with the volume turned high at one end, but much quieter at the other. They united in cross-table chat over Christmas pudding, with everyone agreeing that Granny had surpassed herself this year.

The children, as dutiful as ever, helped carry dishes to the kitchen whilst the adults set about restoring pots, pans, plates and cutlery to its rightful place in cupboards and drawers – just in time for the Queen's speech. As the Queen addressed the nation from the small screen in the corner, the children fidgeted and looked bored, but the adults were glued to the TV. Alex nudged his cousins and pulled faces that made them giggle.

'Keep quiet,' from all the adults, put paid to their moment of merriment but their ordeal didn't last long and disorder was swiftly restored to the lounge.

Hungry Hippos were unleashed to chomp up marbles as fast as their players could make them go. Shouting, cheering and the occasional, 'Boo resounded around the room.' All having the sort of fun that was replicated throughout the land.

Despite the substantial lunch they were all feeling peckish by six o'clock. The feeding station was replenished with turkey and ham sandwiches, Moira's Dundee cake and Aila's mince pies.

'Come and get it!' had barely left Granny's mouth, before the children were back eating. The adults joined them and chatted about the day and their good fortune at having plenty.

Roddy and the children shouted and cheered as they continued marble gobbling, while the ladies took their mugs of tea to the sofa and with heads together began putting the world to rights. It wasn't long before Iris said:

'Those poor souls on the Harmony.'

'What's to become of them?' Aila asked.

Alex's ears pricked up at this and having just lost his second game, plonked himself on the carpet in front of them and listened intently. He told them his tales of charitable works, of his running around collecting clothes, and then remembered the bar of chocolate. None of the ladies could wholly believe that this one boy chocolate-eating-machine could have done such a thing but were convinced by the seriousness of his face that it must be true.

Aila called to Roddy: 'Did you hear this. Young Alex gave his bar of chocolate to two of the men from that stranded ship, wasn't that a great thing to do?'

'Don't know why you did that?' Roddy retorted.

'What's got into you Roddy Cameron,' Iris said, 'don't you do praise anymore?'

'Well, I suppose it was a worthy thing to do, but why do it? I expect they are better provided for than they make out you know, and as to giving them clothes, well there's those that live around here that could do with them. Charity should begin at home.'

Aila aimed a ball of rolled up paper at him, 'Oh all right Roddy, don't go on, we don't need you giving us all a headache.' He caught the ball, threw it at Aila – missed – and hit Alex on the nose.

The resultant paper fight distracted everyone and Moira whispered to Aila, 'Well that shut him up.'

'Sure did,' Aila replied, and the pair set about rounding up Christmas presents, avoiding balls of paper as they did so until they were all running around dodging and throwing as they went. Iris collapsed into the chair just as Roddy scooped Fiona and Flora under his powerful arms and carried them into the hall. 'Put me down! Put me down!' they screamed, but all to no avail. Hugs, and kisses were passed from one to the other, much like the earlier presents had been, they put on their coats and left. Peace was restored and Alex settled himself in front of the TV, while Mum and Granny nattered in the background.

Iris smiled, 'I do so love these family Christmas days. It seems odd that we never had them as children. I wonder why the Church of Scotland didn't want us to celebrate Christmas at home?'

'God knows.' Moira replied and giggled: 'Oops. Maybe I shouldn't have said that. At least it all changed when I was eight. I still remember that day as clear as anything Mum. We were all so happy, our first fun Christmas. Just you and Dad, Roddy and me.'

'Yes, it was such a happy day.' Iris sighed. 'But we've got another new holiday tomorrow, so no work for you Moira. What are you going to do?

'You know what Mum, I haven't got a clue. Let's wait and see.'

Chapter 12

In the fell clutch of circumstance
I have not winced nor cried aloud,
Under the bludgeons of chance
My head is bloody but unbowed.

  Invictus
  William Ernest Henley

Moira was snuggled up in bed enjoying an unusual lie in when the
phone rang – who could it be, and why so early on Boxing Day?
Reluctantly she pulled on her dressing gown, trailing the tie belt behind
her, as she went down the stairs and plonked herself on the telephone
seat in the hall.

'It's only me,' Roddy said, 'I've had a report of an injured deer that
might need attention. I'll go out this morning and find it, does Alex
want to come with me?'

'What a silly question. Of course he wants to. I don't even have to
ask him!'

'Ok, I'll pick him up in an about an hour, it'll just about be getting
light then.'

'OK. Bye, see you later.'

There was no rousing to do, the call had woken Alex and the news
of a stalking trip had him up and ready in record time.

Over the years several pieces of country clothing had been passed to
Alex, who could now look wholly the part of a country gent when he
embarked on such missions. Thick moleskin trousers – turned up a bit at
the bottom and hoisted with a belt – looked fine underneath his thick
Harris Tweed jacket. No one would ever notice that the pockets, elbow
patches and cuffs did not absolutely match. In fact, it gave him an air of
maturity that implied a knowledge of the animals and plants of the

Highlands. His uncle had taken him out on the moors all his life and they worked together well. Neither was concerned if the wind blew too hard, nor the rain fell too heavy; they were completely capable of becoming totally immersed in tracking deer. A patient, silent work, requiring total concentration; one where time passed surreptitiously and all cares in the world could dissipate on the breeze. As Alex finished the last of his porridge, there was a toot of a car horn. He put on his cap, grabbed his old binoculars, and was out the door and in the car without a backward glance. Moira laughed at his eagerness, it was so good that he had her brother to be a role model, boys need a father figure, she thought, and smiling, waved them off.

It wasn't far to the Glenmore Estate, where Roddy lived and worked. They parked up, and set off along the banks of the lake, that reflected the light of the rising sun and twinkled in the stillness of the morning. The pair glanced left and right as they moved towards the spot, at the edge of the forest, where the deer was last sighted – eyes searching for any signs – binoculars at the ready. After the lake they cut across open land towards the east, where lying snow made looking for hoof prints easy. The wind was getting up and they bent forward. Roddy whispered, 'Our scent is being blown away from the herd, that's good.' Alex nodded his head, raised his binoculars and scanned around. He tapped his uncle on the shoulder and pointed towards an area of churned up ground. There had plainly been a good-sized herd here, and not long ago – the route the animals had taken was easy to follow. They proceeded with caution, each foot poised mid-air before being carefully placed on the ground, avoiding branches that might snap or undergrowth that might rustle. Roddy held his hand up and gestured to Alex to stop, then used his single index finger to wave him forward. They moved, inch by inch, until they came to a small ridge with a clearing beyond. They dropped down, crept along the ridge, and peered out over the edge. The pair focused their binoculars on the herd – a small group of eight hinds and their four calves – grazing away on grass revealed by the rays of the dawn sunlight. The group had separated from a larger herd, so Roddy and Alex moved carefully to the right, totally unaware that each crouching step was being closely monitored by the four curious eyes of a pair of crows in a tree close by. Alex gestured towards a deer that was limping, and Roddy nodded his head. The ageing hind was dragging her rear right leg that was badly damaged and infected. It was obvious that the animal would not last much longer. Roddy silently cocked his gun, looked through the sight and brought the hind down with a single shot to the head. Death was instant. Roddy's shooting skills had been honed over many years and he was confident that no suffering had been caused. The herd darted away, taking cover once again in the forest edges, and the two of them walked down the ridge to retrieve the deer that lay motionless on the ground.

They could talk now.

' It's always best to go for a head shot Alex. Done properly, it's as pain free as we can make it, and easier than a shot to the heart.' Alex nodded.

'That looked like an easy shot. Was it Uncle Roddy?'

'She was stood still, and her close proximity made it as easy as they get. But despite all my years as a gamekeeper, it's still a sad moment when confronted with death, even one as necessary as this.' They bent over and inspected the leg which was badly bitten.

'By the look of it she might have been struggling for a few days. Bloody dogs, why can't their owners control them? It makes my blood boil.' Roddy said to a tearful looking Alex.

'I bet it was that group that was in Ullapool on Christmas Eve Uncle Roddy, they didn't seem to be bothered about anyone other than themselves.' Roddy patted the hind,

'That's true Alex, they come here with no consideration of others, no concept of the damage they cause. Ignorant. That's what I call it. Come on let's get this deer up and home, give me a hand.'

Roddy was strong and used to carrying heavy loads, but he manoeuvred the beast to cause the least strain on his back, hoisted it onto his broad shoulders and adjusted it around his neck like a thick scarf with legs and head dangling down. Then they climbed back up the ridge and to the open land beyond, where Alex remained with the hind and lovingly stroked her head, whilst Roddy fetched the Land Rover. They swung the stiffening animal into the back of the vehicle, and set off back to Roddy's home on the estate.

Its location in the heart of the Glen with mountains rising at the rear and the river flowing in front was as perfect as any Highlander could wish for. The white building with its grey roof had been added to over the years and now sprouted an office and a sunroom at the front, and work rooms at the back. It was to here that they drove and took the animal to the preparation room. Being cold the carcass could be hung to tenderise, but first they must prepare the animal. The damaged leg was removed so as not to infect the rest of the carcass and as Roddy did this, Alex carefully took his hunter's knife and opened up the body to remove its innards, then wiped it out with salt water. He had done this before and needed no instruction from his uncle, and thus they were able to hang the animal, skin still on, from one of the hooks on the rafters. With most of the rear leg gone, this was not as simple as usual, but with the use of ropes they were able to leave the animal, head down, to tenderise. It would take a good few days for this ageing hind to be ready for butchery, but as little as possible would go to waste.

They left coats, hats, and boots in the adjacent boot room from where they could directly enter the warm kitchen and receive a cheerful welcome from Aila.

'I expect you're ready for a drink Alex,' Aila said as she cut a slice of gingerbread and handed it to him. 'How did it go this morning?' Alex nearly spat the crumbs from his mouth in his rush to answer.

'Oh, Auntie Aila, we found the deer, it was a hind that had been bitten by dogs. It made me a bit sad.'

' I expect it did,' Aila replied, stopping him before he could continue. 'Let's look in the back to see if there's space for all of this.' She opened up the lid of the huge freezer in the boot room. 'That's good, there's more room than I thought, and you'll be taking some home with you when its ready won't you?

'Oh yes please, ' Alex said, as he peered through to the hanging carcass and smiled.

Alex was now boiling hot and shed another layer before joining his cousins in the sitting room, where little sitting was actually going on. They were running around like dervishes, playing a game known only to them until all three collapsed on the chairs, totally out of breath, and laughing so much that, clutching their sides, they said, 'It hurts,' over and over again. Aila popped her head round the door to remind them that Herbie Rides Again was about to start on the TV. There would be time to watch some of it before lunch and this brought about an instant calm, and it became a sitting room once again.

There was never a suitable time to interrupt the viewing of one of their favourite films, so Aila used her firm hand and simply turned it off. The turkey soup, crusty bread and cheese stopped their protestations and indeed all backchat. Lunch was wolfed down, and the TV re-joined in the shortest of times. The kitchen was set to rights and Roddy went to his office to study the requirements of the next group that would be spending New Year at the big house. Probably southerners he thought, although the Americans were also frequent visitors, and their dollars and large tips were often more welcome than their loud voices that made stalking difficult. Meanwhile Aila sat in the kitchen, took out her knitting ready for a short spell of peaceful time all to herself.

Moira was similarly occupied, sat by a roaring fire, watching a film that she had missed at the cinema, and sang along as the characters declared themselves, hopelessly devoted to you and that they were the one that I want on these summer nights. Alex bounded in followed by his uncle, just as THE END appeared on the screen. The pair detailed their successful mission to an attentive Moira, who beamed with pride as Roddy commended Alex's stalking prowess. They both silently wondered if this could be his future.

'I'll be back for him in a few days,' Roddy said.

'Best ring first, he could be anywhere in the holidays.'

'Will do, we've got a big group in over New Year so I'll have to fit it in with them. Some of them might even want to watch. We'll see how it goes.'

Alex was halfway up the stairs, turned his head and mouthed a quick, 'Bye,' as Roddy departed.

***

The day at sea had been a somewhat different affair. A reasonable breakfast – the first for many weeks – preceded their fishing plans and the anglers had a distinct bounce in their normally leaden gait. The captain, true to his word, had found some nylon twine that might make lines, wire to be bent into hooks, and some old metal nuts that could be used as weights. Only six of the men thought these endeavours worthwhile. So, whilst two pairs of hands were bending wire into a variety of shapes and sizes, the rest tied lines to metal rods they had found earlier in the bowels of the ship. So engaged were the men in discussing the merits of hook sizes and shapes, ideal lengths of rods and line, that a good deal of the morning had passed in a flash and they were ready to try out their handiwork. Wrapped up like arctic explorers, the six ventured onto the deck with their bait box of bread and cast the longest lines over the side. The wind whipped the lines into the air and blew them back onto the deck, clipping the anglers heads with the inadequate weights. They tried again and a couple of lines stayed over. Two of the men clambered down the ladder to cast off closer to the water. Then they all waited, waited, and waited some more, but there was no sign of anything. The lines ravelled into a mangled mess of nylon and twine as they were pulled up with no fish in sight.

Lunch had reverted to gruel and dry bread, but it was hot and warmed them from the inside and revived their spirits. The original six – now swelled to ten men – resumed talk of rods, fishing and what to do. Each of them – according to their own references – were experts in the field of fishing and loudly declared the merits of their own suggestions. It was unanimous that flexible rods and floats were required, spools needed to be made, and that a boat nearer to the actual water would be advantageous. By some miracle there appeared to be consensus on who would do what and they split into pairs for a foraging mission. Jim and

Samuel were urged to see the captain – so that Jim could practice his English – they humorously declared, and they set off hesitantly to the officers' quarters.

The pair were unsure of the protocols for approaching the captain and hesitated at his door like two miscreant school boys.

"Hello what can I do for you two?" The captain asked.

'We are going fishing; can we boat have?' Jim replied. Ivan the captain smiled,

'And what sort of boat do you require?'

Samuel took over. 'We have tried to fish this morning, but we are too far above the sea. We need to be in a small boat, so that we can use short lines. Can we use the lifeboat please?'

The captain tapped the side of his face, peered at the two men who stood watching his facial muscles, their heads drawing closer to the captain as they anticipated his reply. 'Yes. Why not,' he said. 'We can use it as drill practice; something else to occupy you all.'

Jim and Samuel slapped each other on the back and went to shake the captain's hand as he looked at his watch. 'It's now past two o'clock and too late to start today,' he said. ' I'll inspect the fishing tackle in the morning and arrange for the lifeboat to be lowered then.'

The foraging group returned from their forays into hidden corners and cupboards, with their less-than-ideal materials, and received the boat news with jubilation. The abandoned kit was retrieved from the deck and work started in real earnest, ready for inspection after breakfast when it became light.

Chapter 13

Life is what happens to you while you're busy making other plans.
John Lennon

All manner of rods and lines, but little in the way of reels, were laid out in the bowels of the ship. They took the place of the thousands of fish that should be there – the irony was not lost on any of them. Grown men fishing for a single fish when they should be cutting and freezing thousands. The Ten, as they now called themselves, inspected their handiwork, nodded their heads at the ingenuity of some products, and looked away in embarrassment at the inadequacies of others. Compatriots stood around and made less than complementary remarks and laughed out loud – but The Ten took it in good humour. The captain managed to steer a path between praise for jobs well tried, whilst avoiding too much mirth at the obviously useless, but imaginative juxtapositions of twine, wood, and pipe that the group had laid out. Some efforts were generally agreed to be superior, and these were selected for use. The onlookers were allocated launching tasks by the captain, who handed a small tin to the fishermen saying,

'Something that might help.' They crowded round to look at the contents – small pieces of meat that he had retrieved from the galley. Nothing special, more gristle and fat than anything else, but he anticipated that it would prove to be a more effective bait than bread. The anglers, grateful for the protection afforded them by the ship, clung to the ladder as they descended into the lifeboat that bounced around on the swell. The sea spray cut into their skin and the salty taste filled their mouths. Spectators stood and watched from above, as others withdrew to the shelter of indoors – a bit of reading, more cards or lonesome depression.

The Ten cast off their lines. It got colder. They waited. Nothing. Smiles were replaced with frowns as their bodies shivered in the cold. But then, there was a shout. Then another. Two lines were pulled up, and there, dangling on the end were two fish – little bigger than sprats – it was a start. The men threw the lines back into the sea, using their catch as a much more adequate bait and spirits were lifted once more. But the cold permeated their cores, until they could tolerate it no more; their mission would have to be abandoned. Lines were pulled in by hands that could barely flex, yet two of the men detected tugs and pulled out a mackerel each. Not big, yet not too small – about ten good mouthfuls. Success! The fruits of their endeavours were rushed back to the galley and displayed with pride. The ensuing banter was, for the most part, good-humoured mocking, but The Ten didn't mind, their pride had been restored. They felt victorious. The captain inspected the catch, nodded his head in approval of their endeavours and couldn't have been more fulsome in his praise. The aroma of cooking fish soon wafted into their nostrils and The Ten ate their portions with relish, as others watched with regret.

Their elation didn't last long. During a miserable lunch, their jollity declined to the level of their crewmates, and all of them were back to the vivid reality of their imprisoned state. Discussion could neither elevate their spirits, nor devise plans to make their escape. None of The Ten had funds for flights, boats, or trains and gloom descended on them again. Others chatted in ones or twos, or disappeared to their quiet places. Christmas was over and their own version of normality had taken over. The captain broke the mood when he appeared at the mess door, and said, in a much less officious tone than usual,

'I would like to see each of you privately to discuss our situation. If you would prefer to come in pairs that's fine. It's entirely up to you.'

Being a methodical man, they were called in alphabetical order and Jim and Samuel agreed that they would go together when the first of their names was called. The pair sat around waiting, watching the faces of those who returned – they neither looked happier nor sadder – so nothing could be read there. By mid-afternoon it was their turn, and they approached the officers' mess with a degree of trepidation, knocked, entered and sat down in the two chairs waiting for them.

'Well Jim and Samuel, we all realise that we are in a bad position, and I don't know if any more funds will ever reach us. Promises are made and not kept. The money that arrived just before Christmas, frankly, came as a surprise. Is there any way that your families could fund your return home?'

'No, that isn't possible,' Samuel said, 'both of us were helping to support our families. We lost our livelihoods in Nigeria, that's why we are here. His face took on a look of abject misery, he swallowed hard and looked the captain in the eye. 'It seems that we are never meant to have money or a decent future.'

The captain nodded sympathetically, 'I am so sorry, I had presumed that was probably the case, and you are not alone. I am doing absolutely everything that I can to sort this out, but must warn you that it may take some time. You can rest assured that I will stay here until the last man has been repatriated, I will not desert you.'

'But what will we do without money, how will we eat or keep warm?' Samuel asked.

'I have kept some of the money back as an emergency fund,' the captain replied. 'So we will be able to eat, not well – but just about adequately – for a few more weeks yet, and I should have found help before then.'

'What are we to do, day after day after day?'

'I will keep rotas of works going so that physical activity can be maintained and I am trying to get some books, games, radios anything that can occupy you all. I know that isn't what you want, but for the time being it is possibly the best I can manage. To end, on a slightly brighter note, I have been given permission to go ashore whenever we need to collect provisions. So we will do more runs, for just a few bits at a time. This will give you a break from being at sea, allow you to walk around and have a change of scene. I must, however emphasise, that your behaviour on land must be excellent, if any of you cause trouble, then we will all be stopped from doing this, so you have been warned.'

'We wouldn't dream of causing trouble,' Samuel said indignantly. 'We are honest men and grateful for the help given by the people of this town. You can trust us captain.'

'I'm sure I can. Will you tell the others that I will see them later, as I have some duties to perform now?'

Jim sat expressionless as Samuel explained the position and said not a word. The pair looked mournfully at each other; they were numb with sorrow, unable to find words or actions to improve their lot. They had always wondered what hell would be like and they were rapidly finding out.

Elsewhere, ships were refuelling, taking on more water and sending tenders to collect stores – the harbour was reverting to its normal winter buzz. Sailors milled around, some chatted, a few wandered the streets, while others made minor purchases and locals wove their way around the visiting hoards. A group of Russians, swathed in layers of clothing, made their merry way up Quay Street from the inn; their good humour was infectious and passers-by grinned as they walked by. The group all but fell into the chandlers and greeted Angus like a long-standing friend. 'Dobroye utro' they shouted, slapping his back and thrust a list at him, then in broken English, one asked:

'Is it true the ship stranded?'

'Yes it is. It's a long and sad story I'm afraid.'

'Have food they got to eat?'

'Well they have some, but it's not sufficient,' reported a rather subdued Angus, who watched the group pull coins and notes from their pockets and place the cash on the counter.

'We help, what they need? Tins of meat, beans and flour. You know. Just use this money for them.'

'Oh, that's generous,' Angus said as he counted out the cash and collected everything together and placed them into a crate, marked up – The Harmony. The Russians left, much as they had arrived, clearly pleased with their actions – a show of solidarity between mariners. Language and race were no barrier to supportiveness when fellow seamen were in distress. Their parting words: 'We will tell others,' were nearly knocked from their mouths by Alex rushing in. A booming Russian voice advised him to be careful and Alex greeted them: 'Dobroye utro,' and they all laughed. Encouraged by their response, he continued with a couple more sentences in nearly fluent Russian, and was rewarded with a few coins, popped into his pocket, and several hearty slaps that all but winded him.

Alex was getting good at languages and could now manage a few words of greeting in about the same ten languages he had mastered in swearing – but the rewards were infinitely better for the former – and his latest haul was counted and safely put away. He had not been aware that his business acumen was being observed by his mum and Angus, who cheerily returned to their work and asked why he was there.

'Oh, I've come in for some shopping for Gran. She said the snow is too deep for her today.'

'Did she give you a list?'

'Yep, here it is.'

'Not much then, does she want it now or can I drop it round after work?'

'No rush,' she said. He dashed back to the door, 'I'm off to the duck pond, see you later.' Moira had long ago given up on telling him to wrap up and to keep his gloves on. He didn't seem to mind getting chilblains, in fact play had the apparent effect of removing all feeling from his extremities.

Moira and Angus sighed in relief at the sudden lull when the ship to shore radio crackled into life.

'Good morning this is Ivan Lyudmil, is that Angus?'

'Yes it is, good morning to you too. How can I help?'

'I have official business to sort out on land and will call in with a small order for collection on New Year's Eve. I am also looking for anything that the men could use to occupy their time. Not gifts you understand. Just loans of some games, or radios, even books. Anything to break their boredom. Is this an acceptable request?'

'Of course it is Ivan, I will ask around, I'm sure we can sort that out for them. Bye for now'

So it was that word was passed around the town by mouth, and ship to ship by radio. Residents pledged to do what they could, whilst sailors discussed the situation as they hung around at the pier. The grapevine wove itself through the communities on land and sea, it was much more efficient than the telephone. Cupboards were rummaged through, drawers were emptied and contributions taken to the shop. This was not a land of plenty, people could ill afford to give away much, they were canny, but they were equally understanding. By lunchtime two unused board games were placed in another Harmony crate and by mid-afternoon casual shoppers had added a little of this or indeed that to both crates. But more was needed to feed them into the new year.

Chapter 14

A random kindness can repair a wound that only tenderness can heal.

     Anon

The days between Christmas and New Year are strange. Neither work nor rest for many, normal for some and as busy as ever for others. Ullapool was no different. Children played out, enjoyed the snow that was now deep, but neither crisp nor even. Many stayed beside fires and televisions, some continued their winter crafts, while others were at work supporting communities on land and at sea. Turkeys had been eaten hot and cold, curried and stewed, and the last remnants made into soup. Fridges housed the odd slice of gammon wrapped in foil and bowls of leftovers lurked behind jars, where they could fester undisturbed until the New Year. In short, more food was required – to tide them over until Hogmanay when the serious partying could begin.

A steady trickle of customers came to purchase eggs, milk, a few tins or frozen items and some fresh bread. The grapevine had not yet reached some of them and they asked fellow customers about The Harmony crates that now stood where Christmas Specials had previously been stacked. Most then purchased an extra tin or packet, or popped their change in the tin marked up for the purpose. Others came marching in with their generosity held high and proud; ensuring that they would be recorded as benefactors for months to come. It was too cold for many of the elderly, who sent in neighbours or relatives for their few bits, but asked for their change to be added to – the fund.

Miss McKay arrived, just as they were about to close for a bite to eat, and deposited two large bags on the counter:

'For the men, they need to be occupied and these will help,' and off she went. Not like her at all, she generally liked a chat, but then Moira remembered that Miss McKay's brother was going to stay with her over Hogmanay and that she was probably in a rush. She liked to be organised, everything 'Ship shape,' though she never went to sea. Headmistress was written through her like a stick of rock, which is exactly how she carried herself – she wore her superiority like a starched ruffle that kept her head held high.

Angus and Moira sorted through her offerings. Some primary school readers carefully tied together with string and marked: For language improvement. A tin of paints and two large pads, along with a whole roll of lining paper, crayons and pens. Two How To Draw books, balls of string along with Macrame For Beginners – slightly dog-eared but still usable. The pair looked at each other and laughed; if Miss McKay had left the bags anonymously on the doorstep, they would have intuitively known who had left them there. They folded the bags ready to be collected in due course and their contents were placed in the appropriate crate – now labelled ACTIVITIES.

Moira didn't need to worry about Alex, her mother was on lunch duty this week. Iris liked seeing more of Alex in the holidays and loved his company and his cheeky humour. Their lunch would be spent with Granny doing a lot of chatting, and Alex either contributing nothing in the form of dialogue or taking over the proceedings with a monologue on whatever had taken his fancy today – one could never be fully sure which.

The last-minute ship to shore requests were sorted, ready to be picked up before Friday. Not as bustly as Christmas but still busy. The streets were now quiet, the wind was up, it was fairly unpleasant and Ivan's arrival was greeted with genuine pleasure and the proffered cup of coffee was gratefully received. His face became animated as the drink flowed through his body, then he noticed the crates labelled: THE HARMONY.

'Oh, what's this?'

'They're for you. There's been a good response for activities, but I expect we will get more. There's tins and packets as well. They've been given by other trawler men and from locals.'

'What?... It's all for us?'

'It most certainly is,' Angus replied.

'You've already been good to us. But this will mean so much to my men.' The captain's eyes watered, and his voice crackled with emotion. 'I would wish that it weren't necessary, but unfortunately it is.'

Angus gave him a reassuring tap on the knee,

'Don't worry yourself about it. People like to help, so please don't be embarrassed.'

'I know, but I'm meant to be in charge, in control, and some days it's all I can do to control myself. This was to be my last such trip, and for some it is their first. The situation isn't good for any of us, but especially for those who have no money in the bank nor relatives that can help.'

'Look, Ivan, we – that's the whole community – will help wherever we can. What's happening to you is awful and we want to help. We can't sort out all the bureaucracy, but some officials are trying to do that. We just want to show that we care. If you need anything in particular just let us know and we will do our damndest to get it.' The captain smiled,

'There is one thing. It seems trivial, but one of my men is trying to improve his English and I want to help him. Do you think anyone might have some old children's books they could spare?'

'Well blow me down, someone has just brought these in,' Angus said, as Moira passed the neatly tied bundle of books to Ivan whose face showed disbelief.

'There are some other bits for you as well, but you might like to take them all when you pick up your order. A sort of New Year treat – well hardly a treat – but you know what I mean.'

'I agree, that would be better, and it will give one of the men a valid job to do. I don't know how to thank you, I don't have the words, but this will never be forgotten,' Ivan said as he placed the bundle under his coat and left saying: 'I will collect our order on Friday morning, if that's all right.'

'That's fine, we look forward to seeing you.' And he was gone.

No more words were necessary, Ivan's sad look and his slight shake of the head said it all.

The captain walked wearily toward the harbour, the wind biting at any exposed skin, and it was all he could do to keep his eyes open as he untied the boat. He started the engine, and returned to his floating prison, where he would once again need to hide his own fears and cover them with a veneer of calm authority. There was no other way to stop them all slipping into even deeper despondency.

Many of the crew had seen the captain leave for shore and had been surprised to see two of their own with him and were confident that they would return with good news. But they were to be disappointed. The captain returned alone, unseen, in the gloomy darkening winter afternoon and braced himself for the evening briefing. The men gathered in the mess, all eyes facing their captain in anticipation of good news – bad news was more than any of them could bear.

'Good evening, you might have seen two of your crew mates leave with me this morning and now realise that they have not returned. Their families, after much effort, managed to fund their passages home and they are now travelling south by train, on their way to catch flights from London.'

Bedlam broke out, voices were raised in anger and sheer frustration. Men pushed and demanded:

'When are we going home?'

'What about us?'

'Why didn't the men tell us they were going, were they too ashamed to say goodbye?'

'We have been with them for weeks. They were friends, or so they made us think, yet they slunk off like thieves. How could they?'

The captain's raised hand and stern look quelled them. He explained: 'They didn't know what to say to any of you. It was too awkward for them, so they decided that this was the best way. They were probably right you know. What could they have said to make any one of us feel better about the situation we all find ourselves in? They will be thinking of you and offering their prayers for your speedy returns, so don't judge them too harshly. On a more positive note, I met with some officials from Immigration today, and this should move matters forward. In the meantime a few extra supplies will come aboard in two days. I will not desert you. Remember, we are all in this together.'

As he left, he signalled to Jim, 'Come with me, I have something to show you.' Jim followed with hesitant feet; his face creased into a look of concern.

'There's nothing wrong Jim, no need to look so worried,' the captain said as he indicated for him to sit on the chair in the corner. There was a pile of books on the adjacent desk and the captain handed the top one to Jim. Speaking slowly he explained that:

'Someone in the town has given us these books to teach you English. They are for children, but we must begin somewhere.'

'Thank you very much, you are very kind. Do the books have a name?'

'Yes, this one is called Play With Us. I will sit next to you and show you the words and we can practice pronunciation.'

Thus the captain of the Harmony, sat next to Jim, a twenty-eight-year-old Nigerian sailor and started to teach him – Peter is here. Here is Peter. I like Peter. I like Jane. Jim repeated the words and with some hand gestures, some smiles, and a good few giggles, they covered book 1a. Just a further thirty-five to go.

Jim had seen these books in Nigeria and had always wondered why there were never any pictures of people that looked like him. Now he understood, they had never been written for anyone like him. That didn't bother him now, he just wanted to learn, to improve himself, and he sat repeating and repeating the words until he could say them perfectly, then asked if there was paper and pen. The captain found an old pad and left Jim on his own studiously copying each word numerous times. Jim would have had to have been exceptionally naughty to have received so many lines from Miss McKay, and she would have applauded such endeavour.

'You mustn't do too much learning at once,' the captain said on his return. 'Take it steady, a little at a time. The books and paper will be available here all the time so that you, or any other of the crew, can use them. I will try and run daily classes, they will be short and at different times, depending on other ship commitments. Meanwhile, dinner is ready.' Samuel arrived just in time to help with the translation of all of this and the pair returned to their own mess, and another just adequate meal.

The next day passed like all the others. Groups of two and more continued to work out ways they could return to their homelands. However, for many this was not only financially impossible, but it would be considered a disgrace. Returning without money was not an option. They were fearful of being judged as failures. In their own eyes they saw themselves as such, so had no reason to believe that family and friends would see them any differently.

They had been told that they wouldn't be allowed to settle in Scotland or further afield in England; they didn't have the paperwork, the money, or the connections. Misery overwhelmed them, as it would time after time, until the situation was resolved. It was not a good day for any of them and the captain and engineer were feeling increasingly isolated and alone.

Chapter 15

If anything is worth doing, do it with all your heart.
    Buddha

Moira drove slowly through the soup of grey slush that splattered unwary pedestrians as she delivered shopping to the frail and elderly. Alex fidgeted beside her,

'Can't we go faster Mum?' Moira laughed at his earnest expression, 'You should know better than to ask that. Of course we can't, the roads aren't fit.'

The village disappeared into the rear-view mirror as the van followed in the snow plough's tracks towards Roddy's house. Alex cried out, and pointed to the right 'What's that mum ... at the side of the track?' She slowed down to a near standstill and followed his gaze into the distance.

'It's a Ptarmigan! Well spotted Alex. It's difficult to see in its winter-white plumage.' He peered through the windscreen,

'It's amazing, I've only ever seen one in its summer brown.' The bird, disturbed by their presence turned and raced away to the forest edges from whence it had come. But they weren't the only ones to see this sudden movement of a bird that should be on higher ground; a Golden Eagle circled above, whistling a high pitched kee-kee-kee after the prey they had just scared away. They could almost feel the bird's frustration as he swooped over them and then soared up and away, higher and higher until it became a mere dot in the sky.

Alex dashed into the house babbling away, telling them all about the scene they had just witnessed, and then he calmed down, bid his mother a quick goodbye, and was off with his uncle to the preparation room.

'Don't go rushing ahead young Alex,' Roddy said. 'Some of the guests at the big house want to watch this, so I'll have to fetch them, it won't take long, but just you wait.'

'But I can still skin it?' Alex asked in a panicky voice.

'Of course, you can. You show those Yanks what you can do.'

'Oh, I will ... but they won't laugh at me will they?' Alex said with a seriously anxious expression.

'Of course they won't. Don't be silly. It's not your first time. But it will be for them. You'll do us both proud, I'm sure. What are you planning on doing with the hide?'

'Oh, I'm not sure yet, I've not thought about it. Oh, do hurry up Uncle Roddy, I want to get started.' Alex said, jumping up and down.

'I won't be long. You get kitted up,' his uncle answered, and was gone.

The four hefty Americans arrived like extras from a vigilante movie, and looked shocked at the overalls Roddy handed to them. 'Gee, we gotta wear these?' asked one in a southern drawl as they twisted and contorted their bodies into the snugly fitted garments.

'I'm afraid so,' Roddy explained, 'Health and Safety. It's only one deer, but it's going to be eaten after all.'

'Guess so, can't be too careful when it comes to chow,' said another, patting his corpulent belly as the overstretched overall pinged open, much to everyone's amusement.

Roddy took them through the process to be carried out and introduced them to Alex, who appeared through the door, skinning knife in hand, as if he were the leading man in a Shakespearean play. The deer's head had already been removed and Alex carefully made incisions around the three whole limbs: just above their knees. Then it was straight down the body: a careful line down the sternum from neck to groin. The men made appreciative comment, and commended him on his skill. They discussed the procedure as he removed the hide carefully from underlying tissue. Some parts separated easily; others needed careful use of the knife. He remembered everything that he had been told, and occasionally closed his eyes, to better see what his uncle had done in the past. In some places the hide was not keen to part company from the body and so he sensibly asked for advice, which he followed to the letter. A round of applause marked the final decoupling as Alex proudly held his hands high and showed them his work. One perfect hide – neither tear nor hole – and the audience, as one, gave him a round of applause. Alex beamed with obvious pride and gave a hint of a bow. Roddy brought the curtain down on the performance with a, 'Can I have some help here maestro?' The pair removed the naked carcass from the hooks and laid it on the bench, ready for later.

Aila appeared with steaming mugs of coffee and handed over a bottle of whisky,

'You can add a wee dram,' she told them, which indeed they did, not concentrating too much on the 'wee' part either. The libations warmed the group, who watched the next stage with Alex like he was one of their own.

Roddy sharpened his butcher's knife and the whole became two, then four, then eight and so on until each part was bagged and labelled, a relatively quick process when carried out by practised hands with sharp tools.

'Well gee, that was pretty impressive,' nodded the one called Chuck as they all gave more applause. 'We aren't from hunting backgrounds,' Chuck explained. 'To be honest, I'd never given this whole process much thought.'

'Nor me said another,' I didn't know that one injured animal could provide so much meat.'

'Well, gentleman, I've got a nice surprise for you,' Roddy said as he handed two bags over to Chuck.

'You'll be able to enjoy the best of this beast – the tenderloin and rump are on the menu for tonight.' Their delight was obvious as they departed in the Land Rover which whisked them back to the big house for lunch.

Alex was still on a hide high when he joined his cousins, aunt and uncle for piping hot soup, bread, and cheese. He recounted, in tiny detail, each cut of the knife until his cousins could stand it no more and urged him to:

'Put a sock in it Alex, we've heard enough.' This didn't deflate him, and he was just about to start on a more poetic prose of his skills, when even his aunt declared:

'ENOUGH,' and he finally got the message.

Roddy gave Alex a playful punch, tousled his hair and said, 'I'm going to take the Americans for a tour of the estate now. I've left some bits for you in the prep room, don't forget to take them home,' and he was off.

The children spent a happy afternoon in the snow, until they were so covered that they nearly became invisible in the dimming light, and were called in before they became too cold. The sound of the van alerted them to Moira, who had just drawn up outside. Alex dashed to the prep room picked up the large bag that had been left for him and yelled: 'Bye,' to the kitchen and ran outside to join his mum, who tooted her own farewell from the comfort of the vehicle, and they made their way home.

With a fresh audience, Alex started on again about his skills, until even his own mother grimaced at the detail and playfully punched his shoulder,

'I'm beginning to wish you'd never even seen that deer,' she said, then gave him a motherly smile and he started all over again.

Alex unfurled the hide and displayed it for his mum – as if it were a fine fishing net after careful repair. 'Well you did a good job there,' she said, and gave him a hug that he accepted willingly – such was his ecstatic state.

'Can we start the curing mum?' Moira gave him a raised eyebrow look,

'Just wait a minute, we've got to empty the bags first. Goodness, there's a lot in here and look there's a note.'

What does it say mum?'

'For my favourite hunting partner and my sister' Moira read. 'Isn't that lovely Alex? What a good man Roddy is. Let's get some of this meat in the pot and the rest in the freezer, then you can start.'

The large Formica kitchen table was finally clear, and the hide could be salted. Fortunately, Roddy had jet washed the flesh side, so much of the debris had been removed and this made rubbing salt into every nook and cranny much easier. When the entire pelt had been covered, Alex carefully folded it into half, placing salted sides together, rolled it up and stood it – to drain away moisture – in the bucket waiting under the rear porch. The process would be repeated daily, but for now Moira was pleased to tidy up the mess and get her kitchen back.

Chapter 16

Ring out the old, ring in the new,
Ring, happy bells, across the snow.
The year's going, let him go.
Ring out the false, ring in the true
        In Memorium (Ring out wild bells)
        Alfred Lord Tennyson

New Year's Eve – Hogmanay was here and anticipation spread through the air. Excited children whirled around the streets like dervishes, the sound of their voices elevated to deafening. Mothers scurried around their houses completing chores and even the dogs caught the mood and wagged their tails more. Small boats moved around the pier like ducks on a pond, jostling for moorings so that they could offload men or load up produce. Others prepared to go fishing – not for herring and mackerel, but crabs, prawns and lobster, to be caught in baited creels. These were the prizes for the local men; this was their area of expertise, and their highly prized catches would be easily sold. There would be no fishing in the morning; there was too much celebrating to do tonight.

Tills in the shops rang out the old, as crew from the large trawlers and factory ships emptied shelves of souvenirs and day-to-day items scarce in their homelands – whether Russia, Poland, Bulgaria or west Africa. Many would be leaving in the next few days. Some would stay, hoping to scoop up the last of the departing mackerel; shopping was not urgent for them. They relished time on shore, a break from routine, something to lift their spirits at the end of 1987.

In Angus's store, the staff were assembling orders both large and small, and had no time for resting on laurels, or sitting on chairs. It was a short day, but a busy one. Alex had been enlisted to help with deliveries and ran around town, dropping off deliveries, ducking and diving through the groups of hefty mariners meeting up with their compatriots from other ships. His face glowed red with his efforts and he let out an audible sigh as he reached the store. The place was so crowded that he could barely squeeze through the door. Men were sitting on the floor waiting for their produce; others perched on the empty lower shelves or leant against patches of bare wall. The air smelt of stale tobacco and the odour of hard physical work; the noise was ear-splitting as everyone spoke at once.

Angus, calm as ever, took it all in his stride. He guided men to their purchases stacked up in the corner, or in the overspill area outside. He answered the phone, took payments, and still found time for a few words with everyone. Moira scurried around on sensibly shod feet, gathering together orders, and continually twisting her skirt back into place as it went on a mission round her thighs. After stretching to reach the highest shelves she exhaled loudly then rubbed the small of her back, all the time looking longingly at the stool in the corner.

The arrival of Captain Lyudmil and four of his crew, Samuel, Jim, Ade, and Yomi, went unnoticed; the captain's usually booming voice was lost in the hubbub.

'Why don't you go for a wander,' he said to the men, 'this could take ages. Come back here in half an hour.'

The throng of customers gradually dispersed, but so did much of the stock, and Captain Lyudmil bit his bottom lip as he glanced around at the depleted shelves. He looked relieved when Angus ushered him into the office and pointed out the goods he'd ordered stacked outside.

'This shouldn't take long, Ivan,' Angus said, and handed over the paperwork to the captain, who carefully counted out the payment from the Harmony's dwindling reserves.

On cue, two of the crew, Ade and Yomi returned and gathered up the piles of groceries. Next through the door was Samuel, crying with laughter at Jim, who stumbled in behind him like an Egyptian mummy – his long woollen scarf had coiled itself bandage-like, around his face. Samuel's hilarity was infectious, and they all began giggling. The sound drew Angus and Alex from the office and they all watched as Jim, eyes twinkling with mirth, escaped from the scarf and hung it loosely round his neck. He was a tall man and he stood erect as he looked at Alex and – enunciating each syllable – said:

'Hello, Alex, how, are, you?' In response, Alex pointed at each in turn and said,

'Oh, hello, you're Jim ...and... you're... Samuel aren't you?'

'Yes, that's right,' nodded Samuel, 'You remembered our names; we won't forget yours.'

'So – famous are you now Alex?' grinned Angus.

'He gave us a bar of chocolate for Christmas,' Samuel said, 'one he probably wanted to eat himself. It was a thoughtful gesture.'

Angus nodded his head and gave Alex an appraising look, 'Well done, Alex, that was a kind thing to do, I bet your mum is proud of you.'

Alex shrugged his shoulders, 'Maybe,' he said, and turned away. Angus directed the men's attention to the crates saying:

We've got some more donations for you in here, gifts from the community. There are some tins, and a few bits and pieces to help you all pass the time.'

Jim and Samuel tentatively looked at the contents, some of which caused smiles, others quizzical looks. Alex reached in and took hold of a game of Connect Four, held it briefly to his chest and looked around – oh, I've always wanted this game, he thought, then solemnly placed it back in the crate – just as Moira returned from the cellar, and gave him an understanding nod. Alex touched his mother's arm and she hastily smoothed down her wayward skirt as he said.

'Mum, these are my new friends. This is Samuel.'

'I'm pleased to meet you, Alex's mum. You have a polite son,' Samuel replied. Alex then introduced Jim, who looked down from his six-feet, two-inch height, to the upward turned face of five-feet, two-inch Moira, and held out his hand. Moira blushed as his eyes connected with hers.

'Hello, Jim,' she said, 'pleased to meet you.'

Without losing focus he replied, 'I am pleased to meet you too.' Moira turned away, and with a face glowing bright pink, passed the receipted paperwork to the captain, then stepped away.

The crates were hoisted on to Samuel and Jim's shoulders and they left with Happy New Year ringing in everyone's ears. At the door, Jim turned and put his hand in his pocket, then reached out, and placed something in Alex's hand.

'Happy New Year, this is for you,' he said and then they were gone.

Alex unfurled his fingers and there cupped in his hand, was one Quality Street – the red one, his absolute favourite. He yelled out, 'Look what I've got Jim gave me a sweet.'

They were all surprised at the gesture. Jim had virtually nothing, yet had given his only sweet away. They were not to know that it had been carefully kept, for this moment, and had been taken from its little hideaway in Jim's drawer just this morning, ready for such a meeting. The giver had carried that sweet as if it were a jewel, and was delighted to say his thanks in the best way he could. The small item had now been replaced with a crate of games – a strange swap – but another generous gesture from the people of this village.

What Jim had not expected were his confused feelings. His gloominess had been overturned by one glance from a woman he had never met before. She had looked at him with eyes as blue as the sunlit sea, a flush of pink on her cheeks, and her blonde hair tousled around her lovely face, and he didn't even know her name – just that she was Alex's mother. You're being stupid, he told himself, been away from a woman for too long. A dialogue between his rational and emotional voices that carried on his head all the way back to the ship. So intense was this discussion that he had no words to say. Samuel asked why his friend was so quiet, but received no answer.

It would have astounded Jim to know that a similar discussion was going on in Moira's head; except hers was coming down distinctly on the side of: Don't be ridiculous. But something had changed. Her mind carried the image of a face looking down at her, shiny like mahogany with brown eyes that glistened under long curling lashes and a smile that revealed the whitest, straightest teeth she had ever seen. 'I am pleased to meet you too,' she whispered under her breath. Angus asked what she had said.

'Oh, nothing, just thinking out loud,' Moira answered.

Together they closed up the shop and returned to their homes.

Everyone was to celebrate that night. Land-based or sea-based, surrounded by friends or isolated with near strangers – they would all make the most of the cold clear, moonless night, to say goodbye to one year, and hello to the new.

On the Harmony, once the provisions were unloaded, cook went speedily into action. The captain and engineer would join the men – it would be crowded – but this was no time for divisions of rank. The ageing Christmas tree was now adorned with bottle tops on strings tied to branch ends, and someone had fashioned a more angelic angel out of a cereal box for the top. It caused a great deal of mirth to see Cornflakes written across her wings, and her crowning glory was the cockscomb that appeared to balance, halo-like, on top of her splendidly drawn face. It was now a tree for all occasions but, like the ship, was unlikely to last another season. The crew sorted through the activities box, studying instructions on games that were alien and expressing pleasure at seeing favourites they played at home. Some relished the paints and paper which were included, others preferred handicrafts;

some could not stir themselves to even look.

They all squashed together appreciating the best meal since Christmas. Although Mr Kipling had not contributed to these festivities, there were large bowls of jelly and sufficient shortbread to give them all two biscuits each – these were a generous gift from Mrs McTavish. The crew were unaware that her husband had persuaded the local landowners to chip in for two bottles of whisky – this would be a surprise for later.

In Ullapool, families finished meals, wrapped themselves up, and wended their way to the ceilidh. Moira and Iris locked arms with Alex and tried to swing him in the air, but could barely lift his feet off the ground.

'Think you've grown a bit since last year!' Iris said, as they joined up with others, all on the march to the village hall.

'It's a shame Roddy can't join us,' Moira sighed.

'Still they'll all have a good time at the big house,' Iris nodded, 'and I bet their festivities will last longer than four hours!' They all laughed. They wouldn't miss this night for the world.

Alex joined the pipe band on the stage, and played his chanter. The lilting tunes washed over the crowd as they watched, or listened as they made their way to the bar, returning with rounds of drinks. There was no sign of the alleged Scottish meanness tonight. Next it was time for the bagpipes – instruments that pleased and disturbed in equal measure. Like every year it was a night of singing, drinking, music and dancing – a totally traditional Hogmanay.

As midnight approached, the men on the Harmony wrapped themselves in all the outfits they could find, clutched tots of whisky, mugs of hot drinks, and assembled on the deck to greet the New Year. They shivered. The salt-laden spray of the sea left their faces as cold as the night air as they lined up on the deck and looked out to the shore. The steaming drinks gradually thawed cold hearts, and eventually most could greet the freezing weather with a smile.

Much the same was happening on land. With coats on and glasses in hand, every man, woman and child made their way to the pier and looked out to sea. As the clock struck twelve, the loch lit up. The vessels moored as far as the eye could see turned on their lights – white, red, green and blue. Some twinkled, some blazed, but the night sky was illuminated, and the sea shimmered in the reflected light. Every ship's horn, hooter and bell joined in and greeted the bagpipes playing from

---

* Recorder like instrument used by beginners learning to play the bagpipes.

land. Shouts and cheers resonated as village folk hugged and linked arms for Auld Lang Syne. The old words and actions were more successfully rendered on land than on the Harmony, where arms got tangled and lyrics were unknown.

1988 had arrived, and for most it would be little different from its predecessors but for others who knew what lay ahead? All their destinies were in the hands of strangers.

Jim remained on deck as the others drifted back inside. He rested his arms on the rail and looked out into the distance; lights on ships going out one by one and barely any were visible on land. The night was now black. There was no moon, but a green light rose above the invisible horizon. It flickered and grew, gliding across the sky, turning it blue, then purple, then all three colours together, wafting from left to right and up and down in a perpetual motion of shimmering colour. Another stunning Scottish sky became imprinted on his mind, around the face he could not forget. Slowly, he made his way below.

Moira and her neighbours directed their steps homewards and, just like Jim, stopped to watch the sky perform its psychedelic dance. The sky stayed lit for so long, that they were illuminated right back to their front doors.

They had barely taken off their coats when there was a knock – John, their first footer* stood at the door. He crossed their threshold, handed them a lump of coal, a tot of whisky and shortbread, then wished them a happy New Year and departed, to complete his seasonal task around the close.

Sleep wouldn't come to Moira. Like someone else, she had pictures of different colours washing through her mind but, in the centre, was the face of the most stunning man she had ever seen.

The first person to enter a Scottish house on New Year's Day – a bringer of good fortune for the coming year.

Chapter 17

Only a night from old to new;
Only a sleep from night to morn.
The new is but the old come true;
Each sunrise sees a new year born.
    'New Year's Morning'
    Helen Hunt Jackson

There were sore heads aplenty on land and a fair few at sea. Some expressed regret at the overdoing of things, whilst others considered it the price to be paid for a good night and a fitting end to the old and welcoming of the new. Moira and Alex's day would, like all previous 1st Januarys, be spent on the Glenmore estate.

Moira set off in her trusty old Ford Fiesta that slid around on the glass-like-surface of the roads, but with no overnight snow, she was able to access the estate with relative ease. Total silence met them as they wended their way along the track, only the engine disturbed the tranquillity, so Moira stopped the car and turned it off. The pair sat motionless and listened, and watched. Nothing – absolute quiet – no movement anywhere; the moment apparently suspended for all living creatures. Just Moira and Alex, alone and at peace, at the beginning of a New Year. The cold began to permeate the car and they gave each other a knowing look, it was time to move on and the moment was gone.

They soon reached the house and, with perfect timing, Aila pulled open the front door and the pair dashed in. Moira and Alex shuddered as the roaring fire in the lounge enveloped them with warmth and removed all vestige of chill from their bones. The smell of pine emanated from the flames as the logs crackled behind the fire guard, and the room took on the sharp and sweet scent of the burning resin.

The sun soon emerged from its blanket of clouds and illuminated the winter wonderland outside – much too good an attraction to keep children cosily indoors. They were dressed and out in a flash, leaving the two women to chat as they prepared the meal. The two had gotten on well from the first day Roddy had brought Aila home. She was a good fit for him and the family; kinsfolk even before they were married, and now close like sisters. They didn't look like sisters though. Aila was tall and willowy with long dark hair that framed her serious face and was usually tied back in a low ponytail. They were complete opposites. But when Aila smiled she could bring a glow to the coldest of places.

The children, with only three years between them, played and argued like siblings. The girls couldn't help ganging up on their cousin, who was better able to retaliate with strength than words. This could result in tears all round. The boy who could talk adults into submission was left voiceless when confronted with a few taunts from two young girls. The adults couldn't help but laugh at this, but fortunately today was harmonious, and they could be seen playing happily outside.

Aila was regaled with all the details of the Ceilidh – who had behaved, who had not. Moira listened to details of the festivities at the big house – the visitors had celebrated to the maximum and had brought the New Year in outdoors. From their elevated position they had been able to see the ships' lights in the distance, hear the cacophony of the ships' horns and bells and then witnessed the most spectacular northern lights seen for many years. So good that the Americans had returned to the house for more celebratory drinks and retired to bed incredibly happy. They were unlikely to see much of the morning. Fortunately, Roddy had been able to leave just after midnight, not long behind his wife and daughters who were fast asleep on his return.

A buffet lunch of leftovers from the big house was laid out in the kitchen, so that within a moment of Roddy's return with Iris, they were all sat down and tucking in. Alex, now less constrained by chatty girls, started on yet another of his monologues, describing how his now called, friends, had returned to the shop, and remembered his name.

'Well you are difficult to forget,' Aila said.

'And the one called Jim gave me a sweet, a red one, my favourite, I wonder how he found out. I like him, he's got a kind face.'

'Steady on there, young Alex,' Roddy said, 'you can't always tell a book by its cover you know.'

'What's books got to do with it?' Alex asked quizzically.

'It means you can't tell the inside of something by looking at the outside silly. Some lovely wrapping paper hides rubbish presents, and sometimes old boxes contain delights. We've being doing this at school dumbo,' added Fiona – a year his junior but in her mind infinitely superior.

Alex looked deflated but wasn't going to let bossy Fiona have the last word.

'Well I KNOW he's good on the inside. He gave me a sweet, didn't he? You like him don't you Mum?' Moira glanced downwards, as a flush of pink enveloped her cheeks.

'I don't know him Alex, you've known him longer than me, but I would agree he does have a kind face.'

'What's his name?' asked Flora.

'Jim,' Alex replied.

'Huh!' Roddy snorted. 'If he is from West Africa he'd have some unpronounceable name like a jumbled-up alphabet, not a simple one like Jim. Probably stole the sweet as well.'

'Roddy Cameron, wash your mouth out with soap and water. I'll not have you defaming people like that, especially to children!' was his mother's retort.

'Oh … OK, but there's something not right there, just you wait and see.' And off he went to lay some more logs on the fire.

The conversation appeared to be forgotten, but not by Moira. She had heard her brother's words and understood his caution. But her instincts told her that he was wrong. These were good men caught in appalling circumstances and she found herself strangely defensive of them all – but especially Jim – as she retrieved his image from her mental memory box.

With kisses and hugs all round, three generations made their way home before total blackness settled for the night. Alex followed his usual routine of Meccano, eating and TV while Moira pottered about before settling herself with volume sixteen of Encyclopaedia Britannica. She had bought these many years ago from a local jumble sale hoping that they would be of help for Alex's schoolwork, but he had made little use of them until recently. Over the years she had dipped into them, and now with MUSHR to OZON on her lap, she searched through to find Nigeria in its midst. She intended to know more about this country of which she currently had zero knowledge.

The cause of this curiosity was meanwhile alone in the officers' mess, which had become the school room, library, and quiet place of the ship. Not available all hours – the Captain liked to have his own time there – but it was being put to good use. The more raucous pursuits could be carried out in the crew mess.

Jim had spent some time each day with Samuel, the Captain, or both and was proving to be an able student. He was already on book six: 'I Like To Write,' and was assiduously practising both the words and the deed. He reflected on the lost years of learning brought about by his father's early demise. There had been no money for school and in such circumstances even seven-year-olds had to contribute food and money to the family. He had caught fish with a line, run errands for neighbours and helped with household chores. Book learning had little relevance as he grew into manhood.

His studies now had added impetus, and words learned all those years ago were remembered – useful building blocks for a pupil determined to succeed. Others might mock his schoolboy sentences, but they didn't know how important it was to him . They did not have access to the recesses of his mind, where a face that had no name rested, and was only visible to his closed eyes.

Chapter 18

For my part I know nothing with any certainty,
but the sight of the stars make me dream.
    Vincent Van Gogh

The long dark nights and pitifully short days of January pass slowly in the Highlands, with little discernible difference between one day and the next. Only the wind, rain, snow or dry weather to comment on, and occasionally the sight of the sun. The village busied itself with normalities, trying to condense a day's worth of work into the six hours of daylight; not possible for all, and certainly not for the businesses that provided goods for the ships. Some trawlers left at the beginning of the month, but others would be there for a few weeks, and they needed food, oil, and water. Men took opportunities to shop and even grab a short break in a local hostelry. Pupils returned to school, sad to lose their days of play, but pleased to see classmates and settle into routines they did not even know they needed.

Immigration and maritime officials from Inverness visited the Harmony and discussed the situation with local agents. Rumours circulated that some of the crew were to be repatriated, but not how many, or whom, or exactly when. The villagers cared what happened to the stranded men, but in a remote unemotional way – they were strangers in need, a transient charity case that would eventually be gone – only to be replaced by other concerns which would tug at their hearts and open their wallets and purses. But, in the meantime, they would do what they could, and some would do much more than others.

Amidst all the darkness of those days there was meaningful activity too. Handicrafts were started and plans were made ready for the bicentenary year of the village. The British Fishing Society had planned the new port all those years ago, and it now lay at the junction of croft land and loch, as if it had been there for ever. The white and grey buildings were reduced to model village proportions by the towering mountains that hinted at the land beyond. All of this was to be captured in a commemorative quilted wall hanging to be made by the women, who discussed details as if their futures rested on their choices. Squares of fabric became the focus of intense work and friendly rivalry brought the women together. The men kept their plans closer to their chests, as if releasing details would, in some way, diminish their efforts.

The men on The Harmony had no activities – meaningful or otherwise. The captain tried to keep them occupied, but uncertainty was a cruel task master and drained their spirits of enthusiasm and replaced it with nervous anger that couldn't help bubbling over. Pushing and shouting was the least of it, and physical altercations were becoming more frequent. A visit from officialdom came at just the right time – they had to behave if they were to get out of this horror.

One-by-one over the whole of Wednesday they were interviewed by two officials from immigration with an interpreter in attendance. Notes were taken, financial statements made, contact numbers and addresses in their home countries recorded. Most of them were given little information, just informed that they would hear from them later. No date, just a waiting game.

For some there was better news, a businessman had stepped in to resolve the situation for his Igbo kinsfolk and they would be flying home, with tickets paid for by him. There were few words that could describe their jubilation, but they couldn't rub their happiness into the wretchedness that already traumatised their less fortunate friends. And so, they kept their voices low until they burst onto the deck, where they hugged, danced and shouted for joy.

'We are going home, we are going home,' they said over and over again. Their good news couldn't be kept from the others for long, and when it reached them, they made a pretence of goodwill and expressed feigned delight at their good fortune. But it was almost impossible for them to disguise their true feelings – their overwhelming bitterness at being left behind. Never had the highs and lows of man been so visible. Whilst the lucky packed bags, the remaining Yoruba* men sought their own refuges where they sank further into the despondency that coursed through their veins. Jim went to his books, to fill his mind with words, to push forward, but it was difficult. A Day in the Sun had many appeals but not when it was only on paper and had to be shared with two tiresome children.

* Igbo and Yoruba are two of the four main ethnic groups in Nigeria.

The departing men were up early the next day, their packed bags ready to be loaded onto the launch. But all the crew was surprised to hear that the ship would be moved into port, so that they could take on some water, and pick up a few items – the authorities would inspect the ship from top to bottom when they were all on land. As they pulled up alongside the jetty, the ecstatic ten were down the gangplank as speedily as Olympic athletes and jumped onto the waiting minibus. There were some hugs, a little backslapping but there were few words. What could they say?

'Goodbye and good luck,' was about the limit of either side. Hands waved and smiling faces beamed at depressed ones, as the bus drove along Shore Street and disappeared away to the left, on its way to Inverness.

'Those Igbo* living up to their name,' snapped Yomi, one of the remaining men at no one in particular. Jim touched his shoulder as if to calm him,

'They were our friends yesterday, don't make enemies of them because they had good news.'

Yomi turned towards Jim, his face set like stone.

'That's as maybe...' his face loosened... 'we all know Igbo is slang for I go before others. Seems like it's been taken as a truth.' Jim took Yomi's arm and led him towards the others who stood dejected, unsure of where to go and what to do.

Surrounded by cold and snow when all they could think about was the climate, tastes and smells and colours of home, the men stood as statues, barely able to find the motivation to move a foot, a leg, or an arm. Gradually two, then four moved away and these smaller groups dispersed; they had a whole day to fill and would attempt to make the most of it.

Jim was happy to accede to the captain's request to collect the order from the store, in fact he nearly whooped with joy. With Samuel by his side they managed to amuse themselves by pretending that they were Peter and Jane having Fun at the Farm, and deciding whether they liked Mummy better than Daddy. Anyone listening in would have guessed that they had learning difficulties, but would nevertheless have laughed out loud at their childish gestures and mannerisms. So carried away were they, that they appeared at the shop door laughing raucously, and Moira grinned at their laughter, and wondered how they could find humour at this difficult time.

'Have.... you.....come.....for.....the.....supplies?' she enunciated.

'Yes, we have,' Jim replied, his voice soft like velvet. This took her aback, she had expected him to have a resonant voice that matched his size, and the surprise made her blush again.

'I've got them ready for you, do you want to take them now or fetch them later? I think that your ship will be in the harbour for some time, so you would have time to walk around town, stretch your legs.'

'Can we take them now please? The Captain will pay for them later.' Samuel answered.

'Of course. How are you going to fill your day?'

'We will wander around. It is just good to be off the ship.'

Moira's innate kindness came to the fore as she asked:

'And for lunch?'

'We will eat tonight on the ship.'

'That's too long to wait. Come and have some lunch with me, I'll be pleased to have the company.'

'Are you sure?'

'Absolutely sure, come straight back here and I will be waiting for you.'

Much of this conversation was above Jim's current language skills, but he had understood that this was not only a beautiful lady, but a good-hearted one too, and he suspected that he had better move on from Peter and Jane with great rapidity.

The order was gathered together, a few more tins were added from the Harmony crate, and were hoisted onto shoulders, or tucked under arms and back to the ship they went, with Jim pestering Samuel all the way for a word-by-word account of the conversation that had just taken place.

There were several official-looking people on the deck who asked who they were, and, on explanation, they were allowed to deposit their loads in the galley and then had to leave. The captain was just returning to the vessel and saw Jim and Samuel walking along the pier with a surprising spring in their step and they regaled him with the details of their invitation to lunch. This met with his approval and a certain knowing little smile. The look that had passed between Jim and Moira on New Year's Eve had not passed him by.

Moira was serving Miss Mackay, when they returned and introduced her to the two seamen, who responded with a polite:

'Hello, pleased to meet you.'

She peered up at them from above her glasses, her face devoid of emotion and her voice crisp with authority.

'I'm well thank you,' was her less than fulsome reply as she placed butter and cheese in her basket and promptly left.

Moira grimaced at the departing back and turned to the men, 'Sorry about that, she can be a little curt sometimes.' The men did not show any concern and Jim asked,

'What is this …. curt?' She laughed,

'Brief … too brief … rudely so.' His expression spoke volumes, it was clear that he still had no inkling what curt meant, and Samuel came to his rescue with an explanation in Yoruba.

'Ah, I understand. She busy, no time to talk.' Moira nodded, smiled and grabbed her coat.

The walk to Moira's house was short and there was little in the way of conversation. It was all slightly awkward with no one knowing exactly what to say, or indeed in Jim's case – knowing exactly what to say – but with insufficient vocabulary to actually say it.

Once inside the house, Moira took full charge, instructed them where to leave coats and boots, showed them where the toilet was and busied herself heating up a giant pot of soup made from scraps of venison and loads of vegetables. Angus had given them a large loaf and she had cheese, so they wouldn't go hungry. The soup lubricated their voices, and conversation became easier, with simple chat of the village and its generosity – nothing personal – this was not the time. The men asked about the weather, the long dark nights and were cheered to know that it did get better. Samuel said,

'It's good that the weather will get better, but we want to be going home before then.'

There was so much Moira wanted to know, particularly about Jim and his life, but it would wait, there would be other opportunities of that she was sure. Surreptitious glances gave her an opportunity to better study him, only to find herself on the receiving end of similar looks and so they both averted their eyes, as if caught in a terrible crime.

None of this escaped Samuel who could only see heartbreak ahead for them both. Their lives should not have touched, it was an aberration, an accident of time and place, or was he little envious? Of that he could not be totally sure.

The men sat relaxed in the kitchen, enjoying the moment, the comfort of full stomachs, the first total relaxation in months, but they could not stay long. Their gratitude was heartfelt and unfashionably polite.

At the door Samuel offered Moira his hand and for one embarrassing moment she thought that he might kiss hers rather than shake it, and the very notion crinkled her face into a smile. That smile radiated towards Jim as he shook her hand, and, for the briefest of moments, they could communicate through their eyes – they were both sure of what went unsaid. She closed the door behind them, and stared into space. Her mind a flurry of thoughts and emotions, then told herself, Don't be so silly, you're acting like a schoolgirl, and busied herself with chores to focus her mind on the more practical. By the time Alex had returned from school, her oven was spotless, the ironing done and the kitchen floor gleamed. Nothing like a bit of foolish nonsense to get jobs done she mused.

The men wandered to the harbour, joining up with others who spoke of feeling cold, their hunger, and their eagerness to get back on board for something to eat, however inadequate. Jim and Samuel just kept quiet about their more fortunate circumstances – it would be cruel to do otherwise. The officials would not let any of them on board, so they huddled up in a tight group, stamped their feet and clapped their hands to keep their blood circulating in their fingers.

'This is my ship, I should say when you come on board,' said the captain on his return and he marched up the gangplank, with an air of authority the crew had not seen for some time. In only a matter of moments they were called on board and were back in cabins, or in their own private places, when the captain gave out a tannoy message.

'I would like to meet up with you all this evening to appraise you of the situation. I will see you in the mess after dinner.' Once again, they had no way of knowing if this was good or bad but all tried to be optimistic.

Jim had English words running through his head, and practised simple, silent conversation whenever he was alone. Each day the learning became easier, and he settled into a routine. He took himself to the officers' mess, gave one gentle knock and entered, only to find the captain in thought, so deep, that for a moment he was unaware of Jim's presence. Jim cleared his throat, Ivan looked up and he forced a smile,

'Do come in, did you have a good day?'

'Yes, I did thank you.'

'I'm pleased for you, just be careful. Your circumstances will make you feel close to anyone who shows you friendship and compassion. There is no likelihood of a future for you here, but these are good people and friendship with them is to be encouraged. But not too close you understand?'

'I think I know what you mean, can we use the dictionary please?'

The captain laughed at his own stupidity. 'I'm sorry Jim, you've done so well with your English that I forgot you're not fluent yet.' They poured over the English / Nigerian dictionary and phrase book he kept for his own use.

Jim cleared his throat, 'I understand that you are ... what's the word... concerned for me, and I thank you.'

The captain reached over and offered the book to Jim, 'This is for you, you have greater need than me,' and left him to plough through the rest of the Peter and Jane books; two equally irritating cousins – Simon and John – had joined their daily activities and Jim did not fancy an Adventure at the Castle, or indeed anywhere else with any of them. He was done with these children. He now had a book that would enable him to converse properly and gave the dictionary a little hug. So wrapt was he in his work, that only the smell of dinner alerted him to another meal, which was followed by cards and Ayo boards and filled the time until the briefing.

Uncertainty once again caused their anxiousness to ebb and flow into a tsunami of emotions and, as the door opened, the look on the captain's face did not lift their spirits. It was blank, a frozen face that expressed nothing. His words were little better:

'The inspectors have confirmed that the ship is to be condemned. It can neither easily, nor cheaply, be made seaworthy and the owners will not provide funds for this work. In order to pay the harbour fees, some of the fish processing equipment will be removed and sold. Any surplus funds will be shared amongst you, whilst your futures are sorted out.'

'It seems that the paying of harbour fees is more important than us,' Jim whispered to Samuel.

The captain continued, 'Our engineer will soon leave for Bulgaria, and consequently, I will, whenever possible, eat my meal with you all.' Mutterings turned to loud voices, but he continued, the power of his voice rising above any of theirs. 'As to your futures, I have no further information, but the ship will return to the harbour tomorrow so that the equipment can be removed.

Jim wondered out loud, 'Maybe we should rename the ship, Limbo?' A couple of men responded with glares, a few more with frigid blankness, but Samuel managed a giggle and three joined him – they were all on a never-ending melodramatic roller coaster. Jim took himself away, to let the night air blow away the misery, and to peer into the gloom of the night.

He was not the only one who stood on the deck looking out into the black beyond – no magic skies tonight – just darkness, with the occasional twinkling lights of the trawlers and factory ships visible through the mist. The other men were scattered around, all deep in their own troubled thoughts. Jim concentrated on the lights that came and went, it gave him a focus and brought to mind the bible: John 1:5 The light shines in the darkness, and the darkness has not overcome it. He was not given to memorising the bible and wondered where this had come from: must be some litter bin in my mind.

As the mist dispersed, the lights continued to shine and became brighter, and were joined by twinkling stars in the sky, their luminosity overwhelmed the trawler lights that appeared to fade away. Jim wondered if it were an omen, and chose to see the stars, that spread as far as he could see, as specks of hope, of better times ahead and wondered what they could be.

Chapter 19

And I have asked to be
Where no storms come,
Where the green swell is in the havens dumb,
And out of the swing of the sea.
     Heaven-Haven
     Gerard Manley Hopkins

The twinkle of the night stars gave way to an unfolding sky of red as the sun rose to heat the day and draw people from their homes. Activity at the harbour continued unabated as nationalities mingled easily during the cold sober light of day. The sallow complexions of the eastern Europeans stood out against the swarthy skins of the Spanish, who contrasted with the much-tanned Danes and Norwegians and in this mix were those from West Africa – a real melting pot of nationalities – and indeed sexes. It came as a surprise to many, that there were female crew on several of the eastern ships. These were not frail beauties, for they lived a hard life, and had to be a match for the men. Some worked with the fish, but others were medics, officers or experts in their own fields. Trawlers and factory ships were no place for shrinking violets nor indeed flowers of any sort. This was the life of beer, vodka and Polish white spirit.

Squawking swooping gulls accompanied the voices of nations; creating a discordant ensemble that pierced Moira's ears as she delivered supplies to the harbour for the captain of the huge Russian owned factory ship that was moored way out in the distance at the entrance to the loch. The captain had traded with Angus for the last three years and a friendly connection had been built up between them. He reminded Moira of the visit to his ship that had been arranged for the next day. It was to be a boys' day out, Angus and Roddy plus two others were to take a group of young pipe band members to visit the ship and see its inner workings. There was absolutely no fear of Moira, Roddy or any of Alex's family forgetting when it was; they had been reminded, daily, for the last week. He had even started a Meccano model and was using the ageing Britannicas for some fairly dated guidance in this. The Russian laughed at this tale and helped her to transfer the goods from van to launch and bid her goodbye. They would depart in three days' time, and he looked forward to seeing her again when they returned in the Autumn.

The encounter was watched by several eyes on the Harmony as it drew to its specially reserved space at the pier. Most of those eyes saw animated conversation and smiles, but one pair saw only a figure wrapped tightly in a thick coat. Her smile, even though directed at another, made him smile too.

Reality took over as Jim jumped onto land to catch the mooring rope that he pulled tighter and tighter, winding it around the capstan, as the same was done at the stern. The ageing ship creaked and groaned as it succumbed to these efforts and came to a halt against the pier. Onlookers inspected the vessel – its rust and rotten wood and shook their heads – no expertise was required to classify the Harmony as doomed. They watched as six of the twelve crew disembarked and ambled away. Their leaden tread and bowed heads spoke volumes and the onlookers looked away as if ashamed.

Jim and Samuel were among the six. They had no instructions, no chores to carry out and no money. Just empty hours that they didn't know how to fill. So they walked, well more of a shuffle – there was no destination to lengthen out their strides. A white van drew up at their side and a voice asked:

'You two in town again?'

'Yes, we have to be off the ship for two hours and then we must help to remove equipment for sale.' Samuel replied, as he bent to see Moira at the wheel. She wound down the window.

'I've heard about the sale, it's awful.'

'We don't know what to think these days, the only news we get is bad, never good.' Moira gave a knowing nod and opened the van door,

'Are you allowed to come into town in the evenings ever?'

'I'm not sure. But we have no money, so there is no point. We do at least have a little to eat and some heat on the ship.' Samuel said as Jim watched on.

'Would you like to come and have a meal with me? Alex is out to visit a ship and you would be most welcome, both of you, and it would be company for me.'

'Oh, I don't know. I don't think that we are allowed out at night,' Samuel said hesitantly, 'but if we are, then yes, we would like that.' and Jim nodded.

'Of course it's allowed, you aren't prisoners you know, not on land anyway. So, about five o'clock, is that OK? Let me know through the ship to shore radio at the shop if that isn't possible, otherwise I will see you both tomorrow.' And off she drove.

Jim was getting more fluent by the day and had needed little help in understanding that they had been invited for a meal. The sudden uplift in mood showed on both their faces and put a spring into their steps as they continued along Shore Street, chatting away in Yoruba:

'She's a lovely lady,' sighed Jim, 'should we ask the captain if we can use the lifeboat to come ashore?' Samuel's face took on a pensive air,

'Well, that's probably the right thing to do, But what if he said no?' Jim looked shocked at the thought.

'Surely he wouldn't do that?'

Samuel's pensive face took on a defiant air, 'Let's just do it! what can he do, give us the sack, stop our wages? We know he can't send us home.' At this, Jim shook his head, not in anger, but mirth, and the pair laughed at each other and continued their debate as they walked along the loch towards somewhere signed – the Braes of Ullapool – but they never made it. The town clock struck ten and the sound carried on the wind straight to them. They spun round and with heads bent down retraced their steps, and pushed their bodies into the might of the wind that was trying harder, with each step, to push them backwards. The weather here turned as swiftly as the seagulls that swooped over their heads, and for once they were pleased to reach the shelter of the Harmony. They made it just in time and were ushered down to the factory level where equipment, selected by various buyers, was waiting for them to carry out on deck and be taken away. In the end it didn't take too long and there was little emotion in the so doing. It might have been the end of an era for the old vessel but there was not a man aboard that had any allegiance – except maybe, for Captain Lyudmil.

Moira, now back at work, pondered on how easy it had been to invite the men for dinner; she was rather impressed with herself and stood taller, as if she were a woman of the modern world, not a Highland lassie that had seen little of the United Kingdom – let alone the world. Stretching was not her strong point she decided, as, in so doing, her head brushed against the sign saying – Special Offer – which flew through the air and landed on the minister's rather bald head as he walked in. Fortunately, he found the funny side and remarked:

'God certainly does work in mysterious ways. I wonder if this is a direct message and he's trying to sell me off cheaply?'

They all laughed, no harm was done, and the sign was restored to its rightful place. He left with a twinkle in his eye, a barely disguised chortle, and a parting,

'Maybe he wants you to come and see the offers we have in church, perhaps we will see you sometime?'

Neither Angus nor Moira were wholly sure whether he gave a last little wink, or was just a nervous tick, but it tickled them, and they were laughing out loud when in walked Mr and Mrs McTavish and that put an end to their frivolity. They were stalwarts of the church, not noted for their sense of humour; religion was much too serious a matter to be taken lightly, and they saved all their energy for singing, never aware that their duets caused mirth to so many. They passed pleasantries, commented on the wind getting up, selected their groceries and returned to their car with all the seriousness of a military operation. They would have been mortified to see the hysterical reaction their visit had caused, but the two people inside were able to lock up for the day, return to their homes and still be smiling. So he does seem to work in mysterious ways, Moira said to herself, as she walked through her front door and laughed out loud again.

No Alex – he would be at her mother's four doors away. It wasn't a day for playing and it was now nearly dark outside, still she expected they would notice the lights on, and he would return as hungry as ever. She pulled out a large piece of venison from the freezer, Alex and Roddy should be proud of providing for people in need. Today is going rather well she thought, just as Alex dashed in, wanting a meal as usual.

Moira's friend, Doreen, who lived next door would pop round for a drink, film and chat later. She was always cheerful and able to lift Moira's mood when life took on more serious moments, whereas Moira was good on sensible advice, they were perfect foils for each other, even though Doreen was fifteen years older. And so these evenings had become a regular fixture, something they both looked forward to.

Alex had lit the fire and was comfortably ensconced in his prone position in front of the TV when Doreen popped her head round the door:

'Hello, Alex how are you?' to which she got absolutely no reply, so left the room and joined her friend in the kitchen. They would claim the lounge as their own when his beloved programme was over.

All the post Hogmanay gossip of the last two weeks was dissected. Moira recounted some of the more humorous goings on at the shop and pier but was unsure whether to confide in her friend about the more personal. She decided to keep quiet; there wasn't much to tell, just possible juvenile feelings that Doreen might laugh at, and Moira didn't want to have her new found happy bubble burst.

'I've been asked to help with the anniversary quilt, have you?' Doreen asked.

'Yes, Mum and I are going to do a square together. I think we might do trawlers, but it could just as easily be one of the hills, or even the memorial clock, what about you?'

'I don't know, I've been busy at work sorting out the school admin and haven't had time to think about it. I'm not as creative as you two. Perhaps I should just do one of the sea, what do you think?'

'Well, to be fair, I reckon much depends on the fabric we've got. Shall we just let the colours and textures guide us?' Moira asked as she finished wiping out the sink.

'You're right, of course. Maybe we should throw it all in the air and see how it falls!' laughed Doreen as she grabbed a tea-towel and cast it aloft.

'You know what, that might not be as daft as it sounds,' Moira said, 'Let's all get together next week and make some sort of start.'

'I'm all for that,' nodded Doreen, 'Shall we see if Alex is ready to give us a look at the TV, his programme must have ended by now?'

They had timed it to perfection and Doreen popped the rented video cassette into the machine as Moira poured their little treat: Cinzano and lemonade. Alex was welcome to join them in their fortnightly viewing, but he always decried it as mushy stuff. Meccano held a much greater attraction – he had a ship to finish and sped off to his room.

Comfortably settled, the film started, and Meryl Streep came into view. Moira could barely believe her eyes at the title – Out of Africa – and she watched with such intensity that she barely touched her drink. They were mesmerised by this huge adventure. Doreen was fixated on every scene with Robert Redford, but Moira was totally engrossed in Africa, trying to remember all the sights and sounds of Kenya and wondered if Nigeria was the same. She had discovered that they weren't, the encyclopaedias had taught her that much, but now she had an image of Africa that she could store away. The emotional ending left tears washing down their cheeks, and, after much sniffing and tissue wiping, the pair declared the film,

'Wonderful,' and it was time to end their evening.

As Doreen was being blown home, the Harmony was rising and falling in the increasing swell, a storm was brewing, and this would be a rocky night. Many people were hoping that it would have abated by dawn, there was fishing to be carried out, last trawls for some, but others had social events and wanted nothing to stand in their way.

Chapter 20

Be the change you want to see in the world.
      Mahatma Gandhi

The storm continued through the night, then gradually, as daylight broke through the leaden skies, it abated. Calm was restored to the loch; boats stopped rising and falling; seagulls could fly again, and trips were still on. The Russian skipper of the factory ship had been adamant – his launch would pick them up at two, and refreshments would be served on board – they would be returned around six. Just as the memorial clock struck two, the launch berthed at the pier, and they all piled in under the close supervision of Roddy, Hamish (The Seaman's Mission volunteer chaplain), Angus and John the publican at the Ferry Boat Inn.

Alex and some of the other boys were used to travelling on launches, but this was a first: to actually see the inner workings of a massive factory ship with two hundred people on board. Their excitement was palpable, and chatter reached a crescendo as the launch took them a circuitous route around the mouth of the loch. Many other vessels – of varying size – swayed in the water as they passed, until the sparkling and enormous Irena towered above them. It was quite the spectacle – the captain had known exactly what he was doing when he had prescribed this route.

They were welcomed aboard like honoured guests and, after much handshaking, were ushered down to the bowels of the ship, to the refrigerated zone where boxes of frozen fish were piled from floor to ceiling as far as the eye could see. It was difficult to believe that there was room for another sprat let alone a mackerel. Men and boys stood with mouths agape, and more than one wondered if there were any more fish left in the sea. Once they'd overcome their amazement, the adults asked technical questions about size of the hold, tonnage of fish, value of the cargo, whilst the boys were more interested in how the boxes were lifted in and out of the hold, and did they make their own ice? The overwhelming cold overtook them all, and they were pleased to climb the scrupulously clean stairs to the floor above. Here, machinery whirred, and men dressed in orange waterproof dungarees and hairnets worked at full pelt; the smell of fish was overpowering and the noise deafening. They watched as fish advanced along the conveyor towards the guillotine machine, then onwards to the men who gutted and washed them. The boys were mesmerized as they observed the filleting machine, then the skinner, and finally the men at the processing benches who trimmed the fish and removed any last bones. Other machines then sorted, weighed and packed the fillets into wrapped portions, which were conveyed onwards to the huge freezer. When frozen solid they were packed into boxes and sent down the conveyor lift to the hold for storage. Fish that not long ago had been swimming in the sea, scooped up with their cohort and made ready for sale in a matter of a few hours. It was an astounding spectacle – and the noise was overwhelming. People had to shout to be heard; most wore ear defenders – as did their guests – so conversation was impossible; it bore absolutely no resemblance to the fishing that they did with a rod and line or pot. The guests realised that this was indeed a factory, with a cargo worth a fortune. No wonder they were called, 'klondykers'! They had searched for mackerel gold and found it – without even having to catch it themselves.

The visitors removed their ear defenders, clambered up yet more steps, into daylight and the near silence of the top deck. Questions flowed like the fish they had seen on the conveyor, asked one after the other and occasionally all at once. Finally, they were shown where the fish had arrived on the ship earlier that day. They learnt that they been caught by European trawlers who dropped their netted catches straight onto the deck receiver, which now lay clean and unused. No sign that, just a few short hours ago, this deck had been a crush of men labouring to usher a seething mass of fish on their journey to the freezers below.

The exuberant boys almost stood to attention when the Captain joined them. His broad smile and crinkly eyes were infectious, and the boys beamed back at him, all attention now drawn to his face and especially his hat, which was the largest they had ever seen. The peak was absolutely normal, but the top was as large as a giant dinner plate and nearly twice the width of his head. There was a hint of more than one giggle, but mention of gateau and sandwiches distracted them. The men were invited to join the captain and some of his officers in his quarters for refreshments, while the boys were to eat in another lounge below. Roddy and Angus were a little unsure about leaving the boys unattended – they might get up to mischief – but their fears were assuaged when the Latvian first mate and the ship's physiotherapist, who would take care of the younger members strode into the lounge. These two women had all the attributes necessary to take charge of any number of unruly children and the men separated happily. An afternoon tea of buns and some unidentifiable bits and pieces that the boys declared, rather dodgy looking were laid out for them to help themselves and they did so with gusto. Meanwhile, the men were receiving the famous Russian hospitality, which always started with a shot of vodka, regardless of what was to follow.

Jim and Samuel, however, had a different mission in mind and were setting off for shore under cover of rapidly approaching darkness. The lifeboat was now kept permanently tied to the side of the Harmony and it was easy for them to step into without being seen. The journey was short, and the little boat was tethered in no time; they walked briskly under the snowy sky, and were indoors at number four at exactly five o'clock. Smiling, she dismissed their offers of help and ushered them into the lounge.

'Oh no, I don't need help. Take these two drinks; make yourselves at home and I'll join you in a minute.'

With a roaring fire in front of them and a beer to hand, the two men smiled at each other, sank back into their seats, and relaxed. They remained totally quiet until Moira joined them and blurted out: 'Tell me about your names – they don't sound Nigerian.'

'Oh, that's not unusual in our country,' said Samuel. 'Many of us are Christians and have names taken from the Bible. Mine means, of God.'

'I should have realised that,' said Moira. She felt totally ashamed of the sudden way she had interrogated them and covered her embarrassment by topping up their glasses.

'What about you Jim? I don't think that your name is in the bible.'

'My name is Ejimgietochukwu,' said Jim proudly, as Moira nearly choked on her drink.

'Oh my goodness, it's a good job it's been shortened to Jim! I don't think I'd ever be able to pronounce that. Does it have a meaning?'

'Oh yes, I praise God because of you,' he explained, looking her straight in the eye.

'I'd better see to the dinner,' she stuttered, blushing, and hurried from the room. What had happened to the confident, modern woman she'd assessed herself as just yesterday?

Her self-possession was restored whilst tending boiling saucepans and a pot of stew, she cleared her throat and called the men to join her in the kitchen. Between mouthfuls she asked about their seafaring lives and their homes; they wanted to know about her family. Samuel asked about her husband and Moira wondered if Jim had put him up to this. She was quick to confirm that Alex's father was long gone, and that there was no contact, and Jim gave a slightly audible sigh. Moira asked if Samuel and Jim were married, and she smiled at their 'No.' They told her of the boat they used to own in Nigeria and were about to flesh out the details when there was a banging and crashing at the front door. All three jumped up and were astounded to see Alex struggling to keep four men upright; Roddy, John, Angus and Hamish were absolutely drunk – laughing like fools and walking like marionettes on strings of odd lengths. The surprise worked both ways as they took stock of the two large Nigerians standing in the hallway with Moira.

Angus broke the moment with his rousing, 'Hello Jim, hello Samuel. Good to see you,' as his legs gave way and his rear hit the bottom stair.

'Hello Angus. It looks as if you have had a good time?' smiled Samuel.

'And who they hell are you?' Roddy shouted as he squared up to the two men.

'They're our friends,' Alex said, moving towards Jim.

'Friends? They'd better not be,' roared Roddy. His face turned puce with anger. 'We don't want people like you here. Get back to where you came from.'

'Go inside, Alex,' Moira urged. 'Roddy, you're in no fit state to be looking after the lad, or to come here insulting my guests,'

'Come on Roddy, let's get you home,' John said, as he staggered towards him, and tried to steer him towards the door.

'I'll go when I'm good and ready and that will be when these two are out of here.'

Roddy raised his fists, swaying as he did so and threw a punch that hit fresh air. As he was about to fall, Angus staggered from the stairs and grabbed his right arm, just as John grabbed the other, and Hamish pushed them all through the door. They left as noisily as they had arrived, with parting shouts of, 'Good to see you again,' 'Nice to meet you,' and 'Leave my sister alone, you bloody......,' ringing through the night sky.

Moira couldn't stop shaking. Roddy had always had a temper, and they'd obviously all had far too much to drink, but he'd never behaved like this before. As she stared after the men, a couple of curtains twitched in her neighbours' houses across the road; no doubt the whole town would be talking about her soon. The years rolled back and she saw herself remonstrating with Alex's father, after he'd drunk his week's wages away on a Friday night, and tears rolled down her cheeks.

'Moira..?' Jim touched her arm and led her gently into the lounge. 'It's just the drink talking.'

Her tears washed away the memories just as surely as Jim's reassuring presence did, and for just those few private moments, they both found an inner calm and all the bad words flowed away. Roddy had meant to drive them apart; in fact, his actions had drawn them together.

Jim and Samuel were fantastic – they made her a mug of tea, cleared the kitchen and restored it to full sparkling order. Alex sat with his mum and held her hand and patted her back saying,

'It's all right Mum. They were just drunk. I'm sure Uncle Roddy didn't mean it.'

'Probably not son,' she responded, knowing full well that he did. Roddy was usually a happy drunk; the alcohol couldn't be blamed. She'd always believed prejudice to be the result of fear, caused by ignorance, but her brother didn't have that excuse – he'd mixed with all nationalities. It had to be the colour of their skins that had provoked this response. How could he? she said to herself, repeatedly, only stopping when Jim and Samuel staggered back from the kitchen, pretending to be worse for drink, and made them all laugh. They clearly thought that her brother was just a bad-tempered drunk trying to protect his sister, and she was not about to disabuse them of that.

The evening had been ruined as far as Moira was concerned, but not so for the men. Drunken incidents were hardly a novelty; the words had hardly registered. Their concern was only for Moira – both of them could see how hurt she had been by her brother's behaviour.

As Moira regained her composure, Alex reverted to his normal chatty self and gave them a detailed – VERY detailed – account of his trip – what he had seen, the strange eats, what he had learned, and the hilarious journey home. It sounded as if the men had been plied with Russian beer and vodka – and who knows what else – and had finally left the captain and crew after much vigorous backslapping and bear hugs. The effect of all that alcohol had hit their legs immediately they tried to get off the launch at the pier.

All four men had been determined to see the boys home safely, not realising that in fact it was Alex who was supporting them and leading the way. Alex considered that the whole episode had been hilarious, so for the moment that was the end of the matter.

Moira turned the TV on, hoping it would take all their minds off the incident and they passed a pleasant hour wondering how Paul Daniels managed all his magic tricks, and the evening ended on a happier note.

'You must come again,' insisted Moira, 'I might not always be able to give you a meal, but at least you'll be cosy and relaxed. Life on your ship can't be pleasant.'

'We would love to visit you again,' replied Jim and Samuel almost simultaneously.

'Why not Monday?' she asked and was given a gentle kiss on her cheek by one, and a handshake by the other.

'I'll see you about six then?' and off they went.

With Alex now in bed, she sat alone in front of the fading fire, thinking unpleasant thoughts about her brother, and imagining the bad heads they were all going to have tomorrow. 'Serves them right,' she said to the embers, and simultaneously hoped that her brother's was the worst of the lot.

Chapter 21

Long is the night to him who is awake;
Long is a mile to him who is tired;
Long is life to the foolish who do not know the law.
  Buddha

Hurt and anger make poor bed mates and after a fretful disturbed sleep, Moira rose to take out her emotions on dust and dirt wherever it could be found – it was a therapy that worked for her – she was not one for sitting and moping around. Moira must confront her brother; matters couldn't be left unaddressed. But what if he couldn't actually remember what had gone on? she thought, then dismissed the notion as foolishness, they had all seen it. It could not be disregarded.

The hangovers were scattered across town and the worst was just pulling itself out of bed to go to church. Hamish was used to an occasional dram, but drunk and disorderly was not a behaviour admired at the mission or the church. His memory was hazy, drowned out as it was, by the thumping of drums and cymbals in his head; in fact, he was not entirely sure that he was even sober. He wouldn't be recounting this story to anyone, and trusted that the others would stay equally quiet. Mind you, he said to himself, it was a damned good trip ... I think. He understood from seamen that came to the mission, that a hearty breakfast was required for such moments, and set about with the frying pan, feeling decidedly nauseous as bacon, egg and sausage sizzled. It was a good job, Mary, his wife, was at her sisters, she would certainly have had something to say, and it was unlikely to have been agreeable, so he thanked his God for some small mercies and struggled off to church, hoping that the sermon would not last too long.

Angus had already been well chastised by Joan, his wife, before she set off for church, so he only had the head and still decidedly wobbly legs to contend with. He was doubly relieved that he never went to church and could therefore avoid a further rebuke for at least another hour. No fry up for him, Alka Seltzer was about the most he could manage, and he tossed a coin: back to bed or brisk walk? Falling tails up, the walk it was. He tried to look totally sober as he braced the wind and cold to walk around the loch. As his head began to feel more normal, he retraced his steps and reflected on – The Incident. His sympathies were entirely with Moira and her guests, Roddy had behaved like the worst of people and should be ashamed; she deserved better than that, and so did the men. He was unsure of how to deal with the situation and decided that it would be forgotten – best not talked about – but his memory was sufficiently clear to be cautious about ever discussing race with Roddy in the future. In short, he would take the cowards way out and was ashamed of himself.

Doors were opening at the pub and the landlady invited in the two waiting customers; opening time was never early enough for some, whilst it was clearly too early for her husband who was doing a more than passing resemblance of a zombie upstairs. He was aware of a fair few cures for his current condition, but none appealed, and least of all – the hair of the dog – even the suggestion of serving alcohol made him feel decidedly queasy, so he plumped for a pint of orange and lemonade to assuage his thirst, which had left his mouth like sandpaper. His head however was surprisingly clear, and he had no difficulty remembering the look of utter sadness on Moira's pretty face and wondered how her brother could treat her like that. John was used to seeing all races in the pub and had long ago forgotten to see the colour of people's skin, he judged on character, liked his people good and true. He heard unpleasant remarks, 'That east Europeans weren't totally white,' or that they, 'Didn't mind their seas being black, just not their friends.' It always surprised him that peoples could work together in relative harmony and then lord it over others because they did not look the same. Best say nothing he thought, Moira deserves better than having people discussing her behind her back.

And so it was that the roots were cut from this potential grapevine, no chance for buds to grow and flourish, any fruit that it might have borne, withered and died before it could see the true light of day. Of course, someone had other ideas, she was unaware of their silent conspiracy, nor would she have cared if they had spoken out. She had nothing to be ashamed of, it was her brother who did, and she felt sickened by him. A telephone call to her sister-in-law revealed that he was in a foul mood, a bit worse for wear and decidedly silent on the previous day's activities.

'I'm not surprised he feels bad, serves him right he was horrible last night,' said Moira.

'What on earth did he do?' Aila asked.

'Not now, I'll tell you later, I just want to talk to him, can I come round?'

'Of course you can, he's not here now, why not come for tea, it'll be good to see you and you can tell me about all of this.'

'Ok, don't tell him I'm coming – keep it for a surprise.'

'Ok.' Aila said as Moira put down the phone.

Alex planned on a bit more animal skinning, but Moira was the only one to be doing that this afternoon. Roddy was out when they arrived. The children went straight outside to play which gave Moira an opportunity to update her sister-in-law.

Aila, stopped her washing up, dried her hands and gave Moira her undivided attention, as she recounted the details of the previous night.

'Well, I'm not pleased to hear that. He can be a stubborn nuisance sometimes, but that's not acceptable. But what I want to know about is your visitors. Where did they come from?

'They're from the Harmony, just two of the crew. I can't help them all, just doing my bit you know.'

'Ah, I see. Makes it worse doesn't it? There's you doing good works and himself comes in and causes trouble, I'm so sorry Moira, you don't deserve that.'

Moira recounted, in the finest detail, the events of the last four weeks. At first, she kept emotions and feelings out of the tale, but as she drew towards the end it all burst out, and she revealed her innermost feelings to her slightly astounded sister-in-law.

'Moira don't take this wrong, but you can't have a relationship with this man, he will be leaving at any time, he won't be allowed to stay here, his home is in Africa, and I don't see you moving there any time in the future. It's good that you are looking out for them, but don't you think they might be taking advantage?'

'No, I don't for one moment think that, would you say that if they were white?' Moira said indignantly.

'Now you are being ridiculous, I would say the same whatever shade their skin. This is not about different colours, it's about different circumstances, cultures and countries.'

'Oh Aila, I know you're right, and I may well be behaving like an adolescent, but it feels deeper than that, I can't explain it to you. If nothing else I most certainly intend to give them support – to make life a little more tolerable for at least two of them – surely that's what we all should do?'

'Of course, you're right, just be careful, eh? We don't want any heartbreak; you've already had more than your share of that. It is time you found someone, but not this one, it's far too complicated. Let's be done with this now and we can set about Roddy later, he doesn't need to know all of this, we will keep it to ourselves.'

'OK.' Moira said, and sat bolt upright as Roddy returned.

He didn't look one hundred percent to her and that made her lips turn up into a nearly smile – Serves him right. I bet his head's thumping like a pneumatic drill – and continued chatting to Aila before breaking off with a quick 'Hello,' to Roddy, who acted as if the previous night hadn't happened.

But his memory was not too impaired, and he understood that his sister would not let the incident rest. She was not one for ignoring problems and he doubted that she would leave matters the way they were. The children joined them, before playing a game in the lounge. Maybe she is going to let it lie, thought Roddy, with the most ludicrous thought since Adam decided that a bite of the apple was a sensible plan. Moira sat erect, turned her chair to face Roddy, and without warning began:

'How dare you come into my house – so drunk that you couldn't stand – then insult my guests, and even worse, in front of the nephew you were meant to be looking after. You ... are ... a disgrace, I'm ashamed to call you my brother.'

'Steady on there, let's take this easy.'

'Easy? Easy you say. You were barely able to stand. You were rude and aggressive, and you want me to go easy?'

'I might have been drunk, but no one got hurt, aren't you taking this a bit too far?'

'No, I'm bloody not! I try and help two people who are in difficult circumstances and in you waltz with your prejudices, assuming that you have a God-given right to be offensive in my own home. I'm decidedly uneasy if you don't mind.'

'Hold on you two, don't take this any further or words may be said that are better quietened,' soothed Aila.

'Well, I've got work to do at the big house,' retorted Roddy, stomping out in a less than contrite manner, with not even a goodbye to his nephew. Moira, feeling the emotion of it all sat and cried, just a few tears but not for long, I should not have to feel troubled by someone's else's wrongs. I'm made of sterner stuff than that.

'I'm sorry for making a scene Aila, but I needed to say it.'

'Don't worry, it's been said now; the boil's been lanced. Let's change the subject. What are we going to do about this quilt making; we've not

104

actually made any progress? Moira nodded, blew her nose and blinked away the last of the tears.

'You could come round to mine on Wednesday, Alex will be at band practice.'

'Good idea, I'll bring my fabrics. Let's get this project moving. The bicentenary will have passed if we don't buck ourselves up!'

' You're right,' Moira said, 'time for me to go home. I've said my bit and we can all move on now.' Aila nodded and leant over to give Aila a hug.

'Yes, it's good to clear this all up and move on. It's behind us now.'

After unburdening herself of the anger that had been pent up overnight, Moira became much calmer. With any luck that would be the end of it, her brother would realise that he'd upset her, and harmony could be restored. Well nearly harmony, there would always be that little wisp of concern, but it could just blow away with time.

The drive home was not silent like the one going there. The pair chatted about the Russian ship. There was no mention of Roddy. Alex had much more exciting stuff to do than spend time even thinking about a moment, that to him, was just a few words, said by a man in, his cups. He had heard this expression used recently and was quite taken with it, and relished the opportunity to use it, if only in his head. Maybe he should make some drunken sailors to put on his Meccano ship, which he set about doing within moments of getting home.

With calm restored to her mind, contemplative reflexion took over and Moira could see that she might have overreacted somewhat. Was it because she had been shocked at her brother's prejudice, at seeing conflict in her home, embarrassment in front of guests, an attempt to protect the vulnerable, or something much more personal – was it out of love? It was all of those, but it was clear to her that it was driven by the latter, the idea made her smile, but it concerned her too, there was going to be a rocky road ahead.

Chapter 22

Day after day, day after day,
We stuck, nor breath nor motion.
As idle as a painted ship
Upon a painted ocean
    The Rime of the Ancient Mariner
    Samuel Taylor Coleridge

Those on the ship had no knowledge of fallings out or ongoing issues. Their concerns were day to day. When would there be news of their future; would they be able to afford more rations? It was all becoming desperate, and the captain was weary of his inability to move forward. His wife was urging him home, but in this he was adamant, he would be the last to leave the ship and he would not return home until all the others were able to do the same. Much of the Monday morning was spent on the radio, attempting to find out when the funds from the sale of the equipment would be released to the men. It was hard going, he was used to bureaucracy, but dealing with so many different agencies, none of which he was entirely used to, was like rowing with brooms, and he was becoming emotionally bruised by the whole experience.

The men had started to find their own routines, and most were currently dealing with laundry, just the same as on land by coincidence. With only twelve of them remaining life became a little easier, they had spread themselves around the cabins, so were now less cramped. Mealtimes were more agreeable, and they had formed groups to play some of the games provided by the locals. None of this actually alleviated their concerns. Most had families that relied on money being sent home. The thought that their children could be going hungry was a hard cross to bear. They could only wish and pray that extended family were stepping in to help, and that this would all be over before long. They couldn't phone home to find out. There was no money for a stamp let alone a phone call, and most families didn't have home phones. The not knowing just made everything worse. Still, they had to get from one day to the next with as much fortitude as they could muster. Some found this easier than others, but overall, there was a comradeship that gave support to those having a bad day or even week.

They had all long ago stopped seeing the beauty of the surroundings. Snow covered hills and mountains swooping down to the loch merely reminded them of the cold, the wind, the snow, the rain – all of which prevented them from spending much time on deck. But they needed exercise, these were strong men used to much physical activity and they could feel themselves losing their vigour. Some tried exercise on deck, but the cold always cut that short, so they tried to do the best they could in the machinery room, which now had much more space. It was Samuel that had the brainwave.

'Let's move the bits of equipment to the ends, and make a sort of cricket pitch,' he suggested. The men, inspired by the best plan for weeks, undid bolts, removed cables, cleared general detritus, until the space was largely cleared. Several paced out a wicket which was marked with daubs of paint, old wooden crates were broken down and remodelled as stumps and bats. Someone made a tight knot of string and covered it in cloth to make a ball. Six-a-side Nigerian style could commence. Neither bowling nor batting was of the highest standard and the few runs made were invariably for six, as grown men crawled under pipes and machinery to retrieve the ball. Still, it broke the monotony, and caused a great deal of jocular shouting which reached the captain's ears. He appeared at the door with curiosity written all over his face and made the best catch of the day. The ball travelled towards him and he instinctively raised his right arm upwards, splayed his hand out into a perfect broad cup and jumped off the bottom step, caught the ball to his side and instantly hit the floor with a thump and great cheering from one side and displeasure from the other. He wasn't entirely sure whether to be assertive and reprimand them for activities carried out without permission, or to just go with the flow. The flow won. He could do little else, his bottom was sore, and he couldn't stop laughing at the ridiculousness of it all. He was declared umpire, a duty he carried out with all the seriousness of a Test match official – it was the best fun of the year and spirits were lifted considerably.

Cook looked at his watch and dashed away from the merriment, shouting out:

'Dinners going to be late!' and the others raced after him, shouting out,

'What can we do?' Even bad meals needed to be ready on time!

For the first time in days there was laughter; pleasures can be found simply when there is little on offer, and today had offered them more than expected. For two of them there was more to come. They silently left the others after dinner, donned their outer wear, slipped down to the dinghy and crossed to the pier. It was dark now and they were able to make their way to number four without being seen, they had agreed that this would be for the best.

It was such a pleasant evening, the miseries of life on board the Harmony were left behind and replaced by conviviality. Alex was keen that they saw his ship, with which they were genuinely impressed, and Jim was able to join in some of the chat about the skill required to do such a good job.

'You have the makings of an engineer Alex,' Samuel said, 'Would you like a job with us?' All three roared with laughter as Jim led the way downstairs.

'What's all this merriment about? Moira asked.

'I've been offered a job Mum – engineer on the Harmony.' She laughed along with him, ruffled his hair and frog marched him into the lounge.

Alex turned to Jim and said, 'Tell us about the boat you used to own.'

'Oh yes do,' Moira added, 'and tell us something about your home, we'd like that wouldn't we Alex?' who nodded his reply.

Samuel began,

'We were both raised in a fishing village on the edge of Lagos lagoon in the south west of Nigeria. As boys we paddled out in canoes with lines to catch fish, it was easy, there was plenty for us all, and we didn't need much skill. As we grew up, we made pots which we put further out to catch crayfish and shrimps. We sold our catches at Epe fish market – it's a bustling, noisy place – teeming with people from all over Lagos. Jim and I have been good friends for a long time and even as young boys we planned to buy a boat together when we were older.' Jim, hesitantly joined in.

'With a boat we could go out into the lagoon and fish with nets. That way we could make good money,' he said with pride and nodded to Samuel to continue.

'We were sensible, saved our Naira until we were able to buy our first boat. It wasn't a special boat, and it was rather old, but we were young and eager to do well. We repaired it, painted it, serviced its little engine until it looked like new.'

'I bet your families were proud of you.' Moira said.

'Oh yes they were,' Samuel replied, 'They helped us to purchase a dragnet, so that we could fish beyond the lagoon.. Each time we cast the net and drew it in there were so many fish. A net heaving with splashing tails and gaping mouths. Ample for our families and for us to make profits at market. Then the government said that the country needed more protein and encouraged fishermen to venture further out into the open seas. We wanted to do this, but we didn't have anywhere near the funds for a trawler. Then we were lucky. The government bought some huge trawlers and sold older, smaller ones off cheaply and offered bank loans to do this. We had to repair and paint it, just like the first one, but we were so proud when we launched it out to sea.' He looked at Jim, who nodded:

'We were the proudest boys in Lagos on that day.

Moira and Alex sat totally still, listening intently as Samuel continued again.

'There were so many fish, and we could pay back the loan instalments easily. We looked forward to when it was our own, then we could use our profits to buy good homes.

'So what went wrong?' Moira asked.

'Well, the catches became smaller and profits harder to make. We went out into deeper waters, but we could not match the sheer size of the foreign trawlers that were there. They caught so many fish that local people, began to suffer. These giants of the sea had come from, afar. We learnt they were from Russia, China, Eastern Europe and not long after, even Spanish and French trawlers arrived. There were rules on catch sizes, but no one obeyed them, and they were hardly enforced anyway. The dragnets of the world took away our livelihoods and by nineteen eighty-seven there was no money to pay the loan and the boat was taken from us. We received nothing. After years of repayments we neither owned the steering wheel nor the net.'

'That's wrong,' Alex blurted out.

'So we had nothing, no boat, no job, no fish, nothing. That is why we joined the Harmony.' Samuel gave a deep sigh,' We have travelled hundreds of miles because there were so few fish at home, only to find that the same trawlers are taking the fish from Scotland. It seems that we are never going to catch fish again.' Moira looked at them not knowing what to say, but shook her head at the injustice of it all. They all sat in silence before their mugs of coffee lubricated their throats and conversation restarted. The men were keen to hear about Moira's family, then realised it was time to return.

'Why don't you come again later in the week?'

Jim looked over to Moira with great fondness shining in his eyes and said,

'We would like that very much,'

'I've got a ladies night here on Wednesday she replied, 'so what about Thursday, is

that OK?'

'Oh yes that's OK,' he said again, and once more they departed with a handshake from one and a kiss on the cheek from the other. No blushing this time, the glow was inside where it would linger longer.

Chapter 23

If you can dream – and not make dreams your master;
If you can think – and not make thoughts your aim;
If you can meet with Triumph and Disaster
And treat those two just the same;
        If
        Rudyard Kipling

Mackerel were swimming in their depleted shoals to new feeding grounds and trawlers laden with cash departed for home waters. Huge freezers of frozen fish were carried away – east and west – in factory ships that could hold no more. The season was over. Ullapool fell into the calm peace and quiet of winter routines; villagers could claim it as their own again. Some residents travelled to balmier climes for well-earned holidays, to recharge their batteries before the shoals of tourists arrived in the spring. But, for most, they just settled back into daily routines. They battened down the hatches ready for the imminent arrival of February, which was often the cruellest month of the year.

The pavements of Argyle Street were clean and no longer served as a counter for stores. Seagulls no longer swooped over the sea from dawn to dusk – their easy pickings went away with the ships – but they would return for spring chips and summer ice creams. Cafes and pubs could be cleaned and decorated, seed catalogues could be perused, it was a waiting game on land, all in a state of suspended animation waiting for spring to arrive. Those on the Harmony also looked forward, not for spring, all they wanted was home – their animation was suspended too.

Wednesday arrived, Aila brought her fabrics in a capacious tapestry-bag she had made for the purpose, while Iris had merely bunged hers in a carrier bag. Doreen had simply bundled hers up under her arm for the few steps from next door. They had two hours to themselves before Alex returned from band practice, and they settled down for a creative evening. They giggled like schoolgirls as they threw their fabric pieces in the air to create a sea of colour that decorated the lounge floor. When blue fell next to green they all saw a landscape, purple next to orange a sunset, red on blue boats at sea, but black and brown were dreary – only to be used for small detail they were agreed. Some pieces fell remotely, others in piles and had to be cast into the air again, a merry process that resulted in a visual chaos that took on meaning to these four skilful ladies. Iris, being the eldest was given first choice, it would be local trawlers at sea for her. Aila plumped for a landscape of mountains and moors. Moira held her breath and crossed her fingers as Doreen picked up fabric and declared the whites and greys 'Perfect for a view of Shore Street.' Moira exhaled, smiled and picked up the purples, reds and oranges; it would be a mackerel sky for her.

The chosen pieces were folded together and order restored to the floor.

'Did you hear that shouting on Saturday night?' Iris asked. 'I looked out of the window but could only see some shapes. It was a group of people, men I think and it looked like it was near here.'

'I heard something too,' Doreen said, 'But I was too engrossed watching TV to look out. It didn't last long, did you hear it Moira?'

'I most certainly did, it was that drunken brother of mine and his mates. Give them a few hours on a Russian ship and they turn into idiots. They were meant to be bringing Alex home, but seems like he had to steer them.'

Moira turned to give a look to Aila, just a glance, but Aila nodded, she understood – keep quiet about anything else.

'I'm surprised he didn't wake the whole of Ullapool; he was in a real state when he got home,' giggled Aila, 'mind you he suffered the next day.' Moira gave another warning glance as Aila continued. 'He had a terrible head – tried to hide it – but I understood. It serves them all right.'

Their joviality was brought to a sudden halt when Alex burst in:

'I'm starving, what is there to eat?'

'Seems like hunger has made you forget your manners son, what do you say?'

'Oh. Hello, but please Mum, I REALLY am starving.'

Their evening was over, and they shouted 'Bye,' to each other as they made their way home. Moira heated a bowl of soup to feed the apparently malnourished child, then hurried him up to bed, with reminders to have a good wash and clean his teeth. She was never entirely sure if he needed reminding, but liked to err on the cautious side, frequently reminding him – 'That cleanliness was next to godliness,' which was a strange thing to say, given that neither of them believed in any sort of god, let alone The One.

Thursday was busy in the shop as customers ordered for the weekend when most would be celebrating Burn's Night.

'Best to do it on a Saturday,' most customers said.

'Not an occasion for a Monday,' declared Miss McKay. Moira and Angus smiled, neither had the imagination to see Miss McKay any other way than ramrod straight and in total control of her body. No room for inebriation there. They kept their serious faces when she agreed to make a concession to the celebratory nature of the event, and were barely able to contain their mirth when she said:

'I will be joining The McTavishes for dinner, and afterwards a little recitation and singing.' For such a momentous occasion she took half a pound of best cheese and a pack of oatcakes.

'Hardly lavish party fare,' Moira commented after she had left, and the pair's shoulders rose and fell in merriment at the idea of such an abstemious celebration.

Several events would take place around the town. Angus and Joan would be making merry at the Caledonian Hotel which held the most traditional evening, pipers and kilts were the order of the night there – a formal ending to their hectic season. Moira had already arranged to go to her mums, and Doreen would join them for a simple evening, just to mark the occasion. Before then she had her visitors to see and she couldn't wait to get home, feed herself and Alex, then spruce herself up ready for their arrival.

Alex was getting used to Jim and Samuel being around and liked to join in. It was a distraction in the long dark nights, and they had started telling interesting stories. However, he had a lot of homework to do, and it couldn't wait any longer,

'It MUST be handed in,' his teacher had warned, and Alex realised he could delay it no more.

Moira paced around the house, but there was no sign of them. Perhaps they couldn't make it? What if they were preparing to go home? Her face looked anxious with its furrowed brow, then sad at such thoughts, but beamed when the doorbell rang, and they were there. Samuel explained. 'The Captain gave us a briefing. It was a waste of time. He had nothing to tell us. There's no news on when we can go home, nothing on money from the sale of equipment. It seems that matters will get even worse. It would have been better if he'd said nothing.' Moira's face mirrored their dejected looks as she rose and left the room, then reappeared with two beers,

'I think you two need one of these. Why don't you tell me some more about Nigeria,' she said as they sipped their beers and licked off the foam that covered their lips. 'Tell me about your clothes, do you wear traditional dress at home?'

The men burst out laughing, spraying the foam into the air and catching it in their hands: a choreographed display of quick reactions.

'Oh, no we wear just the same as you,' answered an increasingly confident Jim. To which Samuel added.

'We are Yoruba and have our own language. Our culture goes back thousands of years and spreads over several countries, and we do wear traditional outfits, but only for special occasions like weddings.

'Oh, do tell me what you wear, I'd love to know.' Moira asked, as Samuel continued.

'Well, many men chose the colourful dashiki, and a kufi.

'What on earth are those?'

'A dashiki is a brightly patterned shirt, with no collar. A kufi is a hat that sits close to our heads. It's not like your caps and hats, it doesn't have the bit that sticks out.'

'Oh, you mean the brim,' laughed Moira, 'What about the women, what do they wear?'

'They wear a long dress with a scarf draped over the shoulder, and long lengths of fabric twisted around their head to make a sort of hat. It's most elegant,' Samuel assured her.

'Some chose the brightest possible colours, but many chose grey for weddings, or purple and lavender – the colours of royalty; blue means love, peace, and harmony.'

'It all sounds so elegant, but I don't think it would be right for me. It sounds as if the headgear alone would cover most of my body!'

They told tales of festivals that could last through the night, with huge banquets, dancing and always music and always LOUD. They described the drums that were famous throughout Africa and explained that their rhythms provided a backdrop to their lives. Jim and Samuel began to beat out a rhythm on their thighs before moving on to the arm of the chair and the fireplace, then the singing started and all three were transported to a foreign land only to be joined by Alex who descended the stairs in a flash and tried to join in. An African moment in the Highlands of Scotland. A roaring fire was not conducive to all this activity, and before long they were all aglow and sat with arms swung wide as they lolled on couch and armchair in an attempt to cool off. It was a long time since Jim and Samuel had been so comfortable and it made them feel good.

Alex looked startled to be told: 'Bed for you young man.'

'But I've only just come down mum, that's not fair.' And immediately turned to the men and asked,

'Do you have Christmas and Hogmanay like us?' Jim nodded and spoke.

'Oh yes, we are Christians like you. Our culture may be ancient, but we are civilised people, and we take our religion seriously. So, we have the best of all worlds – holidays and festivals like you – but local Yoruba events too. One day you might be able to visit Nigeria and we will show you all of this.'

'Do you eat the same things as us?' Alex enquired.

Jim continued, 'Oh no, ours is completely different, we like it spicy hot and have dishes called moon-moon, Akbar, Amal, ekuru and jolly rice.' Alex's amazed look made them all smile,

'What on earth are they?'

'We use lots of peas, beans, cassava, yam, and meat, but it gets harder to buy meat, that is why we take home mackerel from your seas. We love soup and have many types, but always served spicy with pepper and a spice mix called Pima – that makes it tasty.' Jim explained.

Moira looked as mesmerised as her son and passed around coffees. ' I could try and make something similar to what you eat at home. But then, maybe, perhaps not. I don't think a yam or cassava has ever been found up here. To be honest, I don't even know what they are, so, I'd be best to stick to what I know,' Moira chortled as she passed round a plate of biscuits, and gave Alex a final countdown to get to bed.

It was time for them to return to their ship, and once again the pair were almost over grateful for her hospitality. The handshake and kiss marked the end of another evening, but before they left Moira said. 'Will you both come and join us for a meal on Sunday? I'll make it a traditional Scottish meal and teach you about Scottish customs. Would you like that?'

They nodded and smiled, pleasure written on their faces as they left, but Jim walked back into the house, bent over and gave her a kiss on the lips, smiled and went on his way.

She was stunned, it had been so unexpected. Her finger tips touched her lips, as if to hold the kiss there. Then gently, she kissed her fingers in response, kept her eyes closed, and gave an imperceptible shudder as her thoughts turned to what could be. Fearful of losing the moment, Moira stood fixed to the spot, only moving when a neighbourhood dog barked her out of the spell.

Chapter 24

Some hae meat an canna eat
And some wad eat that want it.
But we have meat, and we can eat
And sae the Lord be thankful.
    Selkirk Grace

No half-day this Saturday, but Moira didn't mind; villagers were in good humour and looking forward to Burns night celebrations that would break the winter gloom. Some remembered the men out in the loch and left tins and boxes in the crate, but the community's generosity was waning. It's easy to forget others' needs when you are tied-up with your own lives.

'This is looking empty,' Angus said as he rearranged the crate, 'Should we remind people that the men are still on the ship?'

'Yes, probably,' Moira said, peering in. 'It doesn't look particularly generous does it? and I'm sure they all need more. I've got Jim and Samuel coming round tomorrow; I've promised them a traditional meal, so at least they will be well fed.'

'It's a good job you told me that.' Angus said as he rearranged the shelf. 'I'll have a look round and see what I can find – my contribution to the proceedings.'

Moira continued cashing up as Angus rummaged around the store and returned cradling a box in his arms.

'Here's a few leeks, a haggis and a chicken, they all need eating, and I wouldn't want them to go to waste.'

Moira gave an enigmatic smile; she knew that it wasn't entirely true – they had only been delivered the other day.

'That should help the proceedings,' he nodded adding a tin of shortbread, 'and what about a couple of these?' as he popped in two bags of sweets. 'They've got a sweet tooth that lot, so let's give them a feast.'

Moira usually hurried home, but the box was heavy and slowed her down. Fortunately, her contribution for tonight's celebration was already made, so there was still time to deal with Angus's offering, some of which was speedily turned into cock-a-leekie soup. She'd always got pleasure cooking, especially for others and in the dark dank days of winter, when daylight was in short supply, eating became a focus. Something to look forward to – if you had enough – but another source of unhappiness if you did not.

Moira's thoughts turned to Jim. Meals had become her way of pleasing him, to ensure the visits continued. But now, their friendship had moved on, and once again she held her finger tips to her lips: the kiss was still there, and she quivered at the memory. But she was brought back to reality by the bang of the front door and Alex bursting in like a hurricane.

'I'm absolutely fed up with peeling vegetables,' he shouted, 'I never want to see another potato!'

'Well, you might be bored, but you're certainly punctual,' Moira laughed, 'I bet you had your eye on the clock all the time you were at Granny's. Did you actually finish your chores?'

'YES I DID,' he asserted. 'I finished just as Doreen came round – she had a large bowl, covered with a cloth. Do you know what was in it, Mum?'

'We-ell, his mother said, securing the lid on a large saucepan, 'she was on pudding duty and said it would be a surprise, so a surprise it will be. But you'll never find out if you don't get yourself changed; I've left your things on your bed.' His grimace didn't go unnoticed, and Moira smiled to herself as she followed his leaden steps upstairs.

A last-minute look in the hall mirror: not bad, she thought, as Alex jumped down the last three stairs and they were ready for the short walk to number 12. Moira carefully held the large pan of cullen skink in her gloved hands as the smell of smoked haddock wafted over them and lingered in frozen suspension in the icy air. The biting north-easterly wind threatened to deposit yet more snow on the already white landscape and the pair quivered with relief as Iris opened the door.

The house, identical to Moira's, was full of family furniture. Not exactly antique, but solid, it had after all stood the test of time. This was not an occasion for eating in the kitchen, only the extendable oak table that took pride of place under the front window of the lounge would do for tonight. The Burn's night tablecloth lay, in all its red tartan glory, over the polished wood. The cutlery gleamed under the rays of a single candle held erect in a brass candlestick of enormous proportions – everything ready for the evening. The Cameron cloth, of which they were all so proud, had been used for this occasion throughout their lives, it might even have belonged to Iris's grandmother, and would probably be passed down for many more years to come. There were no pipers to play in the haggis, but a tape of the Ullapool pipe band lay ready in the machine, waiting for them to finish their soup. At a nod from Iris, Alex turned on the music. She held the haggis aloft and paraded it into the room with a flourish, along with the neeps and tatties, without which no Burns night would be complete. They laughed, chatted and commented on the superior nature of the haggis as they savoured each juicy mouthful.

'I don't know about you, but I'm already full to bursting,' Iris declared.

'Me too!' Moira and Doreen said in unison. 'I can't eat another thing,' they both groaned.

'I can eat more, what's for pudding?' Alex said as he leaned forward in anticipation.

'You'll have to wait for the rest to go down first, we're in no rush,' his mum said and they all laughed at his sulky face. So, as Alex moped, and the ladies chatted, time passed, until Iris, who had the smallest appetite of them all announced:

'I think that I could probably manage a bit of pudding now.'

' At last!' Alex said.

Doreen needed no further urging, and rushed out. She returned with a huge Typsy Laird trifle which she presented with all the flourish of a major-domo.

'How many have you made that for Doreen?' Moira exclaimed.

'I think I might have got carried away,' Doreen admitted, 'but I expect it won't go to waste,' as she looked at Alex and gave him a wink.

When the meal was over Alex lost interest in being with three women and asked if he could watch the television, and was turning on the controls even as the confirmation reached his ears. They left him in peace and withdrew to the kitchen. They chatted about the summer bicentenary plans and the squares they were to make. As none of them were committee members, they had so far relied on word of mouth, but were sure that rumours of famous singers attending, and a band competition, were probably wide of the mark. But all were agreed that the committee was, competent, and that anything they were involved with, would be well organised and to a good standard. So agreeable was the evening that the sherry and whisky were passed round again, and they all had a second pouring. Not an excessive amount, but unusual for these ladies, none of whom were great drinkers, as they had witnessed the horrors it could bring about. It did however loosen their tongues, and each became a little more voluble with each sip and Iris asked what news there was of the Harmony and the men on board.

Moira, feeling somewhat braver than when completely sober, knew that the time had come to tell her mother and her best friend about the current situation. They listened intently, as she appraised them of the meetings, the lack of stores on the ship, and all of the day-to-day tribulations the men were enduring. Then – after a deep breath – she told them of Samuel and Jim.

The questions followed in a rush:

'You should have told us before,' Doreen said. 'We could have helped to feed them you know; none of us have a lot of money, but surely we could all contribute to keep those two well fed.'

'You're so considerate Doreen, but I must be honest; I get as much from this as they do. I so look forward to seeing them both, but especially Jim. You'll think me foolish, but I've become attached to him. I can't put it into words, but there's a completeness when he's just in the same room. He's physically strong, yet gentle, with a voice that calms like gentle waves lapping on a beach. There's a depth to him that becomes clearer with every improvement in his English.'

'Sounds like you've managed to put that into words rather well my girl,' Iris said. 'Seems as if you've got the love bug, but you go careful, there can't be any future there, so don't go getting yourself hurt. Keep a cool head, you'll be thirty-eight this year and he'll be back in his own country.'

'Oh, I know it sounds like a schoolgirl story Mum, but it's not. You are right, it's difficult to see a future, but I won't stop having them round, can you both support me in that?'

'Of course we can,' Doreen said.

'Why wouldn't we?' Iris asked.

'Well, you might react like Roddy, he is plainly less than pleased.' Moira responded, twisting her hands together nervously. 'The noise you heard the other night, it was Roddy. He was so drunk, but he said some hateful things and would have hit Jim and Samuel given half a chance. I was ashamed of him you know. Ashamed and embarrassed.'

'I'm shocked, Moira,' said a visibly distressed Iris. 'I never raised him to be like that, we're all the same in my eyes and they should be in his. I expect it was just the drink talking. I would just forget it my girl, he probably can't fully remember it himself, let that sleeping dog lie.'

'You're probably right Mum, let's keep all of this between ourselves for now. No one is likely to see Jim and Samuel calling round on these dark nights.'

'My lips are sealed,' Doreen said.

'Mine too,' Iris said, patting Moira's knee. 'When are you seeing them again?'

'They're coming round tomorrow Mum. I said that I would make them some Scottish fare. Angus has been his normal generous self and given me some goodies, so the soup is sorted, I have a little haggis, so just the veggies and pudding to sort.'

'No, you don't,' said Doreen, 'that must be why I made such a large trifle, I'll add a little more to it and there'll be ample for everyone.'

'Are you sure? It's not necessary,' said Moira, 'I know, why don't you join us, it will be good for them to meet someone else?'

'Oh, I don't think so, wouldn't they think it strange?'

At this Moira burst out laughing.

'Nowhere near as strange as two Nigerians, traipsing through the snow under cover of night to participate in a Burn's night celebration being hosted by a dumpy little Scottish lady!'

'You're not dumpy,' her mum admonished, 'And I think it's a good idea. I'm helping out at the community centre for the next couple of days, but I could join you another time, if that's all right. Meet this fellow that's swept you off your feet.'

'Ok, I'll come,' Doreen said, 'but only if you let me bring the trifle, don't want them thinking you're the only provider in town.'

And so, it was agreed, Sunday would be Burn's Night mark two and no one knew how it would pan out.

Once safely home, with Alex in bed, Moira reflected on the evening. There had never been any doubt in her mind that her mother and friend were good people, but she was heartened to have their support; to know that they didn't judge on anything other than character, and she was proud to have them in her life. It's true, she thought, I will be thirty-eight, and perhaps I should be looking for someone to share my future, but there's no one here to fill that role. I've been out with a couple, but they were boring, added nothing to my life. I don't go further than Inverness, so how would that happen? Jim's face sailed across her mind, and she smiled, sure that she had done all the looking that was required.

Chapter 25

We are here to awaken from our illusion of separateness.
Martin Luther King

Overnight the wind had blown in snow that covered the landscape in a duvet of white. It was Sunday and only the most devout were likely to be about; It seems as if God expects more than he should, Moira thought as she drew the lounge curtains and saw a stooped figure clutching a bible and forcing itself through the snow, spoiling God's handiwork as it went. She shivered at the sight, drew her cardigan tightly across her chest,

'Thank goodness I don't have to go out,' she said to the empty fireplace, then retrieved the broom and spade from the understairs cupboard and called:

'The front path needs clearing Alex, and the pavement too. Can you do it please?

'Oh Mum, I was going to the pond, it'll be frozen and my friends will all be there.'

'I'm sure they will be Alex, but you're not going until the paths have been done. It won't take you long, here take these.' He grunted something indecipherable, grabbed the snow clearing tools and proceeded to swoosh snow away from the path with the vigour of a human snow plough.

'Can I go and play now?'

'Of course you can, you've done a good job.' Moira said to his receding back.

The wind had dropped, and the clouds were dispersing, it would be a perfect winter's day and she was optimistic that Jim and Samuel would be able to make it later. She rushed around the house like a whirling dervish with hoover and duster to hand. So fast were the chores completed that there was even time to have a bit of a soak and generally spruce herself up. Inside she seemed like a teenager again, getting ready for a date. Then she looked in the mirror and saw someone that was clearly not that. For a brief moment, image and person looked at each other, one saying inaudibly to the other: Well, you might not be a teenager, but you don't look too bad, a bit of padding, but the face is … OK-ish, best bit is the eyes for sure. Satisfied, they turned from each other, and the silent conversation was over until they met again – the best appraisal she had made of herself in a long time, and it made her feel good.

The Burn's night cloth was to get a second airing – probably the first time it had done so since it was made. Moira ran her fingers over the smooth cloth, coaxing minor creases to disappear over the edge, and set about laying out the cutlery just as Doreen appeared. The pair discussed seating – should men sit next to each other or opposite – which would feel the most relaxed for them? If next, they may feel awkward just looking at the women, opposite it might feel segregated, or best of all they decided, was diagonally opposite, and Alex could be at the head with Jim on one side and Moira on the other. Doreen burst out laughing,

'Look at us, silly fools, anyone would think the queen was coming to dinner. We'll be measuring the place settings next!'

Despite a day of play, Alex rushed to the door at the first note of the doorbell, and had Jim and Samuel ushered in, their coats and boots put away, before the ladies had barely taken off their pinnies. Introductions were met with handshakes all round and a single kiss on Moira's cheek, which she took with all the aplomb of a starlet.

Samuel and Jim were placed in their allotted seats and the others slotted in around them. The addition of an extra person initially stilted conversation and they all sipped their soup in silence. Then Jim looked at both ladies in turn and asked Moira: 'This cloth is colourful and cheery; it reminds me of home, is it a special one?'

'Oh, yes it is. We use it for Burn's night and special occasions. This pattern is called tartan, and different clans have tartans in different colours.' Jim asked hesitantly:

'What are clans?'

'Oh, they are families I suppose. Big families who share the same surname.' Moira answered.

'You are like us then. We have tribes, you have clans, and they all wear different colours.'

'Yes, you're right. That had never crossed my mind before.' Moira said, 'And your English is getting better day by day.'

'I learn every day with Samuel here, and with our captain, but it's easier here, loosening to you all.'

When the laughter had subsided, they explained the meaning of loosening and the new word listening, which he took in good part, and continued practicing as Alex removed the soup bowls. A sound drifted through the door as Alex marched back in from the hallway blowing his chanter. It looked like a cross between a stretched flute and a fishing float and Jim and Samuel had obviously not seen one before. They looked startled, then raised their eyebrows in clear astonishment at the sound. Moira and Doreen giggled at this response and Alex appeared a bit offended by it all.

'What is that?' asked Jim pointing at the offending instrument.

'Well,' answered Alex. 'It's called a chanter, and I like it. We learn to play this before the bagpipes. If you don't like this you will NOT like the bagpipes.' And he blast out more notes and made them all smile.

A full-blown tutorial on the traditions of Burn's night followed and they learnt how it had started on the fifth anniversary of the poet's death. With the chanter now silent and ears just about recovered, Doreen stood and recited in her broadest accent:

'Fair fa' your honest, sonsie face,

Great chieftain o' the puddin race!

Aboon them a' ye tak your place,

Painch, tripe, or thairm.

Weel are ye wordy o'agrae

As Lang's my airm. '

The men looked at each other in yet further astonishment. Samuel could only mutter,

'What on earth was that?'

'There's much more if you want it,' grinned Moira as Doreen took a deep breath.

'No more Doreen, one verse will do, we don't need the other seven!'

Moira was unsure whether haggis, neeps and tatties were entirely to Samuel and Jim's taste, but they certainly ate it all with gusto, and expressed appreciation of the meal, if not the poetry. The whisky was passed round but no one took much, a first sip nearly sent Jim into orbit as it hit his throat, but Samuel was made of sterner stuff and declared it, 'Excellent.' Moira had her usual sherry and they sat and explained how the whole country would celebrate Burn's life in this way. Some of the evenings would be grand, the men in kilts made of their clan's tartan with sporrans, jackets and waistcoats; the ladies in velvet and tartan with a tartan sash pinned with a Celtic brooch. Quite a sight: massed pipe bands and dancing, whisky flowing, much reciting of poetry that could become less understandable throughout the evening.

The men appeared overwhelmed by it all and Doreen was eager to divert attention towards her trifle, which she flamboyantly placed centre stage. Dining continued with almost complete silence, just a, 'Yes please,' by all the males when offered seconds. The bowl was scrapped clean, and they all declared themselves full. An excellent dinner they agreed and each acknowledged that it was the best night in ages.

Jim and Samuel were quick to do the washing up, they could not give anything else they said other than their time and effort, and would not be dissuaded from this. Moira and Doreen were ushered into the lounge where they were to sit:

'Until we are finished.' It was a refreshing change for both of them to have volunteer kitchen help and they did not resist too much.

'Have you got any pictures of people at Burn's nights or any of kilts and the like?' Doreen asked. 'I think that would make the whole thing much easier to understand.'

'You're absolutely right, why didn't I think of that ages ago?'

And so as Doreen rummaged through the bookshelves in the corner, Moira nipped upstairs to pull some photograph albums from under her bed. They were spreading them around when the men re-joined them with Alex tagging along behind. He had become, One of the men, tonight and had listened to them chatting in their own language as they worked, and he even managed to put the crockery away unasked.

'What are these?' Jim asked.

'Photographs for you to see,' Moira said as she passed them around.

Some that were crinkled and faded, showed her great-grandmother, stood in front of the little croft house that had housed their family of eight in much harsher times. No central heating at the end of the nineteenth century, but:

'So many people in the house that they could heat it with a simple range and their body heat,' Moira reasoned.

There were great-aunts and uncles – known and unknown – all looking remarkably similar. The women with shawls around their shoulders and men stood tall in tweed suits and often a cloth cap on their head. A baby in a pram was probably Iris, but they couldn't be sure. There was a good record of Alex growing up and he was intrigued to see himself as a toddler and in another album sat in a row for his first school photograph.

'That's me,' as he pointed at the boy third on the left, back row.

'And here's your first shepherd,' Moira indicated as she passed over the nativity play of 1981.

'Is this you?' Jim asked.

'Goodness, yes, it is, that was taken a good many years ago,' Moira replied. 'And these are when I was a little girl, I haven't looked at these in ages.'

The rest of the evening passed in discussion of photographs that had laid unlooked at for several years. For some it was reminiscence, others an insight to local life, but for one, it gave an intimate view into the life of the lovely woman sat next to him. So engrossed were they all, that when Doreen exclaimed, 'Goodness have you seen the time?' Alex was rushed off to bed

Samuel and Doreen rounded up the photographs, as Jim and Moira took the glasses to the kitchen, where he thanked her profusely for a, 'Wonderful evening,' cupped her chin with his hand, raised her head, bent over, and kissed her gently, but in a way that demanded her response, which was willingly given. His friend's, 'Are you coming Jim?' broke the spell and he ushered her towards the front door with a gentle hand on her back. Doreen joined in the handshakes and watched them depart. Just in time Moira remembered they hadn't agreed another visit and called down the path,

'Tuesday, same time? No meal I'm afraid, but please come.' Their affirmative response was a forgone conclusion and they disappeared into the night.'

As the days grew longer through the rest of January and into February, these visits were continued, sometimes twice or even three times a week. Conversation became easy, Jim's English improved immensely, and Alex remained fascinated to hear tales of their homeland as they helped him with his model making. In short, they slipped into an easy routine that could not continue for ever.

No progress was made in getting the men home, it was as if their problems had been frozen in time along with the weather, but they did at least all have a little money from the sale of the equipment. They were, with increasing regularity, allowed into town, usually in groups so that the ship remained manned. It gave them a break, but with little to do, no real happiness. The captain continued to teach Jim, and they began to converse well and in so doing became friends. He was aware of the attachment that had developed and turned a blind eye to the evening trips. He even ensured that Jim was included in any party selected to fetch supplies, it was his way of bringing some happiness to at least one of the increasingly desperate crew on board. But he was careful to include Samuel so that his friendship with Jim didn't become strained.

The townspeople became used to seeing these men walking around, struggling to fill their days and continued to leave the odd item in the Harmony crate. Some would attempt conversation, others, not knowing what to say, would give a little nod or a 'Good morning,' or 'Good afternoon,' before passing swiftly so as to avoid an embarrassing encounter. And there were those who walked past as if the men did not exist, or, even worse, muttered unpleasantries almost within earshot. Not everyone in Ullapool welcomed this group of men on shore.

As February came to an end, residents returned from their holidays, the sprucing up of buildings took on an impetus in the lengthening days, and evening visits to number four could not go unnoticed for much longer. Moira was not sure if they had been seen arriving, but nothing had been said by neighbours.

Doreen had joined them on a few occasions, and it was clear to her that a romance was developing with each passing day. She didn't pass on the cruel words uttered by the bigots of the village and wondered what these people would say when they found out about the liaison.

Chapter 26

Let us go then, you and I,
When the evening is spread out against the sky
Like a patient etherised upon a table.
>   The Love Song of J. Alfred Prufrock
>   T. S. Eliot

Soggy March followed wet February. Only the mountain peaks were left with snow that matched the white-washed walls of the little houses. The sea, the air, the sky were enveloped in a dreary grey and it dampened the spirits of even the most optimistic of the crew huddled away on their ship. Two of the crew could bear it no more and took the first opportunity to use their hoarded cash, departed on the ten-thirty bus to Inverness and were never seen again. There were ten left, and the captain of course, unlucky thirteen had been reduced to eleven and they all trusted that this would improve their lot.

Jim had become totally engaged with his studies, spending hours reading, writing, and talking to himself. His ship mates sometimes laughed behind his back, but that was no deterrent and he took it in good humour. He wanted to be more fluent and become word perfect so that he could converse properly with Moira. The tall, confident, and handsome man was reduced to a marshmallow core of teenage angst and uncertainty, over a few sentences that he practised over and over again.

Samuel continued to accompany Jim on his visits to number four. It was clear that his services as interpreter were no longer required; he never offered to stay behind, nor did Jim ask him to. They were both well aware what it meant to Samuel, and Jim would never deprive his friend of a few hours of home comforts. Their friendship had already endured through the ebb and flow of life in Nigeria and would not be rent asunder by the difference in their current situations.

They were due to visit Moira the next day – the first Wednesday of the month – when Alex would be at band practice. So at home had they become, that they merely knocked and walked in now, then settled down for a family evening. The three sat around the kitchen table – Jim and Moira opposite each other and Samuel on the other side – all sipping their drinks as conversation turned to the two escapees. Samuel began.

'None of us knew that they were leaving. They gave no clues, no hints. Just disappeared!'

'But where would they have gone?' Moira asked. 'This is such a remote area.'

'No one's certain, but there was mention of a distant relative in London, they could have gone there.' He shrugged his shoulders and continued, 'No one can be sure.'

Jim made no contribution to the discussion just sat, listening and occasionally looking at Moira, then glancing around as if he were carrying the weight of all the world's problems on his shoulders. Samuel carried on:

'The Captain had to tell immigration that they had gone. He didn't want to. Good luck to them that's what we all thought, but we don't know how they will cope.'

Jim continued to wear a worried look, occasionally wringing his hands and fidgeting in his chair, but still took no part in the conversation. Samuel saw his friend's discomfort and the slight flick of the eye that indicated he should leave the room and so he asked Moira,

'Can I watch some television please?'

'Of course you can,'

Samuel strolled into the lounge, eased himself into the armchair and mused, I don't think they'll be joining me for some time, as he gave a knowing smile and turned on the TV.

Jim cleared his throat, like a spokesperson readying himself for a speech. Moira couldn't see that his legs and body were quaking like jelly, but she sensed his continuing tenseness and asked,

'What's wrong Jim, you seem nervous, are you all right?'

He gazed into her eyes,

'Oh yes, I'm OK,' he whispered. Then cleared his throat again. 'Moira, you have been good to both of us. And I do not have all the words to properly say how much this means to us. But, for me, it's more than a meal and comfort. I come across the loch, in the dark, to see you, and I hope that you welcome this as much as me, but I don't want this to be a secret any more. Will you please let me take you out on Friday night?' His shoulders relaxed, the strain on his face disappeared and he gave Moira a look of affection that totally disarmed her.

'I'm not sure what to say,' she said as she reached out and placed her hand lightly on his. He looked bewildered,

'Have I misunderstood. Don't you feel the same?'

'Oh no, you haven't misunderstood, it was unexpected that's all. Yes I would love to come out for a drink with you.'

Jim picked her up and held her face to face. Moira wrapped her arms around his neck snuggling up against the warmth of his body. She tilted her head upwards as he bent forward and they cemented their date with kisses that flooded their bodies with tingles of delight.

The pair strolled back to the harbour and this time it was Samuel who remained quiet as Jim told him of his forthcoming date. He would have sounded out the news with drums or even bagpipes if he could, but as it was Jim only had words. He couldn't contain the happiness inside him. One look at Samuel's face told him that his friend was hurting, and he instinctively knew that he was missing his fiancée back home and abruptly changed the conversation.

Meanwhile, Moira sat having another conversation between lobes of her brain:

Why did you agree to that?

Because I wanted to, silly.

Don't you know what people will say'

What do I care about that?

Well you should, these men will surely be gone soon, and you don't want folk talking about you behind your back when they've gone.'

Talk behind my back? Why? I'm only going for a drink.

People will think there's more behind it.

They can think what they like, I know the truth.'

You'll be accused of all sorts, you don't want to be called another Dollar Diana,

Well, I'm not bothered, it's the right thing to do. I can't walk away from this. I'm doing the right thing.'

Then she marched into the kitchen – there would be no further debate – and she beamed with happiness and gave herself a tight hug.

It was so long since she had gone on a date that all the practicalities had been forgotten. Should she ask Doreen or her mum to sit with Alex? He was old enough to be safely left but she would be happier if someone else were in the house. Best keep it in the family for now, said her common sense, she would ask Mum tomorrow, it was a bit late now and she needed her beauty sleep. The dreams came thick and fast and, as sleep wafted over her, the future appeared as if in a flash of light, then dimmed, and she was back in a sleep so deep that morning arrived as a total surprise and for a moment she wondered where she was.

Angus found her a little more cheerful than usual and could only surmise the possible reasons – it most certainly was not the weather which continued as miserable as the days before. He wouldn't pry, that was not his way, any news, if indeed there was any, would reach his ears from her, or the grapevine, in its own good time. In fact it only took until the next day for her to break the news of her impending date. Just a drink she assured him, but they both knew that it marked a sea change in the relationship. Friendship had moved onto the scale of romance; where it would end was, as yet, unknown.

Alex was surprised to see his mum waiting at the school gate and chuckled when told it was:

'Because I've been let out early for good behaviour.'

'I doubt that!' he laughed back. They walked briskly through the dreary grey as she explained that she was going out, and that Granny would come round to keep him company. His face scrunched into a question as he peered into her face and asked about all the wheres, whys and whats of the evening. When fully informed, he merely asked:

'Can I come too?' And looked a bit put out at the reply.

Iris joined them for dinner, a quick affair to give Moira time for the titivating required for a night out and, at precisely six o'clock, there was a ring of the doorbell, no walking in tonight. Alex rushed Jim through the door in a flash and urged him upstairs to see the latest model making. But Moira interjected and ushered Jim into the lounge to have a few words with Iris, who he had met only briefly before. There was little chance of more than a cursory conversation as Alex pestered,

'You can't go out yet, you MUST see my model,' and finally pushed Jim to the stairs.

Moira and Jim walked down the road, side by side, in the fading light; two people who had known each other for two months, yet had never walked down a road together. It seemed simultaneously strange, yet very right. Like any first date, conversation came in fits and starts before it settled down to a conventional flow, and when he took her hand and gave hers a little squeeze, she responded with a barely visible smile, moved closer, and they walked hand in hand along Shore Street, thankful that the rain had cleared and they could take the long route to the pub near the pier. The Ferry Boat Inn was the town's favourite watering hole and being Friday would become packed. There would be no hiding away in dark corners there. He pushed open the door for her, and they were greeted with:

'Hello there, to what do we owe this pleasure, Moira?' from John the publican, 'and it's good to see you too, it's, Jim, isn't it?'

'Yes, it is. Well remembered,' as Jim went to shake the landlord's hand.

'What can I get for you both?' John asked as he looked at Moira.

'I'll have a port and lemon please.'

'And a beer for me.'

The only free space was in the centre of the room – a stage on which they could be seen from every corner of the room – and as they sat down, faces, which a moment ago had stared agog at the pair, turned back to drinking mates, partners and even the wall, it was as if a local lassie was seen out with a towering Nigerian on any Friday night of the year. Jim and Moira relaxed into their seats, only partly aware of the frequent glances sent their way, of gossip continued behind pints and packets of crisps, and by the occasional double take by newcomers to the night.

Jim relaxed his body into the chair and extended his long legs under the table and said, 'That was easier than I thought,'

'Easier in what way?' asked a somewhat confused Moira, as she watched Jim sipping his beer like an old timer.

'Well, I've never taken a girl out to a Scottish pub before. In fact I've never ordered a pint before.'

Moira smiled, her face lit up and Jim leaned over and spoke.

'All those weeks on the boat have been so miserable, then you came into my life. It's made such a difference. When I am with you all my problems disappear and I feel safe. When things are bad, I think of you, when things are good, I think of you, when the sun shines, I think of you and when it rains, I think of you. With all this rain it must mean that I think of you always. You are at the very centre of my thoughts, next to my heart.'

Moira, covered her mouth with her hands, then managed to say:

'Oh, Jim you do say lovely words, I wish that I were so eloquent.'

'What does that word mean?'

'It means you use words well, speak from the heart with genuine feeling.'

'Then that's a good word, your eloquent, I will write it down and try always to be like that.'

He took a small pencil from the inside pocket of his jacket that lay over the back of the chair, and with her help, wrote down this new word on a beer mat that he secreted into his pocket.

'Your drink's nearly gone, would you like another?'

'Oh, no I'm all right,' Moira replied, but saw the look that washed over his face. She had dented his pride.

'You haven't got much money Jim, let me buy another one.'

'Oh no, I asked you out and I will pay. I have some money from the equipment sale and where I come from it's the men who buy the drinks. Do you want the same?'

Moira watched in admiration as he strolled to the bar, still not noticing that others did the same. Neither did she see the looks of displeasure, and if she had it wouldn't have mattered, her newly found confidence was a match for any disparaging looks or words.

They sipped their drinks, inordinately slowly this time – a little like the conversation – each word to be listened to and savoured like it might be the last. As closing time approached they wandered back, his arm around her shoulder with her body nestled at his side. The clouds had cleared, and stars twinkled brightly, with the moon lighting their way.

'Starry-starry-night, paint your palette blue and grey,' Moira said, 'I just wish that I could sing it for you, it's a lovely song, you would like it.'

'I'm sure that I would, but I don't need songs, not when I have you by my side.'

The kiss lasted long. Two people clearly in the first throws of love, illuminated by a single shooting star en-route to an unknown destination – just like their romance.

Iris looked amazed when her daughter walked in alone,

'Where's Jim ?'

'He wouldn't come in, even for a coffee. Apparently people might find it, not proper for me to entertain a man at this hour of the night. It might rewneed my reputation.' Iris nearly choked on laughter as Moira carried on.

'Well it was a word a bit like that, he meant ruined.'

'There's not many round here who would be so concerned for your reputation.'

'That's for sure, most would be wanting to ruin it as fast as possible!' chortled Moira. Iris's face took on a serious look,

'I don't know what's to become of you two. Whatever, it will be for obvious reasons, a rocky ride, but he seems to be a good man and I can only wish you well. Be prepared for heartache though it's bound to be around the corner, and I'm not sure I'll want to be around when your brother finds out about tonight. Wouldn't surprise me if he doesn't already know.'

'I'll deal with him, it's none of his business. I'm a grown woman who can do what she wants,' declared the newly assured Moira as she gave her mother a hug and watched her safely into the front door of her home.

Moira was aware that there would be challenges ahead. She had seen people's stares, heard their unpleasant comments, and noticed those who crossed over the road to avoid her. But she loved him and was ready for the fight that lay ahead.

Chapter 27

He drew a circle that shut me out
Heretic rebel, a thing to flout
But love and I had wit to win
We drew a circle that took him in.
  Outwitted
  Edwin Markham

The first Saturday of the month, a welcome day off, what to do with it? Moira pondered as she soaked in the bath. Alex had that sorted before she had even descended the stairs. Aila had phoned to invite them over for the afternoon, a bit of stalking for Alex and afternoon tea, and he'd said:

'Yes,' not even thinking to ask first.

'That sounds good, did she mention a time?' Moira asked as she wandered into the kitchen, newly bathed and ready for an easy day.

'No, just afternoon.'

'OK, that's fine, we'll go straight after lunch.'

'Can we eat early?'

'That stomach of yours, we've only just had breakfast! Or is the rush about spending time with Uncle Roddy?'

'Both! I haven't been out with him for ages, we might find something injured then I can get to do another skinning. I want to make a rug for Jim, I think he would like one.'

'That's very thoughtful,' Moira said, with concern that this suggestion would be best not put to Roddy. Certainly, not before she had seen how the land lay there. He might have regained full control of his senses, but you could never be sure. Alex was right, they hadn't seen him for a while, not since January, but then it was winter. Oh, you stupid woman, you do overthink matters, she said to herself and returned to the routine chores, as her brain lingered in the happy part of her mind.

The drive over to the estate was glorious – the weather had changed, probably only a gesture she thought – but the sky was clear, the sun shone bright and her inner depths glowed at the magic of it all. Their arrival was met by Roddy, waiting in his car.

'There's no time to waste, get in there Alex, we're going to the other side of the estate,' and with waves and cheery, 'Byes,' they were off.

The old Land Rover disappeared into the distance and Moira was greatly relieved. Flora and Fiona were off to a party, so there was only time for a quick catch up on their lives, which they had barely done when a toot outside called the girls to their waiting transport, kisses and hugs sent them on their way. Moira was incredibly fond of her nieces; they were bright and cheerful, well mannered, the sort of girls she would have liked for herself, but in the absence of such, she was delighted to be such a significant part of their lives and they equally adored her.

'Did you bring your sewing?' Aila asked,

'No, should I have done?'

'Oh, that boy of yours, he obviously forgot to tell you, another male trait methinks!' Aila said as she plumped up cushions in the lounge.

'But why did you want me to?'

'I thought it would be an opportunity to compare progress and do a little work on them as we chat. Doesn't matter though, how's yours coming along?' Aila asked as she rummaged in her work basket.

'Well to be honest, I've not done a lot, my days have been full of one thing and another, let's have a look at yours.' Aila pulled out a stitched vision of Scotland.

'Oh, that's superb, you've done it in the autumn, not the summer I had expected. The purples of the heather are gorgeous, is that tweed?'

'Yes, it is, a friend bought some bits in Harris and gave me her leftovers, so I couldn't resist.'

'It'll be fabulous when it's finished; I'm going to have to pull my socks up to compete with that,' Moira declared.

'But it's not a competition Moira, and you are exceptionally good at this sort of thing, that's why I had to try hard, I didn't want to be shown up by you! You ready for a cup of tea?'

'Silly question, I'm always ready for tea.'

They settled down in the lounge, with tea and shortbread, ready for exchanges of goings on – they never called it gossip. Aila was quick to start.

'How about that man of yours?'

'No you first, how've you been?'

'Well, there's been little of the, goings on, variety,' laughed Aila

'Roddy has been swamped with work on the estate, there's been a surprising number of winter visitors. I've done the usual estate paperwork and gave a helping hand in the kitchens when required, just normal day to day stuff. It works so well with the girls now growing up. I can leave them safely and sometimes they come and give a hand, they are getting fairly professional at shortbread. What do you think of these?'

'They're excellent,' Moira said, 'well done them. They'll be doing you out of a job.'

'That's enough about us, you're bound to have more to tell than me,' said Aila, ' I take it by the smile on your face that you're still seeing him?'

With that, Moira recounted everything that had happened since Hogmanay, the blossoming of feelings, the worry of not knowing when he would be gone. But for now she stressed her happiness at just being with him.

'What I don't understand is why they can't go home.'

'Oh, don't say that I don't want him to,' replied a suddenly sad looking Moira. 'From what I understand, it's to do with government departments, and money of course. The Nigerian Embassy say it's outside their remit – it should be for the ship owners to resolve – their government seems to have washed their hands of the whole affair. Scottish bureaucracy seems to pass decision making from one department to the other. I'm not sure they know what decisions are, it must be a long time since they made any, from what I hear.'

'Still it seems very unfair and after all it's not the men's fault. Surely it would be cheaper just to pay their fares.' Aila said as she stoked the fire.

'I know, but in the meantime, we make the most of it. Has Roddy made any further comments about them?'

'Well he had a bit of an ear bashing from me. He told me that I didn't understand the world and I accused him of being patronising. Mind you, I've noticed that he can be funny about somethings. You know that he won't fly and says, if God meant us to, he would have given us wings. When I remind him that he uses a car and God didn't give him wheels, all he can do is say that's different!

'That's funny. I remember when he was a boy watching a film set in Africa, he said that it wasn't right for people to live in mud huts with straw roofs. When I reminded him that his own grandmother had lived in a house little different to that, and in the Highlands where the weather is cruel, he just stormed off with a – well at least they used some stones! Mum and I just cried with laughter, which didn't exactly make matters any better either!' grinned Moira as she ate the last biscuit.

The Land Rover could be heard coming from some distance, it clearly needed some attention, but Roddy and Alex strolled in laughing and joking and were at the sandwiches and shortbread in a flash. Whatever they had been doing was obviously hungry work. Alex was at his voluble best,

'We saw a stag Mum, it was huge, even bigger than the one on the biscuit tins – that's only a Royal Stag. OURS was a true Monarch of the Glen, our very own Glen Achall – sixteen points on his antlers, it was this huge.' He extended his arms as far as possible from his sides and nearly hit his uncle. The ladies could only smile at his enthusiasm and newly acquired knowledge. It was for all the world as if he had single handedly, not only found this beast, but had been the first ever person to see one. Roddy was quick to support his nephew.

'It's all true. It was a remarkable stag. I've only ever had fleeting glimpses of it before, so this was an incredibly special occasion,' Roddy acknowledged, as he put his arm round his nephew's shoulders and gave him a manly squeeze. 'There isn't going to be any skinning of that magnificent beast at the prime of its life,' he continued, just as the party goers returned with their little bags of goodies. There was time for a quick catch up with the girls, who announced simultaneously that:

'It was a great party, lots of games and the cake was, TREMENDOUS, just like Bozo the clown.' Which Alex immediately countered with details of his stag, just as Roddy drew Moira to one side, saying,

'Can I have a quick word? We'll be back in a minute.' He led her to the office and closed the door behind her, strange she thought, there must be a secret of some sort coming up. She was right, there was, and it took her totally by surprise.

'Moira, you were seen in the pub with that black man last night, what on earth were you thinking of? Don't you realise that you are making yourself the laughing stock of the village?' I made myself absolutely clear before. I don't approve of his lot, and I most certainly do not approve of your.... association.'

Roddy slammed his fist on his desk, grit his teeth in a snarl and went on.

'They are different to us, live in mud huts, have tribes that kill each other, eat unmentionable stuff, in short, they are savages. They aren't civilised like us, and I do not want my family having any contact with these heathens. If you continue this foolishness, I will have no choice but to forbid you from seeing my daughters. I will not have them tarnished by you and the likes of them.'

With that he opened the door, ushered her out, took her coat from the peg and showed them to their car. He was utterly calm, no trace of the former anger, no sign of his malice. No further words were spoken. It was clear from the pale look of shock on Moira's face that something terrible had been said, but Aila had no sense of the gravity of the situation.

The drive was as silent as a ghost walking on snow, Alex had temporarily used up all his words, and Moira was too angry to barely breathe, let alone speak. Her mind vacillated between acutely intense anger and absolute hatred of her brother. There was no room left within her for sadness, every molecule of her being was directed against the deliverer of such a cruel message. No tears, just absolute determination to get revenge. She would prove him wrong. Wrong on every level, and bring him down from the rarefied air of his moral high ground. He might think that she could be cut out of her nieces' lives by her friendship with someone that didn't fit his blueprint of ideal, but he would not sway her by blackmail and, as she thought this, succumbed to a fit of the giggles at the very word. Ironic, she said to herself.

The phone rang and rang as she opened the door, and in so doing disturbed the volcano of emotion swelling within. She was not surprised to hear Aila on the other end of the line, she had clearly been crying, and with sadness in her voice repeatedly apologised for her husband's vindictive actions.

'There was an all-mighty row after you left. He stormed off to the big house, banging doors and swearing under his breath as he went. I can't bear him when he behaves like this – as if everyone else has lost all reason. There was absolutely no way he would listen to my views, let alone anyone else. It was vile,'

A much calmer Moira was able to console her sister-in-law with soothing words.

'But I should be making you feel better, this is all the wrong way round.' Aila said.

'A bit like everything at the moment,' Moira said as she wriggled in an attempt to get out of her coat.

'How can you be so calm, you must be sooo hurt and angry?'

'Oh, I'm angry all right, but not at you, it's that thick-headed, stupid, idiot brother of mine, he's the one that's lost leave of his senses.'

'I know, he's so bloody stubborn, the whole world could tell him he's wrong, but he wouldn't listen, what are we going to do Moira?'

'For now, nothing I suppose, we need to let some time pass, calm down and see what happens'

'Do the girls know about all of this?'

'Fortunately no. They were watching TV and we were in the office, so I don't think that they heard anything,' sighed Aila.

'Well let's leave it at that for now, and thanks for ringing, I feel a bit better now. You?'

'Yes, I suppose so, but this isn't going to wash over in a moment is it?'

'No, it's not, but we mustn't let it come between us. Agreed?' Moira asked.

'Absolutely we mustn't, and I think it's time I got to meet the source of all these problems, he must be absolutely something!'

'He is, He absolutely is,' Moira murmured. Only to have her thoughts moved on by a sudden change of subject.

'Are you doing anything on Wednesday? Aila asked, 'Shall we have a quilt night?'

'Yes let's, I'll check with Mum and Doreen, it'll do us good to catch up and have a good natter.'

'Good, it'll get me away from that pig-headed imbecile, I'll go now and see you on Wednesday.'

The call ended with both women able to finish the day in a slightly more reasoned state of mind. Still hurt, still angry, still upset, but calmer and one of them, utterly sure that in this, she could win the battle and maintain the moral high ground.

Chapter 28

It is during our darkest moments that we must focus to see the light.
Aristotle

Jim was unaware of the discord between Moira and her brother and
she had no intention of telling him; nor did she have any intention of not
seeing him again either. She was made of sterner stuff than that, and as
the raw anger ebbed away, it was replaced by a calm assuredness that
right was on her side, and that prejudice would not win. It was all
pushed to the dark corner of her mind – the part reserved for
unpleasantness, her mental garbage bin – and it would remain there,
locked away with other painful memories, and only be opened on the
very rarest of occasions. She was back in control, standing as tall as her
five-foot two-inch stature would allow, and ready for the future. Jim
would not have any inkling of what had occurred, and she just looked
forward to seeing him tomorrow.

For once they had the house to themselves, a first for a Sunday. Alex
had a special band practice and wouldn't be home until 9 and so their
kisses evolved into embraces and passion, the inevitable conclusion of
feelings that could no longer be controlled. Their union was frantic, yet
tender, every part of their bodies resonating with the lust and love of the
moment. With their energies spent, they lay in each other's arms, totally
relaxed, the only words necessary were of their love for each other.
Nothing was to separate them now. They could have lain there all night,
but managed to pull themselves apart and were sat drinking coffee in
the lounge on Alex's return. There was no clue from their body language
of the change in their relationship, and both had agreed that this was for
the best.

Alex, as exuberant as ever, detailed every step and breathe of the
stalking he had done to see HIS Monarch Stag, whose magnificence he

described in thorough detail. There was no stopping him. Jim nodded, openly impressed by such an animal, but Moira wanted her son upstairs and in bed,

'It's school tomorrow, time for you to go to bed,' and he did exactly that.

' It's quilt night on Wednesday, will you join us.' Moira asked. 'It'll be good for you to see Mum again and Aila will be here as well.'

' Oh no, I don't think so, I don't sew,' Jim said with a wince.

'We wouldn't expect you to, silly! Aila said she would like to meet you, so why not? It gives us a little more time together, and you should mix with more people.'

Jim looked uncomfortable and didn't reply. Moira gave him a questioning look and he finally said:

'Oh, I'm not sure, it doesn't seem the right thing to do. They won't want me there.'

'It'll be fine, just you wait and see. It will help with your English. Please Jim, it would mean a lot to me, and it'll be better than you think.' Moira pleaded with the coquettish look of a determined woman.

'Oh, all right, but I won't stay long, I know you ladies like to have a good catch up as you call it.' She tipped her head to one side and gave him a flirtatious look.

'OK you win, I'll try and stay for the whole evening, but the way ladies chat, I'll probably not understand a thing.' He took her chin in his hand, leant over her glowing face, and kissed her. A kiss so gentle that Moira felt as if she were a princess, which is exactly how Jim had come to see her.

Aila took to Jim immediately. Initially, she was drawn to him by his striking eyes and glowing skin, but it was the very caring tender way he was with Moira, that set her mind at rest. His melodic gentle voice lulled her into the realisation that there was a hidden depth. It was clear that nothing her stupid husband said was going to separate these two people, they were so right together.

In the end Jim stayed most of the evening. He made coffee for everyone, and made all the right complementary remarks on their handiworks, and even joined in some of the conversation, lured in by Iris's dilemma:

'My fence has blown over again and one of the panels is shot to pieces,'

'Oh, I could repair it for you,' Jim assured her.

'Oh, no. I couldn't ask you to do that Jim. It wouldn't seem right,'

'But you didn't ask. I offered. It would give me something to do, so you would be doing me a …. what do you call it?'

'A favour,' Moira interjected with a squeeze of his hand.

'All right then, you win,' Iris said, 'but we will need to get some more wood and you'll need to look at the job first.'

'I can look on Friday, would that be all right?'

'It would be perfect Jim, I'll see you some time on Friday morning.' Iris's face lifted into a smile as she took in her daughter's blissful face, and Jim's clear delight at having something to do.

Jim replaced broken timbers, sawed and hammered until the fence stood erect – nearly as good as new. Not only did he fix the fence but the gutter that had come loose too and cleared all the detritus into a sack ready to be taken away. He wouldn't accept the few pounds that Iris proffered, so she slipped them into Moira's hand, and whispered:

'Take him to the pub.'

Jim was delighted to do something constructive and that was all the reward he needed.

Life was getting much worse on the Harmony and he kept this from Moira. Meals had become more limited, morale was sinking even further and fuel was running out, bringing them all to the verge of desperation and even the captain had little power to improve their lot. Jim was in a much better position than the others, and he didn't want Moira feeling sorry for him. His pride wasn't entirely intact, and he wanted to preserve what was left of it. Letting her know that he was often hungry wouldn't do at all.

The days were drawing out. Spirits lifted as signs of spring appeared. There was more conversation in the streets, people came out of winter hibernation and more customers started popping into the shop, grateful that they could get out more often. Neighbours who had barely seen each other since Christmas resumed contact, caught up on local gossip and spoke of future plans. In this way Moira heard of one or two elderly people whose homes needed shed roofs repaired, fences stood back to attention and general after-winter maintenance. She offered Jim's assistance, but some were a little hesitant at first:

'We don't know this man, how do we know that we can trust him?'

So Moira explained what a good job Jim had done on Iris's fence and that the work would help fill his time. Gradually, he was given odd jobs to do around town, not for wages, that was not allowed, but the odd note or coins were slipped surreptitiously into his pocket and sometimes titbits as well. He worked himself into the role of local handyman and some even began to rely on him.

Plans for the bicentenary celebrations were moving ahead and a general sprucing up of the town began. Jim offered his services, which were gratefully accepted. His helpful nature and good workmanship became the subject of the grape vine – which in the main lauded his efforts. Of course, there were those who expressed different opinions:

'Should stay on board.'

'Might steal from us.'

'How can we trust him?'

What they actually meant, was that he was different, foreign, black, possibly a threat, and those who were most reluctant to accept him as a fellow human being, were those who should know better. It became clear to Moira that one of the worst culprits was Miss McKay, who steadfastly avoided any discussion that might have involved praising his efforts. She could frequently be seen in close huddles on street corners, with others in the community who were of a similar opinion – their acerbic racial comments sometimes reached her ears, but she remained deaf to their bigotry.

By the end of March, Jim was spending many of his days in the town. He could be seen with hammer and nails, saw and paint pot, up ladders and on his knees. No job was too small or apparently too large and even the bigots couldn't help notice his community endeavours. He began to stay over with Moira. At first, still concerned about her reputation and his religious beliefs he had been reluctant to do this. He frequently asked:

'Are you totally sure. What about Alex what will he think? In fact, Alex was delighted to see more of him, they had become good friends and having Jim around gave him much pleasure. The die was cast, and Jim moved his few possessions from the ship, something that was around the town with the speed of a shooting star and reached her brother within twenty-four hours.

On board the Harmony, Jim left it for the captain to advise of his good fortune, the news being received with mixed emotions by the ten left behind. Even Samuel found it difficult to be cheerful at his friend's improved circumstances. But he still got to visit them, he had not been forgotten in the rush to find their own harmony on land. With no progress on their futures, the men were becoming neglectful of themselves, depression leaves little energy for self-respect and eats away at dreams and ambition: they had endured about all that they could.

Good Friday fell on April first, which seemed somewhat ironic to Moira, who wasn't sure if she should play April fool tricks on her son or carry out more pious works, an easy decision really, given that she had no belief in God. Jim, however, was somewhat confused by the tricks played on him. A metal scourer in the tip of his shoes, so he couldn't get them on. His socks, few as there were, in odd pairs, and he nearly hit the ceiling, when Alex sprang out of the bathroom, just as he was about to enter.

'You have strange ways of marking Good Friday,' Jim laughed, and was reassured that the tricks were for something different all together. After all the merriment had settled down, Alex and Moira were taken aback by Jim's suggestion that they should all go to church on Sunday.

'It being such a holy day.'

Mother and son looked at each other askance, church was generally not something they did, but it clearly mattered to Jim, who couldn't fully understand their reluctance to attend a service that was an annual pleasure to him. To please him they agreed, but Alex was most insistent that Jim should help him repair his bike as his reward.

By the end of Saturday the bike was running well and had been cleaned and polished to perfection, just as Moira, laden with bags, arrived home.

'What have you got there? Jim asked, as he rushed to relieve her of her load. 'That's too much for you to carry,' he admonished.

'It's OK, they look worse than they are, and Angus gave me a lift back, so I've not carried them far.'

'What's in them Mum, that's a lot of bags?'

'Well, I told Angus about our forthcoming church visit, with which he was very impressed,' she said, looking Jim squarely in the face.

'He said that we should make this a very special occasion and handed me all these. I've not had a chance to see what's in them.' Alex rushed forward and had one of the bags in his hands in seconds.

'Mum, mum, this one has got Easter eggs in it!'

'And this cake has balls on the top,' added an equally delighted Jim.

'That's a Simnel cake, a special one for Easter, the balls are made of marzipan which is in the middle as well,' Moira said as she emptied another bag.

'A whole side of salmon – he's just too generous' Moira declared, while steadfastly refusing to see the sticker saying eat by third April – tomorrow.

Angus had certainly put a smile on all their faces and Moira dashed to phone her Mum and Doreen to share the good news. Iris said that she would join them at church, a gesture that overwhelmed Moira, knowing as she did the significance of it. Her mum, like them, rarely went to church, so even going was special, but she recognized that it was her way of openly supporting her daughter, Alex, and Jim. It would be noticed, discussed, and leave no one in any doubt about her position on the relationship. Moira would have given her the biggest of hugs, but that could not be done over the telephone, it would wait until later.

Chapter 29

'Hope' is the thing with feathers –
That perches in the soul –
And sings the tune without words –
And never stops - at all –
    Hope is the thing with feathers
    Emily Dickinson

Jim was up bright and early, Moira just early, and Alex neither of these. 'Sunday is for lying in,' he groaned, but was removed from the comfort of his bed by the smell of bacon cooking. Never fails, Moira said to herself as he rushed downstairs to eat his sandwich, just as Doreen appeared with a coat over her arm.

'For you Jim, let's see if it fits.' And it did. A little shorter than designed but perfect on the shoulders. 'You look good in that Jim.' Doreen said. 'Nearly as good as my late Eric did when he got togged up for church. Give us a twirl.'

Jim duly circled round, like a clumsy ballerina, as everyone nodded approvingly and guided him out of the door. The four arrived at the church a good ten minutes early, but it was already almost full.

'The second busiest day of the year,' the minister explained. 'You are all most welcome.' Their entrance was marked with turning heads, nudged elbows, some raising of eyebrows, whilst the more devout resolutely faced forwards then sneakily took sideways glances, but a loud:

'Hello, there's room here,' from Hamish, surprised each and every one of them. He greeted Jim like a long-lost friend and the congregation settled down, their attention drawn back to the business of the morning, as the organ boomed out a tune only vaguely similar to the one the composer had intended.

Moira was aware of the odd glances in their direction, but generally remained more composed than she had expected and mimed along with the hymns, leaving her mother to cover for the inadequacies of her voice. Alex sort of sang, but not Jim, his voice rose above the congregation, lack of words was no obstacle to him – volume was the order of the day – and Moira just managed to stop him from clapping his hands at a more uplifting part of hymn two. The look in her eyes told him that this was not done, and he settled into the monotony of serious religion. There was no rejoicing and Hallelujahs, just faces that appeared to garner no pleasure from the proceedings, in short, he was disappointed. Where was the fun, the dancing, clapping and smiles he was used to? The service was, in his opinion, grey like the weather, but at least he had carried out his duty to God by attending on such an important day.

The minister was as pleased to see them go, as he had been at their arrival. He shook their hands,

'I look forward to see you all again in the near future.'

'Not likely,' Alex grunted under his breath. Some of the congregation came over for a few words, but Miss McKay was steadfastly holding court with her acolytes under the windswept tree near the Lych gate. The group – church regulars mostly – included Mr and Mrs McTavish and they were deep in conversation. Stood in a circle, heads together, it was clear that this was a private group that had much to discuss. It was only their constant glances towards Jim and Moira that gave an indication as to subject of their discourse. The haughty way they looked over at them gave a clear indication as to their opinions. Iris was all for, 'Knocking the smirks off their faces,' which caused laughter all round and a prelude to a pleasant walk back to the warmth of home.

Iris impersonated some off the stuffier congregation and Doreen was pretty adept at identifying them; of course the trills of Mrs McTavish were instantly recognised by everyone, including Jim. The piece de resistance was Jim's re-enactment of a, proper service Nigerian style. He had them all on their feet, swaying from side to side, clapping and singing so loudly that even Moira could join in, all ending with as many Aaaaaamens as they could muster and a final resounding Hallelujah.

'Now isn't that very much better?' Jim asked, as they all collapsed back into their chairs clutching their aching stomachs and all but crying from so much laughter. No answer was required.

Later, alone in the lounge, Jim and Moira sat close and watched a film, but they were more interested in each other, happy to cuddle, kiss and forget the outside world. Yet Jim's thoughts wandered to his shipmates. They wouldn't have had a day like this and this made him feel uncomfortable. He turned towards Moira and looked so serious that she asked,

'Is something wrong?'

Jim cleared his throat, 'Can I take some cake to Samuel please?'

'Of course, you can, that's hardly a big ask, is it?' Moira replied.

'Maybe not to you, but I don't like asking.' said a very serious Jim.

'Oh for goodness sake, take half and share it with the others, Angus would be pleased for it to go to them.'

'Are you sure? They'll be delighted. They barely have any food left.' His face saddened at the revelation he had kept secret for so long and Moira's expression turned to concern.

'What? Why didn't you tell me before, how bad is it?'

'There are a few tins and some rice, but the oil won't last much longer, then there will be no heat, light or cooking, so everyone is worried.'

Moira's hand covered her mouth in shocked concern. 'Oh Jim. If we had known it was that bad we would have done more. I wondered why we had seen so few of them around these last few weeks. There must be something we can do. I'll tell Angus.'

'You have all been very generous to us already.'

'It's hardly asking for much, no one wants to see men starving on their own doorstep.' Moira said as tears glazed her eyes. At this he scooped her up in his arms and carried her upstairs. All sadness replaced with love and tenderness and then by the perfect sleep of the satiated. They lay like spoons, with his arm tightly wrapped around her as if he were afraid she might escape.

After an early Sunday, Alex was adamant: 'I need a lie in!' so was left undisturbed while Moira and Jim went off to the shop. Murdo – a local inshore fisherman – offered Jim a lift back to the Harmony on his way to check his pots. They left, chatting away as if they were friends of old passing on the tricks of their own watery trades.

An update by Moira on the impoverished state of the Harmony crew sent Angus rushing to the phone as Moira dealt with the trickle of customers that barely occupied her time, let alone her worried mind. She was grateful to leave at noon, it would give her time for domestics which were becoming increasingly difficult to fit in.

Jim's appearance on the Harmony was welcomed by them all, especially the captain, who missed the language sessions and conversations of old, but he gave Jim time with his shipmates before inviting him for a coffee in his quarters. There was much catching up to be done, but little of it was cheerful and Jim was reluctant to share his own happiness too widely in case it distressed the others. Coffees, that looked and tasted like brown water, were passed round and the cake was eaten in an instant. It was obviously much more than a treat to them all. Jim skirted around food issues but in the end decided to ask outright:

'What did you all eat yesterday?' Looks between the men indicated it might be a sore point, but he persevered. The men looked so wretched and were reluctant to say anything. It transpired that meat was now non-existent and they had been reduced to catching seagulls. They lured the birds onto the boat with fish scraps found in the harbour, netted them, and then ate them. But they provided little in the way of meat and so they had searched for beetles, anything that could give them nourishment, there had even been a rat or two. Their discomfort at revealing how low they had sunk was palpable and Jim had to force back tears. He would not want even his enemies to suffer like this and promised that he would do all that he could to get them more to eat by whatever means possible.

The captain confirmed the men's stories and confided that the oil was unlikely to last much more than a week. He had rigged up some old oil drums with grids to make BBQs, and this helped reduce consumption, but the generator wouldn't work for much longer, then there would be no light, heat or running hot water and, as he recounted all of this, tears welled in his eyes and trickled down his cheeks, and he cried out loud. The first release of emotion since this had all begun, and Jim could offer few words in solace, so took him in his arms and hugged him back to normality with further pledges of help.

The captain took him back to land; he looked so despondent, and as Jim disembarked, both of their eyes welled with an emotion more eloquent than any words and they parted with firmly clasped hands and caring looks.

It came as no surprise to anyone that in the following days two further crew members slipped into the Highlands of Scotland, no one knew where they had gone or how they would manage without money. It would seem that they preferred to be refugees in a strange country than starve to death on a boat in the last gasps of life. The Harmony was down to one captain and seven men on board and all they actually had left was hope, and that was in as short a supply as everything else.

Chapter 30

Bodies ravaged by hunger must take sustenance from prayer and psalm
>   Anon

In an attempt to find emergency help for the crew of the beleaguered Harmony, Angus contacted all manner of charities and government departments, but everything took time, so much time, and it made him angry.

'Why do people in agreeable offices, with full plates, take so long to do the very jobs they're paid for?' he asked Moira as she passed the recently arrived chilled perishables to him.

'How would I know? The whole thing is incomprehensible to me. Surely in this day and age we wouldn't let anyone starve in our own country,'

'I agree,' Angus said as he stacked the chiller cabinet, 'Ivan was in the other day – for a hot coffee and a chat as much as anything I think – he looked so unwell, the strain is showing, and I worry for his health. But he never let on how bad it is. Pride can be such a folly.'

'Oh, you're right there, Angus. I'm sure that Jim hasn't told me the full extent of their problems and they might well be much worse than he has described. Surely we can get someone to go on board to see for themselves.'

'We can only do that if Ivan agrees,' Angus said. ' Now that I know him a lot better, I may be able to persuade him. It's in all their best interests if he does. Waiting for the authorities is getting them nowhere. In the meantime, let's have another push for more donations, if everyone gave just one tin it would make a big difference. I'll contact the church and mission,'

'I'll also let all the ladies making the quilt know, with luck all your efforts will produce some official action before long.' Moira said as she passed over the last blocks of cheese, and wiped down the counter surface.

'I do hope so, I'm actually embarrassed that this has not been resolved long before now. It's downright disgusting,' Angus shouted, just as a couple of customers came in and brought the conversation to an end.

Over the next few days Jim chased contacts, made new ones and pushed as hard as he could. Ivan, however, remained reluctant to have visitors, so Moira promised to get as much information as possible from Jim, who was currently painting the railings along Shore Street as part of the bicentenary spruce up.

The minister, on hearing of the declining circumstances of the men announced to his congregation:

'These are our fellow men, all Christians I understand, we must help them as much as we can. It is my intention to hold a special service for them. Maybe not here in church, that may be intimidating for them, maybe on the ship would be more appropriate.'

Hamish from the Seaman's mission stood and added, 'Why don't we have a special gathering near the harbour? Somewhere near the Christmas tree spot, then we could all join in. Good for the community to come together, especially in this bicentenary year.'

'An excellent plan,' the minister replied. 'It'll be uplifting for us all.' Whilst quietly wondering how this would work. His organisation moved only marginally quicker than everyone else's and finally on Sunday seventeenth of April the men arrived by lifeboat to stand with fishermen, housewives, publicans, and the good folk of Ullapool for:

'This special service of unity, to show solidarity with these men and to bless this town of ours in this special year.' The whole experience was a revelation to them all, and not necessarily the most uplifting. The rain stayed away, but the wind did not, and the biblical readings were whisked away on gusts before ears could catch them, hymn sheets flew around like confetti and the Harmony crew had no understanding of what it was all about. The whole affair made all the more surreal by the addition of bagpipes towards the end. In short, it served the pious fairly well, they had done their duty for these stranded men and passed a crate of tins and assorted packets to them – their charitable giving blessed en route – before they returned to the comfort of their homes. Others drifted off to the pub, but Jim and Moira stayed chatting to the crew who wanted to know if this had been a real service.

The box of foodstuffs was carried aloft into the lifeboat and ferried back as the most precious cargo for many a week. Their souls might not have been much lifted, but anticipation of a decent meal was high and they celebrated in song. Hymns sung in a way they understood, loud and cheerful with clapping and praise – the sound drifted back to shore and those standing there were uplifted too.

Moira saw Aila and her nieces at the service, and with no sign of Roddy, took the opportunity to have a quick catch up and discreetly introduced the girls to Jim. Alex huddled up with Fiona and Flora, discussing matters of total irrelevance to everyone else – but apparently as important as matters of state to the youngsters. Iris was delighted to see her daughter with her nieces. Roddy's stubbornness had been obvious from an early age and she knew how difficult it was to change his mind, but the current situation was deeply upsetting and she wished that an end would come to it before long. The strength of the wind increased and bit into exposed skin, making standing still very unpleasant, and so they cut short their conversation and went their separate ways. Jim, with his arms around the two ladies' shoulders and Alex close by his mother's side, walked home briskly. The minister and the trilling McTavishes were once again a source of amusement and unwittingly contributed to another jolly meal at number four.

Jim was full of questions – so many that they laughingly asked if he was studying for an exam in religion. What type of church did the minister come from? Were all services very dull? Why didn't people wear hats and bright colours on Sundays? Could anyone marry in the church or be buried there? The list was endless, so much so, that Iris suggested, with a wink,

'Why don't you make teas Jim, give you time to digest all the answers?' He could see the funny side and laughed his way to the kitchen, where Alex joined him and they started on the washing up.

'I reckon we can do it better than the ladies,' Jim said.

'I reckon we can too,' agreed the tea-towel waving Alex, who didn't even mind this chore now that he had his much-loved companion at his side. They sang and played the Nigerian song Shango together – cutlery and pans were instruments – Jim the deep voice of thunder, and Alex sang melody. The pair were getting rather good, Jim had proved to be an able tutor to the eager Alex. But Moira and Iris began to think that the interminable questions might have been the better option, the volume was loud, very LOUD indeed.

With order eventually established in the kitchen, and peace restored to the house, Iris left for home and Alex, reluctantly, to his room to finish homework.

'He's such a last-minute merchant, it'll trip him up one day,' Moira said, which resulted in questioning from Jim as to how Alex had become, a merchant, and how that would, cause him to fall. Many giggles later:

'I think I understand. This strange language with its funny sayings will take me years to get to fully know.'

'I wouldn't worry about that, you've done so very well, and most of us still don't understand everything that people say: different accents, lots of words for the same thing. Do you know there are hundreds of words for rain in Scotland, can you believe that?'

'Oh yes, I can believe that it seems to be the speciality of the area, rain!' Jim chortled. 'In Nigeria its either wet or dry and if wet, it's a little or a lot, that's it. One day you might see it for yourself,'

'I'd like that, but it's unlikely to happen.'

'You never know, life can have some strange twists and turns,' he said.

'Look at you with your newly acquired sayings, I'll have to get me a dictionary,' laughed Moira, as she poured water into the kettle.

Alex yelled down the stairs:

'Can you two be quiet, you're disturbing my concentration!' This resulted in more giggles, then a:

'Don't you be so cheeky,' from his mother as she took him some hot chocolate before carrying two teas into the lounge. Jim was already settled on the sofa as she pushed the video into the recorder,

'Doreen said this one's very good.'

'Whats it called,' Jim asked.

'Romancing the Stone.' Moira replied as she snuggled up beside him for the full hour and three quarters.

'Oh, wasn't that good,' she said, 'all that romance and action. It had the lot. A lovely end to another good day.' Jim cleared his throat, as Moira turned off the recorder, then he sat bolt upright and said,

'I want to say something,'

'You look serious after such a good film.'

'I want to ask you something.'

'Go on then, ask away,' Moira said with a hint of impatience.

'It doesn't seem right to me that I live here with you, my upbringing told me it was wrong. I have been giving this much thought Moira and today's very grey service made up my mind.' Moira looked concerned and went to interrupt.

'Don't stop me now, let me continue. I have nothing, but I know that I can change that. I'm a hard worker with skills in boat making and fishing and Hamish has told me that there is work available in Aberdeen and that I might be able to get a temporary work permit. But. More importantly. I want to be with you, for ever. Would you be my wife? Will you marry me Moira?'

There was no thought of potential problems. The seriousness in his face, the pleading in his eyes, struck straight at her heart and only one answer was possible:

'Oh, yes, I would like that very much,' she answered, with all the assuredness in the world.

For a moment, nothing was said. Words were superfluous as they fell into each other's arms and showered each other with kisses. They were the stars of their very own romance and it was good. They talked of the future, community reaction, bureaucracy and knew that this maybe the roughest of journeys, but pledged to make it work.

Moira wanted to stand on the harbour wall and tell the whole world, but in the clarity of day, sense prevailed.

'Let's sort out what we are allowed to do first, then we can tell people,' she said. 'I don't want the likes of my brother, deriding us or worse. We must be entirely sure that we can do this.'

So they continued their lives as normal, although a few people commented on her happy face. They remarked that she looked younger somehow, which she put down to better weather and no one said anymore. Not a soul had any idea that they intended to marry – and they didn't intend to wait long.

They chose their times carefully. First to visit the minister who was:

'Very sorry, but wholly unable to marry a divorced person, against the church rules you see.' But Moira sensed an air of relief that such a rule was in place and made a mental note that the minister might share Miss McKay's point of view. A discreet appointment with the registrar was no more uplifting, he was:

'Unsure whether it was allowed,' and would have, 'to check the regulations about foreign nationals marrying here.' But was in no rush to actually check. Moira became increasingly angry at the registrar's intransigence.

'So, have you actually checked whether we can marry or not? she demanded on her fourth visit to his office.

'No need to use that tone of voice,' he sneered as he walked towards her from behind his extensive desk, 'I'm not sure that this marriage should be allowed, I suspect it's a marriage of convenience.' He towered over the seated Moira. 'We can't have foreign nationals abusing our good nature; using our women as aids to passports.' At which Moira stood as tall as she could, stared him straight in the face, widened her eyes, clenched her fists at her side and retorted:

'How dare you talk to me like that. How dare you. I'm a grown woman who knows right from wrong and you're wrong, so bloody wrong. I wouldn't have you marry me if you were the last registrar on the planet. You weasel of a man,' and she stormed out as his jaw dropped in disbelief.

As a consequence, they found themselves driving over to the nearby larger town of Dingwalls to meet the registrar there. The sun had come out, winds had abated and hand in hand they crossed the threshold, full of anticipation – surely someone would marry them? The registrar, a Mr McDougall, had a round florid face, one that spoke of humour and fine living, it rested atop a corpulent body which confirmed the story told by his face. A cheerful man who instilled confidence. Moira crossed her fingers and started on her now well-rehearsed little speech. He listened carefully, urged them to sit in the chairs placed just to the side of his desk, asked many questions, perched a pair of metal rimmed glasses on the end of his nose, consulted a large tome. They sat like statues waiting for his response. After what seemed like an age, he closed the book, looked up, removed the spectacles, stood, walked round his desk and looking at them both said,

'I would be delighted to marry you, it all appears to be in accordance with our rules. I can't currently see any reason why not. Do you have a date in mind?' They could hardly speak, hugged each other, shook his hand, and Moira asked,

'When can we marry?'

'Well there is a six-week waiting period so the earliest date would be thirteenth of June – not a popular date, for obvious reasons – fully booked over the weekends, so any midweek date after then, or if it's a weekend requirement you'll have to wait longer.' It was Jim's turn,

'I would like it to be on twenty-first of June, the longest day of the year, this is a very special day for our family. It was the date of my parent's marriage and my mother's birthday; they have a good marriage, and my mother is a good woman, so I would like the twenty-first.' To which Moira could only say,

'So would I.' Mr McDougall nodded,

'The twenty-first it is then, shall we say noon, split the day into two equal halves? Don't forget you'll need two witnesses, but first let's get the paperwork done.

Chapter 31

In my gifts I give a mine
Down where Lord lies to treasures shine,
Gratitude of hearts oppressed;
Givers' Klondike are the best.
 A song of giving
 Anon

As April progressed the days lengthened, the sun appeared a little more, but it was still cold on a rusty old ship moored in the middle of a Scottish loch. Heat and light were restricted to minimal hours. Cooking, what there was of it, was done on the braziers concocted from oil drums and fired by wood salvaged from onboard crates and from the countryside around town. In this way the oil was eked out until the end of the month; more seagulls made their final flights into disintegrating nets and some provisions reached them from the town. Their nutrition was more diet than balanced, but it was sufficient to keep them alive, and in the end, Ivan had no choice but to fully reveal the indignity of their lot to anyone that could help.

As the oil provided the last flickering light of the night, Ivan received a message from Angus. Officials would visit the ship on the twenty-ninth, to see what help they could give. Ivan barely had any emotional energy left to be reassured by this, but woke the next morning with a slightly lighter heart. The men equally found it difficult to be uplifted; previous dreams had been dashed and they did not see that this visit would make any difference either.

 There were three of them: all dressed in suits, with waxed jackets over the top and their feet clad in sturdy shoes. These bureaucrats explored every nook and cranny of the vessel which, by now, had been denuded to empty spaces. Living conditions were examined, notes taken, and requests to visit the kitchens and store areas made. There was virtually nothing for them to see: a nearly empty bag of rice, three tins of beans, some porridge oats and dried milk formed the main components of what was laughingly called, the stores,

'Surely there's more than this?' asked the oldest of the three, then gave each other shocked looks at the reply. The braziers on deck revealed how the crewmen had been cooking and the large container of feathers indicated what had been caught in the bedraggled nets on deck. No further questions were needed. They left in a sombre mood, caught between compassion and regulations; their earnest expressions showed concern, but little in the way of positivity.

No one expected any immediate progress – there was a May bank holiday weekend to be got though first, but they were to be surprised.

Telephone wires crackled with calls. Smiles broke out on land and on the loch shoulders that had been slumped, pulled back and necks lengthened as good news percolated through. A transport union agreed to pay the crew's air fares home and government departments found funds – not much, just thirty pounds per week – to see the men fed until arrangements were made.

The village was soon buzzing with the news and the spring air became infused with positivity. Moira nearly blurted out her own good news on several occasions, but stopped herself just in time. Family must know first.

The money would arrive on Monday 9th May. But it wouldn't fully resolve the situation. The men would still be on board a cold damp vessel with no heating or lighting and with only a brazier to cook on. No longer starving hungry – but still cold and dejected.

'Surely this shouldn't be the best we can do,' Moira said to Angus. 'They are innocent victims, trapped for all these months in a country that would describe itself as, civilised. But I suppose it's better than nothing, and we'll do the best we can. I'll think of a plan and we can sort it out it in the morning.'

'And I'll get Ivan to come over,' Angus said, 'then he can hear the good news and be part of the decision-making process.'

Being a Wednesday it was ladies' night, not just Doreen but Iris as well. They were to finish their contributions for the wall hanging, ready to be passed to Mrs Stewart the art teacher at the High School for the final joining together. There was a slight possibility that Aila would pop in, but they could never be totally sure. Since Jim had moved in Roddy had forbidden Aila and the girls from meeting Moira. He had instructed her:

'Not to set foot in that house ever again.'

Keen to keep her home life calm she alluded to compliance but took opportunities, when they presented themselves, to pop round and meet them all.

Squares were laid on the floor, suggestions made as to the best way to complete them, and final stitches made. The work was impressive. They would be able to hold their heads up high and stand comparison with the finest needlewomen in Ullapool. As needles flashed, words flowed and they agreed that there must be more they could do to help the crew and gradually a plan was worked out. Moira's suggestion that they could cook the meals for the men, was promptly met by an offer from Doreen to help and Iris offered to prep vegetables and generally give support when required.

'But how will we get it all to the ship?' Doreen asked, almost to herself. 'Could we borrow some insulated containers from somewhere? My school may have some spare ones.' At which Moira nodded her head.

'But then we will have to organise boats to take us, bring us back, and get the containers back to us in the morning. It seems a long-winded way of feeding eight men. Why don't we just cook a hot evening meal and serve it here?'

'But you can't have all eight here Moira, not on top of the three of you already living here, it's too much,' observed Iris.

'I know, let's split the load,' Doreen suggested. 'I could take four, you have three Moira, and maybe Angus would feed Ivan – they have become friends after all,'

'That's a brilliant plan,' Moira replied, 'But we'd better see what Jim and Alex think, about it. This is a big step after all and they should be consulted first.'

'Well it sounds as if it could work, but best word of this doesn't get to your brother any time soon.' Iris said, 'I don't think he's in any mind to see this as the humane act that it is. I'm proud of you both, what good people you are. But ... I'm not sure how to say this ... what will the gossip mongers make of the arrangements? I don't want them thinking that you're taking over Dollar Diana's business.'

'Oh Mum, what a silly thing to say. Do we look as if we ply a trade around the ships?'

'Well, probably not,' Iris chortled into her hand, 'It was a stupid thing to say wasn't it?'

'Sure was, but you're forgiven.' Moira said as she ruffled her mother's hair.

Jim's initial hesitancy was soon overcome, and he even offered to do some cooking if it would be allowed. Alex appeared to be happy and said:

'It sounds like a plan…. so long as I don't have to do the vegetables or clear up the plates.' Altruism was yet to fully flow through his veins.

All of this was put to Angus the next morning,

'I'll check with Joan,' he said and rushed to the telephone to do exactly that. By the time he returned, Ivan had arrived and savoured proper coffee while they dealt with customers and eventually the plans were laid out before him. The first money was due to be credited to the business account by the end of the week, and if everyone was agreed, they would start with a hot meal on Monday evening. Ivan was too drained to do other than accept this hospitality.

As far as Ivan was concerned Monday could not come quickly enough and he left for the ship with some venison scraps and three large onions and some new contributions from the Harmony box – the men would be able to cook a little something to keep them going.

'Operation-caterers was underway,' laughed Angus as he sent Moira home to work out a menu.

The excitement on the Harmony was palpable. The men hugged each other and fist pumped the air. Samuel jumped with the joy,

' At long last,' he shouted out, 'after all these weeks we might be going home.'

'Amen to that.' Was the near universal response.

Good news made even the watery stew and rice seem like a feast – a celebratory meal. No matter the weekend might be as deprived as the previous ones, Monday would be here in no time at all and plans must be made to wash clothes, scrub skin, cut hair – they would not disgrace themselves by presenting a downtrodden look. They were all determined to arrive as smartly turned-out guests, but what could they take as a gift? The answer to this took them all weekend to resolve.

Chapter 32

So, when I hear these poor ones laugh,
And see the rich ones coldly frown –
Poor men, think I, need not go up
So much as rich men should come down.
   Money
   William Henry Davies

The women were all well used to economising, but this would challenge their skills at making a pound do the work of five. The money would buy little more than a family of four might require for a decent diet and this awful realisation left them seriously worried at what they had taken on. How was it to be possible? A call to Angus reassured a little – he would provide everything at wholesale prices. It was the realisation that the money would be paid four weeks in advance that they found most heartening – they would be able to buy staples in bulk.

A four-week menu was devised, and a shopping list drawn up. In a moment of post menu euphoria Doreen declared:

'Thank goodness we've sorted all that out! I think we should rename ourselves the Three Musketeers – one for all and all for one!' At which Iris and Moira simultaneously chortled and started play fighting with two wooden spoons grabbed from the nearby container. They were ready.

It was only later that Moira confided in Jim that,

'It was going to be difficult, it's not anywhere near the money required, but we will do our best.'

'I know you will do your best, that's the sort of woman you are, and I love you all the more because of it.' Jim said as he ushered her upstairs. That night they drifted off to sleep in each other's arms, he into the deep sleep of the contented, whilst she saw sacks of potatoes, nets of onions and carrots, drifting though mackerel skies. The crew meanwhile dreamed of plates piled high and full stomachs – much depended on the second Monday in May.

What a weekend that was, sacks and nets crowded the small entrance hall, and tins were stacked up in the lounge

'It's like living in the shop.' Moira said as she gathered together the ingredients for Monday's meal.

'So, chicken casserole tonight, where's the chicken?' Doreen asked.

'Taking up most of the fridge,' laughed Moira as she pulled open the fridge door to reveal a huge bird.

'Krikey, it's enormous, more like a turkey, where on earth did Angus get that?'

'Not got a clue, I think it must have been fed on waste from the reactors at Dounreay.' Moira said and winked.

'You're such a hoot Moira, only you could think of serving radioactive chicken casserole, it'll certainly put a certain something into the meal!'

Such was their merriment that the meal was prepped and in the oven in no time. Moira wiped her hands on her pinny and said with some satisfaction,

'It'll only need heating up then.'

'Do you think we could manage to make a pudding Moira? I've got plenty of jam, surely we could make a jam tart?' Doreen asked almost pleadingly.

'Excellent idea,' Moira said as she began weighing ingredients. 'You can make the pastry Doreen, you've got much better pastry hands than me.'

Their own meals rather took a backward step as they concentrated on providing for others. But they were happy with their work and early nights were called for – there was a hectic day ahead.

Word of the onshore catering arrangements flew around the town. Some customers were full of praise, and a few offered to help. The community was generally supportive, and those who were not, kept their feelings to themselves. Thus, early on Monday evening, villagers were not too surprised to see the crew dressed as smartly as they could be in misfitting garb, walking along the road from the harbour, looking for all the world as if they were off to a party. It was the tourists that stopped and stared. They had come to this remote part of Scotland to admire the scenery, catch ferries to even more remote places: Isles of Harris, Skye and Lewis, but they had not expected to see a group of tall, strong Nigerians, cross the roads in front of them, and couldn't help themselves:

'Why do you think they are all here?'

'May be on holiday.'

'How odd, do you think they live here?'

Some comments showed the ignorance and prejudice of the utterer and were best not repeated. The men of course, had no sense of this reaction to their presence. They were out for dinner and felt human for the first time in months. But this didn't allay their anxiety at being in a stranger's house and were unsure as to how exactly they would cope.

Squashed initially into Moira's house, introductions were made, and thanks expressed before they split up into their groups to eat. Four followed Doreen, who had found her inner hostess strengths, and ably helped by Iris, had them sat down in a moment. One of the men gave a short recital, which she later learnt was grace, and they set about their meal with gusto.

This was almost exactly replicated at number four, conversation was easier here, Jim and Samuel were familiar with the house and were able to communicate with Ade and Yomi who sat stiff and erect in the homeliest place they had been in months. It was clear that they were overwhelmed by the moment but their tension eased as food was placed before them. Their initial eating gusto slowed down, Jim had been prepared for this moment and disappeared into the kitchen with all eyes following him. He returned with two huge bottles of hot pepper sauce clutched in his hands.

'What are they for?' Moira asked.

'Well, we have our meals hot and spicy in Nigeria, yours is good, but it's not as spicy as these men are used to,' Jim replied as he bit his lower lip concerned that he might have upset her.

'What about you, you never said you wanted spicy, and where did you get those?' Moira demanded.

'I didn't want to hurt you, so kept quiet and used a lot of pepper. I asked Angus if he could find some hot sauce and he got these, I don't know where from.'

'Well, Jim, you could have told me all of this before, you'd better take one of those bottles next door, we don't want them missing out!' Moira said and shushed him out of the room.

Order was restored, sauce passed around and faces smiled in full satisfaction, but one taste of the sauce was all Moira could manage as she declared:

'Phew that's like fire. How on earth do you manage to eat anything sooooo hot? I don't think my mouth will ever be the same again!' She was rather relieved that she had not had to suffer it for all these past weeks.

Once fed, the men relaxed, tried to converse with their hosts, which resulted in merriment all round, the happiest night for longer than they could remember. But they had to leave, and did so reluctantly. They would have happily stayed all night. As Samuel, Ade and Yomi were due to go, Doreen brought her guests round and they stood at the door, all expressing their gratitude in whatever way they could, one passed three parcels, about the size of books, to Jim, who passed them to their hostesses and said:

'The men are grateful for what you are doing and ask that you accept these gifts as a token of that thanks. They are not much, but it is all they have to give.' With that the men were off back to the harbour where Ivan and the lifeboat were waiting for them.

Iris was the first to open her package, the paper had been hand-painted, swirls of colours, reds, oranges, yellows, browns and white, it was such a shame to spoil it and they all proceeded to carefully open their gifts. Inside each was a piece of wood that had been smoothed and painted with delicate pictures: all the colours of the rainbow intricately woven into designs of flowers and leaves, and in the centre were the words THANK YOU – possibly the most moving presents any of them had ever received – and their eyes welled up with tears at the generosity of spirit that had gone into their making. Even Alex, who should have been in bed, peered down the stairs and shouted,

'They're pretty, what are they?' which immediately broke the spell. Calls of:

'Get back to bed now,' cleared eyes of moisture and they went, full of emotion, their separate ways.

So occupied had they been that Moira and Jim had barely had a moment to discuss their plans, but she was not letting him get away with the hot sauce situation.

'You should tell me if something is wrong, how can I know if I haven't been told?' she said, rapidly followed by, 'When are we going to tell the family?'

For once they sat in the kitchen, opposite each other so that they could bat ideas from one to the other. '

We must tell Alex first,' Moira said, as Jim bent forward and cupped her hands in his.

'Of course, he must be first. He will have questions; we must be sure that he's happy. But what about your family?' asked Jim.

'We need to get everyone together, including Aila. There's no point asking Roddy. He's a lost cause, he'll just cause more trouble.' Moira said with a look of determination, then squeezed Jim's hand and said, 'Time for bed.'

The week progressed, the catering became easier, and hot sauce was always available. The guests changed houses, so that they could better know all their hosts and helpers and by Thursday a routine had been established. The men made a porridge of sorts for breakfast, by boiling water on their braziers, and had bread and spread for lunch, but it was the evening they looked forward to, not only for warmth and nourishment, but sitting like a family, with women present and at number four a child. Home was coming towards them slowly, and they could relax.

Moira and Jim, however, were becoming tense with the excitement of their secret and were relieved to hear that Aila would be able to pop round on Saturday evening – after Roddy had gone on a night stalk with some guests. Alex would have to be spoken to before then, and they agreed that Saturday afternoon would be best.

'Give him time to think about it,' Jim said.

'And have questions answered,' Moira added. 'We have never seen any inkling that he might be worried about us being together, but it will be a big change in his life, and we need him to be happy.'

'Of course,' Jim said, ' but I think he will be all right, we are after all friends now.'

'Oh I know you are, but my feelings are all over the place, what would we do if he reacted badly?'

'He won't, trust me,' Jim continued, 'there's nothing we can do about that now,' and he ushered her upstairs to the security of each other's arms.

Chapter 33

The best thing to hold onto in life is each other
Audrey Hepburn

To most people, Saturday 14th May, was a fairly ordinary Saturday in a fairly ordinary month. Nothing remarkable about it at all. But for two people it was a special day – a day for announcements – for happiness to be shared and for congratulations to be given. But Moira was anxious all morning. She busied herself about the shop quietly praying to the god she did not believe in: Please, God, make everything go right and let Alex be happy. Please don't let him hate the idea. At the same time, she was telling herself not to be so silly, a thought that escaped into a mutter, and caused Angus to turn around.

'What did you say Moira?'

'Nothing, just thinking out loud.' She replied, and continued piling up tins of peaches next to the tower of evaporated milk cans that Angus had built. He carefully placed the 'Special Offers' sign above them and faced her,

'You seem to be preoccupied this morning – everything all right?'

'Oh yes, fine. Just thinking about tonight's meal.'

'It's not getting to be too much for you, is it?'

'Oh no, it's good to be active – stops you talking to yourself!' This was so obviously untrue that they both had a fit of the giggles.

'You'd better get off home then,' Angus said. 'You must have plenty to do there.' The words had barely left his lips than she was out of the door, wishing him a final,

'Good weekend,' before speeding home.

Much of the meal had already been prepared, so there was nothing to delay the afternoon talk they'd planned. Alex was bribed into joining her and Jim in the front room with the unseasonable offer of a hot chocolate. He shuffled in, muttering under his breath, and Moira's confidence plummeted.

'Why have I got to sit in here?' he complained. 'What's so urgent?'

Jim and Moira sat bolt upright, their faces fixed like statues. It must have been obvious, even to Alex, that something was up, because he stopped short and just stared at them, They moved a little apart and Moira gestured to Alex to sit between them.

'Alex, we've got something to tell you,' she said.

'Is it bad news?' he demanded. 'You've not broken my new model have you?'

'No, nothing like that. We think it's good news,' said Jim.

'Are we going on holiday then? I'd like to go to Harris. Can we go there?'

'No, were not going on holiday Alex,' Moira said, 'It's nothing like that. Just keep quiet and listen.'

Alex sighed loudly. 'Oh, all right, but it better not take too long – I want to go and play at the pond.'

'Jim has asked me to marry him, and we both want to know how you feel about that?'

Alex took a sip of his drink. His brow creased into a frown.

'Oh, well ... I dunno ... I'll have to think about it,' he said. He downed the contents of his mug, walked around the room head bowed and muttering under his breath. Moira and Jim sat rigid. They watched him rest his jaw in his hand like a young sage, and contort his face into a question. 'When would it happen?' he asked at last.

'In a few weeks Alex – if you agree. But what do you think?'

Alex, shuffled around on the cushion to look left at Jim, then right towards Moira.

'Mmm. That's probably OK,' he said.

'So you're happy about it? Moira gasped.

''Course I'm happy. I like Jim. He's good fun. He tells interesting stories and spends time with me – and I'll have a dad like the other boys now. Hang on, though – does it mean I'd have to change my name to a great long one that I can't spell? That wouldn't be so good at High School.'

'Of course you don't have to silly,' laughed Moira, 'Is that your only question?'

'No – one more. Can I go out and play now?' Without waiting for a reply, he was up and out, leaving the two of them staring at each other.

'Well, that was almost too easy,' Jim said. Moira slumped back into the cushions in relief and he put his arm around her.

'No, it's good.' Moira beamed at him. 'He's obviously not bothered at all. In fact he was delighted. Oh, I'm so happy Jim! I'd been really worried about his reaction,' Jim grinned and clasped her more tightly. 'He may have questions later,' she continued, 'when it has sunk in – but for now the pond is clearly much more important! I've got my fingers crossed that telling the rest of the family will go as well.'

Samuel, Yomi and Ade arrived right on time and instantly made themselves at home. Any previous inhibitions quickly melted away and they joined in as everyone ate. Moira was pleased to see them looking so relaxed, but began to fret that they were staying much longer than usual.

'Will they ever leave, Aila will be here soon?' she whispered to Jim as they cleared things away.

'Don't worry, they'll be gone in good time. Aila's not here yet, so there's nothing to be done anyway,' Jim said.

'I know I'm acting like a girl, but I just want to get this over and done with – to know everything will be all right,'

She walked back into the kitchen. The men had started on the washing up and seemed determined to clean half the kitchen at the same time. They were a little too enthusiastic with the washing-up liquid and Moira wasn't sure whether to laugh or cry at the suds that were cascading from the sink and working their way down to the floor. She grabbed a cloth and started mopping up; order was restored from the chaos, and the men got ready to leave. No sooner had they turned the corner than Iris and Doreen arrived and settled themselves in the lounge waiting for Aila, who was expected at any moment. They had no inkling that the evening was to be any more than a catch-up, and Moira was on tenterhooks.

'I've just passed your guests, walking down the road,' Aila said on arrival. 'A fine bunch they looked too. They must be so grateful for what you're doing. It's a lot of work to feed so many, especially when you don't even know them.'

'But you do that all the time at the big house,' Moira said, as she poured Aila a drink.

'That's different. It's a job and it's not in my own home and they aren't ... well you know ... quite so different to us.' Moira cringed at her sister-in-law's words and gave her a warning glance.

'They aren't that different – except that they like to cover their food in hot-pepper sauce! It's a wonder Jim's got any mouth left,' Moira added, lightening the moment. From that point, a lively argument about the virtues of different sauces ensued and Moira wondered if there would ever be a suitable break in the conversation, but at last the voices fell quiet. Jim gave her a meaningful look and a slight nod. He nudged his chair nearer to her and she cleared her throat.

'Jim and I have got something to tell you all,' she said, a little too loudly.

'Are you both OK?' Iris asked.

Moira couldn't contain herself any longer. 'Yes, everything's better than all right – Jim has asked me to marry him, and I've said yes.'

The surprise was palpable. Nobody spoke and the women all looked at each other. At last, Doreen broke the spell by getting up, marching across the room and hugging first Moira, and then Jim.

'That's terrific news,' she said in an over-enthusiastic voice. 'I'm so happy for you both. Congratulations!'

'Oh yes,' Iris agreed, with the slightest of frowns. 'It is good news, of course – but isn't it, perhaps, a bit hurried?' Her voice implied it might not be absolutely the good news she had acknowledged.

'It does seem quick I agree. But I've known from day one that he's the one for me,' Moira replied, taking Jim's hand.

Jim smiled back at her before turning to Iris.

'I do understand your concern Mrs Cameron,' he said gently, 'especially as I do not, at the moment, have anything other than myself to offer your daughter and I would agree that she deserves more than I can currently give. However, I have been told that I will be able to get work in Aberdeen and this will mean that I'll be able to support her as I should. We Nigerians are a proud people and I take my role as provider seriously. I have been poor before, but I worked hard, and with my friend Samuel made a success of our enterprise. It is only because of matters entirely outside my control that I have finished up in my present situation. I understand, that for some, my colour is a problem, although I do not fully understand it. I love your daughter as you do, I laugh when you laugh, cry when I'm sad, and have good days and bad days, as you do, I help in the kitchen, respect my elders, go to church, eat with a knife and fork and clean my teeth twice a day! The only real difference I can see is that your sauces aren't spicy hot – and that's not a proper problem is it?'

Iris's face softened. 'Oh Jim, I feel ashamed of myself,' she said. She reached up and wrapped her sparrow-like arms round his broad shoulders.

'And I would have loved my pig-headed husband to have heard that speech of yours Jim,' Aila exclaimed. ' It might even have reached the bit of his brain that doesn't work right. I for one, wish both of you every happiness!' And she moved over to join in the hugging.

'I don't want to put a dampener on all of this,' Doreen said, 'but you're not a national Jim. Will you actually be allowed to marry – just like that? Might there not be formalities that must be carried out first?'

'Oh, that's not a problem,' Moira told her. 'We are getting married on 21st June at Dingwalls' registry office. It's all sorted!'

There was another astounded silence. Jim went around with the bottles and poured more drinks. Moira raised her own glass and proposed a toast:

'To my eloquent husband to be.' Everyone dutifully lifted their glasses and Iris added:

'Wishing you both all the happiness in the world.'

The harmony was interrupted by Alex bursting through the door in his usual, boy-hurricane fashion.

'What's going on?' he demanded. Iris, Doreen and Aila looked at their feet.

'It's all right,' Moira said. 'We told him this afternoon and he's fine with it – aren't you Alex?'

'Definitely,' her son agreed.

'So now,' she continued 'all the important people know, and we don't have to keep our plans a secret anymore!'

The village grapevine had always been an amazing way of spreading information. Often no one admitted to planting the seed, yet the tendrils invariably grew faster than Jack's beanstalk, both upwards and outwards until virtually everyone had heard of the forthcoming marriage.

Moira had barely walked through the shop door on Monday, and was about to tell Angus her good news, when Hamish popped in.

'I hear congratulations are in order.'

'Well thank you Hamish.' She smiled. 'But how did you know?'

He gave her a wink and rubbed the side of his nose with his finger.

'Ah, that would be telling,' he said. Then he revealed that only yesterday, he had met up with his friend, McDougall, the Dingwall registrar. 'You don't mind him telling me?' he asked.

'No, it's fine I'd just planned to tell Angus in person.'

'Can someone tell me what's going on? Why are you congratulating her?' Angus asked. Moira rushed to explain and when they were alone, she brought him up to date. It was a good job she did, as the customers who flowed through the door that morning were full of questions to both of them. Some people had already heard the news and were eager to bring others up to date. Many appeared genuinely delighted, but some pointedly avoided the subject. Others – an obviously appalled minority – peered incredulously at Moira from behind the shelves, as if unable to accept that a local woman would consider such a match. Fortunately, Moira was so wrapped up in the supportive words she'd received, that she barely noticed these critical reactions, though at the end of the morning she did feel grateful that there had been no sign of Miss McKay and her sharp tongue.

Although most of the villagers discussed these developments in whispers, there was one house where there was no such restraint. News of the engagement had reached Roddy's ears the night before, though not through Aila, who kept her involvement in the announcement close to her chest. It would probably be the straw that would break this stubborn mule's back, she thought, and kept her mouth firmly shut as Roddy ranted and raved. The tirade went on and on – he raged about the shame his sister was bringing on the family, swearing that he would never cross her threshold if she went through with this marriage, and that she would certainly never set foot in his home again.

'The woman's gone mad; she's been seduced by a man who wants a marriage of convenience. Just you wait and see. When he gets a visa to stay, he'll be off in a flash, and where will she be then? She'll not be able to hold her head up round here ever again,' After this vehement delivery of his opinions, he'd stormed out.

Aila had learnt to deal with Roddy's moods – there was little point in arguing with him – as far as her husband was concerned the only voice in the Highlands worth listening to was his own, and he was the only one speaking the truth. Aila sighed. Normally, she'd wait until the storm had blown out and tackle him discretely when he'd calmed down. But this time was different. The strength and depth of Roddy's prejudice had shaken her and she feared what was to come.

Chapter 34

O I hae come from far away,
From a warm land far away,
A southern land across the sea,
With sailor-lads about the mast,
Merry and canny, and kind to me.
        The Witch's Ballard
        William Bell Scott

Jim carried on helping around the town and became part of the fixtures and fittings – as familiar to the residents as the fishermen that plied their trade from the harbour. He was greeted as a friend by most and joined in quick chats about the weather and the catches of the day – he was becoming one of them. Occasionally, he was asked to join them on a fishing trip, hauling out lobster pots, but never volunteered to dive for scallops in such cold waters. But he never turned down the offer of some as thanks for his help; these little delicacies were kept as treats for the family – there was never any left to give away to Samuel, Ade, Yomi and the others, but they continued to feed them all at night.

The wedding would be a quiet affair, just them, Alex and their witnesses. Doreen had been delighted to accept this role as had Samuel, who wanted to share in his friend's happiness after so many months of misery; it hopefully marked a change for the better for Samuel as well as his friend.

With little money to spare, there wouldn't be any great celebrations – just a tea with family and close friends – the details could wait. There was still much cooking to be done and still no news of when the men's flights would be arranged.

The crew were grateful for the hospitality given to them, but they were now suffering terrible deprivations on the Harmony. The Scottish weather had returned to nearly the cold of winter; the winds had increased, and the rain fell like waterfalls. It was getting too much to bear. The final indignity was the last drop of water dripped from the galley tap into the sink, like a lone pearl, only to disappear down the plug hole and with it, their last vestiges of hope. There was no oil left to move the ship to shore to take on more water, and the sea water that surrounded them was of no help. The captain had no alternative than to seek assistance, they had reached their nadir. More phone calls were made – to the union that was meant to be supplying air tickets, to the Seamans' mission and other allegedly interested parties. Ivan and Angus waited for their calls to be returned – interminable waits that appeared to last forever – but were actually only a few hours. When the union finally got back to Ivan, the news came as a shock – tickets were being purchased for two of the men. The repatriation was underway. But there was no news on water supplies, just another month's money had been advanced.

That evening, first of June, Moira and Doreen made the momentous decision to accommodate the crew in their own homes. The men would have to sleep on lounge floors, but it would be toasty and dry, and most importantly they would have access to water. Any onlooker would have been surprised to see how easily these warm-hearted women rose to the challenge, but they would also have understand their fervent wishes that it wouldn't be for too long.

Angus and his wife Joan agreed to take Ivan. Iris was a little uneasy at having men stay overnight, but offered to help in any other way and immediately raided her blanket box and called on neighbours for more. Three of the men were to sleep at Moira's and four at Doreen's, 'Makes it equal,' Doreen said. Somehow bathroom arrangements were sorted; clean clothes and personal belongings would have to wait until the morning when they could be collected from the ship.

As unconventional as the dormitories were, the men slept surprisingly well, the floor might be hard, but it was carpeted, and their brains imagined that they were still on water and slowly rocked them into dreams of better times. Over the next few days they settled into a routine. The launderette offered to do their washing: which was a relief to everyone. Jim became porridge master, and the men spent their days on board, occupying themselves with this and that.

A local pleasure boat took advantage of a calm break in the weather and took them to the Summer Isles that lie low in the mouth of Loch Broom. The first time any of them had travelled in a boat for just pleasure. They watched sea lion pups playing under the close supervision of their parents, white-tailed sea eagles and dolphins. For two hours they were transformed into happy laughing tourists. They joshed with each other and laughed out loud for the first time in months.

A visit from an official six days later brought the most welcome of news for two of them – they were to leave the next day for London and would be flown straight back to Nigeria. They could all now believe the end was in sight and turned their evening meal into a celebration. No one understood how the two had been chosen, but that didn't matter, everyone was happy for them and the rest were sure that they wouldn't be far behind. They learned that the two crew that had left them in April had been apprehended and were currently being hosted by Porterfield Prison in Inverness. Yomi remarked,

'I bet their days have been more satisfactory than those we have endured on the Harmony throughout May.'

'That's true,' nodded Samuel. 'but it does look as if we will be going home.'

'Oh yes.' Yomi sighed. 'To our own country, to be with our families and friends.'

Iris interjected and sagely advised:

'With the passing of time, this will all become a distant memory. A story you will tell your children and grandchildren, who will listen intently, but of course none of them will ever fully understand how hard it has been.' They all nodded and sat silently, deep in their own thoughts, that vacillated between joy at going home soon and the real fear that it still might not happen.

Two officials spoke at length to Jim the next day, and for one awful moment both he and Moira feared that he was to be sent back. But the officials listened intently and made copious notes. They checked with the registrar in Dingwall and questioned Moira – personal questions she would have preferred to remain unasked – but finally the pair were informed that an initial one-year visa would be granted for Jim. They could marry in the full knowledge that he would not be sent back. But there was no time to celebrate, there was still her job to carry out at the shop, a home to run, a son to be cared for, and homework to be overseen; there was no time for dwelling on anything, other than the immediate jobs at hand.

The lucky two were up early and back to the Harmony where they collected their possessions – few as they were – and stood at the harbour side as the minibus drew up for the first leg of their journey home. The rest of the crew, the captain and several of the townsfolk lined the road to send them safely on their way, much to the interest of passing tourists who couldn't work out what was going on and sidled over to ask. The story was too long to fully explain, and so they walked off shaking their heads, saying that it all seemed a bit weird and asking why they were here in the first place and not going home all together. No one could answer the last question, let alone the men themselves, who were now, along with everyone else, waving the lucky pair off – it was contagious. All along Shore street, tourists started waving at the passing vehicle like the Scottish equivalent of a Mexican wave, and none of them understood why. Still it created a carnival like feeling which induced total strangers to join in and mix. The departing men hadn't left their former gloom behind – they had spread their happiness through those who wished them well – and had they known this, would probably have said that it was the only present they could have left behind.

The remaining five crew and their captain wandered into town to fill their day with whatever they could find to do. Tourists dispersed and residents returned to their workplaces or, like Doreen, walked back with Moira to buy groceries. Angus greeted them at the door.

'I've just had a phone call about the allowance.' Their faces dropped.

'They're not stopping it are they?' Moira asked.

'Oh no, don't worry they're going to keep it at thirty pounds. To help compensate for the heating and hot water.'

'Makes it sound like they are doing us a real favour,' Moira replied.

'Yes, they seem to be funding us as cheap boarding houses,' Doreen agreed.

'Oh well, we did volunteer, and to be honest, I would do the same again,' Moira said. Doreen nodded in agreement.

'So would I actually. I've enjoyed it. It's brought some excitement into our rather predictable lives. Mind you, yours isn't going to be predictable any time soon is it?'

'I suppose not, I wouldn't mind a bit more time to myself though, it's only two weeks to the wedding and I've not even got anything to wear yet.'

'I could do all the cooking for one day,' offered Doreen, 'You get some time off work and go to Inverness and sort something out, is that OK Angus?'

'Of course it is, when would you like to go Moira, what about next Monday? It's usually quieter and Joan can usually manage to help out then.'

'That would be great,' Moira said. 'And thank you both for being so supportive. I've hardly had any time to properly celebrate. Could I take some holiday after the wedding Angus? Just a few days so that we can spend some time together, just the two of us?'

'I would expect no less. Take a week off.'

'No, I can't do that, there may still be crew left here and I must finish what I started, it wouldn't be right to desert them now.' It was only when she turned round that she realised that Miss McKay was stood behind her and she joined in the tail end of the conversation.

'Moira, it is no secret that I do not fully support this impending marriage, believing as I do that such different cultures and colours are best kept separate – to keep blood lines pure.' Moira's face turned puce with rage, but was unable to stop the verbal flow.

'However, I do applaud your commitment to helping all these men, as I do to all of you. I can now accept that I have been lacking in my Christian duty to support others and would be prepared to help Doreen with the catering when you have your few days away. Don't get me wrong, I'm still not entirely happy with the situation, but this Jim of yours seems to be a good man. I have noticed the work he has done around town. It seems that he has made himself indispensable to the village and is liked by many. So, I must applaud him. And now could I have four rashes of bacon, six eggs and a loaf please Angus, and I'll be on my way.'

Her departing back resulted in gasps of astonishment all round,

'Well that was a turn up for the books,' Angus said.

'Certainly was. That God of hers moves in ways too mysterious for me, but he seems to have got the right message through to her at long last. How are you going to like that Doreen, three days of cooking with her?' smiled Moira as she gave her friend a nudge with her elbow.

'Not sure that I will, but I'm not going to turn it down, there could be a lesson for all of us in this. On that note I'd better get on my way and do my bit for tonight,' Doreen said as she rushed out.

Chapter35

Figure it out for yourself my lad,
 You've all that the greatest of men have had,
Two arms, two hands, two legs, two eyes,
And a brain to use if you would be wise.
>   Equipment
>   Edgar Guest

The next few days passed in a flurry of busyness. The days were full, with little planning time for Jim and Moira. For the five men waiting to go home, each new day started with optimism, then ended in their makeshift beds, with disappointment as their blankets. They yearned for their own country and began to sink into the arms of depression again. Jim and Moira would try and rally them, but it was the time they spent with Alex, making models out of Meccano, that cheered them up the most. He had a knack of making them laugh at their mistakes and kept them absorbed making nonsensical vehicles, that might, or might not move. He was becoming the hero of the moment and relished the praise heaped upon him and glowed with delight.

On the following Monday, Moira had an opportunity to feel equally important. It was the big shopping day and Aila had insisted on coming along.

'I want to be part of this, and I'm not letting Roddy stop me,' she said over the telephone and then, to explain her day of absence, fobbed him off with tales of quilts and bicentenary arrangements. Her car pulled up outside number four at the stroke of nine and Moira was out of the house in a shot; this was to be, HER day, and it would be the first she'd had for many months. She was bubbling with the anticipation and her excitement filled the car for the entire one and half hour journey.

They traipsed from shop to shop, she tried on dresses, jackets, coats, and hats, and none were right.

'I'm too big, that's the problem,' Moira complained.

'Oh, don't be ridiculous you're not big, just rounded, a womanly figure,'

Aila reassured. 'There's nothing wrong with that.'

'But I'm so damned short, nothing is going to look right,' Moira said, with a face as long as a blood hound as all the previous happiness drained away.

'Right, let's have a coffee and a bite to eat; get your energy levels up and we'll get you sorted. Let's try that little shop round the back of Debenhams, they're sure to have something.' Aila said with all the encouragement she could muster.

'But isn't that expensive? I can't afford too much don't forget.' Continued the pessimistic Moira.

'Stop worrying about everything, put your optimism back into gear, finish your coffee, and let's do it!'

Revitalised, they retraced their steps, and Moira was trying on again within minutes.

'Oh, I like this one, what do you think Aila?' Moira said as she twisted and turned in front of the mirror.

'It looks lovely, suits you so well. I love that pale grey-blue it enhances your lovely eyes. It's all floaty, makes you look ethereal, not like those padded shoulder types we see on the telly. I think you should get it.'

'Oh goodness Aila, I've just seen the price tag, I can't afford that! It's way too much.'

Aila laughed.

'Oh Moira, you can afford it, didn't you notice the rail we got it from?'

'No, should I have done?'

'Yes, it said thirty percent off everything on this rack, so it's within your

budget. And I've got a dark blue hat and bag at home that would look great with it, so you can use those. You know the ones – I had them at Doreen's daughter's wedding.'

'Oh yes, I remember. I loved that hat, are you sure I could borrow them?'

'Of course. I wouldn't have offered if I didn't want you to use them, grinned Aila as she shook her head in disbelief. Now give me another twirl and let's get that skirt and top wrapped up before you start worrying about something else.'

They laughed and chatted like schoolgirls the whole way home, and Aila was insistent that she would organise a buffet or similar for after the wedding.

'My present to you both. I want to do this Moira, and I most certainly won't take no for an answer. Have you sorted out where to go for your honeymoon yet?'

'No, not really. I wondered if we could go up to Durness or down to Applecross and stay in a little hotel for a couple of nights,'

'Any preference?'

'No, I don't think so.'

'Well let me organise that. You've got so much on and I'm doing little at home, please let me,' Aila implored.

'You're so good to me Aila, and do you know what, I would love a surprise honeymoon – but don't book anywhere too expensive or I'll have to come poaching for meat on the estate, and I wouldn't want to get caught by that brother of mine!' Moira said. and immediately regretted the mere mention of him. They were home, just in time to see Jim and Alex going through the front door. Aila took the outfit: 'I'll make sure it's pressed ready for the big day, then I can pop it over the night before. We don't want Jim seeing it before the wedding do we?'

An overexcited Jim greeted her with words that rushed out like string being pulled out by a magician. Eventually she got him to calm down and he explained:

'Oh Moira, two of the crew were told that they will leave in the morning and Samuel was one of them.' Her face fell.

'Surely not. Why does good news have to be bad?'

'It's OK,' he went on, 'Samuel was adamant that he wouldn't leave until he had seen us married; but the others begged the authorities to take his place. Angus saved the day. He persuaded the authorities to send home one of the men with children.' Relief spread over Moira's face.

'Thank goodness. I don't know why they didn't chose people with children to start with, he must be so pleased. When will Samuel, Ade and Yomi get to go home?'

'We don't know yet. They said something about waiting for prices to fall. It seems that only the cheapest seats will do for them.'

The departure was an almost carbon copy of the week before. Another, two people to wave on their way. Two men intoxicated by their sudden release from months of torment; and for one, the thought of seeing his young family after all this time was just too much. He broke down in tears as he tried to thank them all for their help and generosity, but managed to pull himself together as Moira gave him a hug, and he was on his way.

Happiness, like God can sometimes show itself in mysterious ways, Moira reflected, as she waved them on their way with a lump in her throat, but with happiness in her heart.

They all squashed into number four that night. Iris, Doreen and Moira, Alex and Samuel, Ade, Yomi, and Ivan and enjoyed a sort of celebration – albeit tinged with sadness –at the going of men who had become friends. They were most unlikely to ever meet in the future. None would ever sign up to a factory ship to these waters again. The incarceration had lasted too long and left mental scars. Loch Broom only represented misery to them; they would forever be unable to see the beauty of the area that drew thousands of tourists each year.

The workload was lighter now and Moira and Jim could give more time to planning their wedding, which was by now only a few days away. Moira was concerned about Jim's attire, but he had assured her, that it was all in hand. She had no idea how or by what means.

'I am not taking money from my bride to clothe me at my wedding,' he had asserted, with admirable determination. She equally, would reveal nothing about her outfit, and gave an enigmatic look each time he asked, and then gave him a wink as a full stop.

'There's nothing for you to worry about on your honeymoon,' Doreen told her. 'We've got it all under control Alex will stay with your mum and Samuel, Ade and Yomi with me.' Others were ordering Moira's life, and after the last hectic weeks it gave her a sense of calm.

There was only one thing left for her to do, and only she could do it, and it couldn't wait. It must be done before the wedding, so she got in her car, drove over to the estate, knocked on the door, which was opened by her brother. Moira was in the house before he could even think about stopping her. He drew breath, but it was too late, she had much to say and was not about to let him stop her:

'Roddy Cameron, don't interrupt, let me say my piece. We are brother and sister; as children we played and fought, laughed and cried, shared good times and bad. But we stayed close to each other no matter what happens.'

She fixed him with a piercing blue stare and continued.

'I know that you can be stubborn, but this latest thing is beyond comprehension.' He went to speak.

'Oh no you don't I'm not letting you interrupt. I know you were going to say that I should have thought about my own actions, and let me assure you that I have. Why can't you see people for what they are, why must you see the colour of their skin or the country of their origin? White is not always right. There are good and bad in all communities and yet you will not look for that good, so blinded are you by your prejudice.'

She took a deep breath and softened her look.

'Can you, for one moment, imagine what we look like to foreigners? We are a race where the men wear kilts with nothing underneath, play music by blowing into the skin of a goat or sheep, have evenings reciting poetry to a man long dead. Where dark haired men visit houses with a lump of coal to bring good luck for the New Year. Where men throw tree trunks for entertainment and brush ice to make discs move faster.' Roddy raised his eyebrows and gave her a dismissive look, but she continued.

'Don't tell me that other countries have strange customs, just look closer to home. Take a long hard look in the mirror, what do you see? Almost unwittingly he glanced sideways at the mirror that hung on the wall.

'Do you see the handsome man you can be, or do you see a face full of hate, an inflexible, pig-headed, dogged, perverse man who will eat his soul away with the stupidity of all of this? Roddy, I'm getting married in two days' time, I am not looking for you to congratulate me, nor wish me well, nor even smile at me. Just keep looking in that mirror until you can see deep inside yourself to glimpse the cancer that is growing there. Then destroy it once and for all. If you manage to do that I will be waiting, but until that time I will say goodbye.'

At which she turned, walked out of the house, started the car, drove home and poured herself a large whisky, a drink she didn't like, and proceeded to drink it down even though it was only four o'clock in the afternoon.

Chapter 36

Life is the flower for which love is the honey.
Victor Hugo

The sun's rays burst like an interloper into the bedroom as Moira drew back the curtains and was momentarily blinded by the brilliance. She looked away, and focused on the blue grey outfit hanging on the wardrobe door. This day would start like no other. First a long indulgent soak in a bath full of bubbles, a quick facial and no one to worry about. The house was, for a brief moment in time, hers and no one else's. She was alone. Iris had insisted that Jim stay at her house,

'It's unlucky to see the bride before the wedding, so there's a bed here for you.'

Alex had needed no urging to stay at a friend's house, who had, he assured:

'More Meccano than the shops. We are going to make an AMAZING robot and a space ship to send him to the moon.' And was off with his overnight bag without a backward glance, then returned to give his mum a hug and a quick: 'See you.' All thoughts of weddings pushed to the back of his mind by an infinitely more important moving robot, that would, in his mind, be the envy of the world.

Jim and Samuel were ready and waiting four doors away, the pair of them dressed immaculately and stood to near attention as Iris gave them a final inspection. She stood on tiptoes, straightened Jim's tie, and flicked a little speck from Samuel's shoulder.

'You two look so handsome in your suits. I don't know exactly where Hamish got them from, but he sure did a good job getting the right size.'

'It feels strange to wear smart clothes after so long,' Jim said as he tugged on the jacket bottom, 'but my mother and sisters would approve. I'll be able to show them photographs with pride.' Iris nodded.

'It's such a shame they can't be here. But at least the two men who returned to Nigeria will have been able to pass on your good news, so they will be thinking of you.'

A ring of the doorbell announced the arrival of Hamish who had declared himself chauffeur for the day. He had formed a friendship with both men and done all that he could to make the day special. His car now stood outside glistening in the morning sun and he ushered them forwards, just as Iris pinned heather sprays to their jackets.

'That's better,' she said. 'a proper Scottish wedding outfit now.' Then waved them off at exactly ten o'clock – the time that Hamish insisted was just right to ensure they reached the registry office a little ahead of the bride.

'Are you there Moira?' called Mary – an old school friend – up the stairs.

'Yes, just coming, will be with you in a mo. Make yourself a drink and I'll have one too,' Moira replied as she rushed down the stairs ready to have her hair done. Her friend began blowing and brushing like the professional she was. They chatted and giggled like schoolgirls, with no sign of the nerves that were just starting to wobble around in Moira's tummy.

A wedding clad Doreen in a simple beige dress and little jacket was the next to arrive and then Iris in navy with a splash of red at the neck and shoes to match. The clock chimed ten and the top stair creaked, as Moira made her way down in heels that looked a little precarious on the normally sensibly shod bride.

'You look lovely.'

'Wow that outfit looks good on you'

'Didn't I tell you that hat would look good?' greeted her arrival on the bottom step. Her mother pinned a corsage to her outfit and declared her:

'A gorgeous bride,' moments before Doreen ushered her to the waiting car. The bride and her witness were on their way.

They unknowingly followed Jim the whole way – over moorlands, round lochs, and skirted mountains – across the Highlands to her future. There was little chat in either car, it was a time for reflection on the life journey so far and the possibilities that lay ahead A few butterflies flew through their stomachs and hearts, only to escape unwittingly through their mouths never to be seen again. Both cars drove slowly. They met neither the slow summer traffic nor the decrepit tractors they had planned for and, as a result, both cars arrived in better than good time – they were all early. Moira and Doreen passed the time by driving the streets of Moira's birth town, and she pointed out local landmarks and places that held a significance to her.

Moira's first glimpse of her husband, in the foyer of the registry office, made her blue shadowed eyes glisten, he looked simply magnificent. The dark grey suit and tie, the button hole that matched her corsage and the crisp white shirt that enhanced his glowing skin. This is right, so totally right, thought Moira as she looked at him adoringly.

He felt much the same of her, she looked gorgeous, and he equally silently agreed that they were doing the right thing. He carefully removed a small white flower from his buttonhole and said:

'This is the smallest of flowers, but take it as a token of my love for you.' She took it and put it in her hair, radiating sheer joy as she did so. The registrar broke the moment by calling Jim into his office.

'Shouldn't take long,' he said and whisked him away, for reasons no one understood. For a moment, the group wondered if anything was wrong. A look of panic crossed Moira's face, but she was reassured when Jim returned, beaming away.

'What did he want?' Moira urged.

'Nothing much,' laughed Jim, 'he wanted to practice saying my full name. He wasn't sure if he would get it right, and wanted to apologise in advance, just in case.' Their resulting merriment was brought to order by a call.

'We are ready for you now,' and the four adults and Alex composed themselves and followed the usher in.

Two huge floral arrangements in the colours of summer heather stood each side of the matrimonial desk and turned the bright but functional cream room into something much more celebratory. The pair took their positions in front of the registrar. Samuel and Doreen with Alex sat between them, sat as privileged spectators in the front row of many chairs. Iris and newly arrived Aila, slipped in behind them just as the registrar entered the room. Mr McDougall was looking rather dapper in an unseasonable tweed suit and waistcoat stretched to its limits across his corpulent self. He beamed at them, welcomed them, and set about the business of the day.

It was a short ceremony, no obeying to be done here, affirmations of love, to care, honour and respect were the words that resonated with them. Simple gold rings were exchanged, documents signed and so she became Mrs Ejimgietochukwu. They kissed each other, hugged their witnesses, bade the registrar goodbye and made their way out. Hamish was waiting outside,

'Just happened to have my camera.' And he took on the role of photographer as if he had been born to the job.

'Are there no end to your talents?' Doreen asked.

'You should see my juggling,' he laughed back as he ushered them to their cars.

The return journey was full of laughter. Aila, Iris and Alex led the way and disappeared into the distance as Doreen and Samuel followed on behind. Their closeness with the bride and groom had brought them together as friends; conversation was easy between them and they avowed to keep some sort of contact after Samuel had returned home.

Hamish, meanwhile, had gone into full chauffeur mode again with white ribbon on his car. His passengers sat comfortably in the back, where they held hands, sat close, gave occasional kisses, and held on tight when Hamish took corners as if he were a racing driver, and they both prayed that they would get back in one piece. At one point Moira became convulsed with laughter, which no tight corners would stop. So infectious did it become that Hamish had to brake hard, as tears started to ooze from his eyes. Eventually, taking deep breaths, Moira managed to take control of herself,

'I was just thinking ... I'd better not have to ... write my new name too often!' and started laughing all over again. Jim was laughing as much as any of them,

'I don't think it's a strange name,' which started them all off again, until a herd of cows bellowed their presence in the road and brought their frivolities to an end. Only miraculous avoidance action by Hamish prevented a collision and he could barely find the breath to exclaim:

'Phew, that was close,' before taking a more sedate speed into the village.

'I think you're recovering from that near miss Hamish, you've missed the turning to my road.'

'Not to worry.' Hamish replied, and proceeded without further explanation to Shore Street, where he stopped outside the Ferry Boat Inn, opened the car door and assisted them out.

'But we aren't going to the pub, just to Mum's,'

Hamish shrugged his shoulders and urged them forwards and opened the pub door.

'You have to have a celebratory drink first. Come along, it won't take long,'

Hamish seems to have taken on the role of doorman now, Moira thought, then jumped in surprise as shouts of congratulations greeted their arrival. There were so many people that Jim and Moira could hardly comprehend what was happening. The laden buffet in the corner stayed unnoticed until Angus came forward and gave a short speech:

'Moira and Jim, we all want to congratulate you, and wish you both a long and happy marriage. You have today, taken a big step and we all wanted to contribute to making your day as happy as possible, and so I ask you all to raise your glasses.' Full glasses were raised around the room, all eyes on the slightly bewildered couple. 'To the bride and groom,' toasted Hamish.

The room reverberated to the sound of:

'To the bride and groom,' – who were somewhat overwhelmed by all the faces looking at them. A glass of fizz was passed to them as,

'Speech, speech,' resounded around the room. Moira stood with jelly legs, shaking on heels that were beginning to feel like stilts, she took a deep breath, cleared the lump from her throat and spoke.

'I hardly know what to say, you are all waiting to hear fine words, but I don't have them; I'm in too much shock to think of many words at all – let alone fine ones. In doing this today you have shown the true heart of this community we live in, and we thank you for that. We appreciate you making this day even more special than it already was, and so I give a toast back to you all. I raise my glass to family, friends and all the fine folk of Ullapool.'

'And from me too,' said Jim, who raised his glass like the others, but seemingly wasn't sure whether he should drink from it or not. The moment passed as Moira added:

'Can I take my shoes off now? My feet are killing me!'

The party could begin, sandwiches, sausage rolls, a 'hedgehog' of cheese and pineapple on sticks and other goodies were gathered on plates, and jollity resounded around the room. The pair were ushered over to Alex and Iris who were seated with Samuel and Doreen. Flowers had been placed in the centre of their table and plates, already laden from the buffet, awaited them. It was a long time since any of them had eaten and food took the place of conversation. A cake appeared that they were urged to cut, pictures were taken, more thanks given, and before the proceedings were about to draw to an end, Iris handed a small envelope to them.

'What's this?' Moira asked.

'Well open it and see,' Iris urged. It was a card with a picture of a long white beach, and turquoise sea, it looked as if it were a Caribbean idyll, inside it said:

You are booked into the Sutherland Hotel at Durness for three nights. With much love from Mum, Alex, Aila, Doreen, Angus and Joan.

'We can't go there. It's expensive,' Moira exclaimed.

'Oh yes you can. It's your wedding present from us all, so it's time for you two to depart. Your cases are in the car, all you have to do is drive, and it's not too far,' Iris asserted.

The bride and groom were ushered out to Moira's car which now supported a big white bow on the front. The guests lined up to wave them off along Shore Street in much the same way as the men had been only a week before. But as the engine started a car pulled up in front and blocked their way. Two men in business suits gestured for the pair to wind their windows down, spoke to them, opened the car doors and took the pair to their car and drove off.

The guests stood speechless. Hands covered slack jawed mouths, heads shook in amazement and eyes watered. They knew who the men were – the immigration officials who had interviewed the pair before. Suddenly, voices sounded out in a cacophony of indignation. Doreen grabbed Iris by the hand, pushed her into the car and followed them towards the police station, where they saw the newlyweds being escorted through the door.

Chapter 37

The sun came up upon the left,
Out of the sea came he!
And he shone bright, and on the right,
Went down into the sea.
      The Rime of the Ancient Mariner
      Samuel Taylor Coleridge

The duty officer couldn't help them, said:

'I'm sorry ladies, I'm not party to the questioning you see. He pointed to the bench seat beside the door. 'Why don't you take a seat there and I'll try and find out what's happening.'

The pair sat for what seemed like an eternity. Chipped paintwork, a scrappy notice board, and an unmanned desk occupied their eyes, whilst the smell of disinfectant penetrated their nostrils and covered the smells of ne'er-do-wells who had passed through the premises in the days before. The officer returned with cups of tea.

'It shouldn't be too much longer,' he said, without telling them anymore.

'What do you think they're doing Iris?' asked a furrowed browed Doreen

'How would I know. Whatever it is, I hope my son hasn't got anything to do with it.' Iris responded as she paced the floor.

'I know things have been bad, but what could he do?' Doreen asked. 'They're married now.'

'God knows Doreen, but I wouldn't put it past him. Don't forget they're not legally married until they've ... you know.' She gave Iris an old-fashioned look, which made them both titter.

'I forgot that consummation bit.' Iris said, just as the sergeant returned.

'They'll be out in a minute,' he said reassuringly.

At which Jim and Moira appeared from a side door and rushed over and gave the two ladies big hugs.

It's all right Mum,' Moira said, 'it's all been resolved and look what Jim's got.' He pulled a piece of paper from an envelope and showed it to them.

'Immigration had been told by someone, we don't know who, that this was a marriage of convenience. They took us to separate rooms and asked loads of questions, like they did before. Then it just stopped. They put us back together, disappeared, then returned with Jim's visa. He's all legitimate now, he can stay for the next year. I'm so relieved.' Moira stood closer to her husband, who turned, picked her up, her legs swinging mid air as he kissed her tenderly before gently returning her to earth.

'I bet you are.' Iris said. 'Let's get you two on the road, you've already lost two hours, so there's no time to waste.'

They only drove a little way, then stopped at Knockan Crag viewpoint to look across the headland over the loch out to sea. The cloudless ocean shimmered in the afternoon sunlight and the heathlands glowed with pale shades of purple and lilac heather blooms. – a vast beauty surrounding them. A time to hold each other tight and relish the moment.

Moira drove at a leisurely pace so they could take in the spectacular scenery; the beauty never ceased to take her breathe away. Even on dull days it held a magic but now, in the sunshine, its magnificence was awe-inspiring. Seeing it for the first time was overwhelming for Jim who kept asking her to stop so that he could look at the views that greeted them at each turn. Her hat and shoes had long been relegated to the back seat, there was no jumping in and out of cars on windy headlands in hats, however fine. Consequently they arrived at their hotel, with Jim still immaculately dressed, whereas Moira's blue-grey outfit was now accessorised with a pair of flat brown walking shoes, and hair that tumbled all over the place.

It was difficult to miss the old hunting lodge – which was now the Sutherland Hotel – stood as it was alone, proudly commandeering the surrounding heath. Their welcome, by the owners, was as glowing as the fire that crackled in the lounge where they were asked to:

'Take tea while your bags are taken to your room.' Moira watched a wiry youth carry their dilapidated suitcases up the panelled wooden stairs to a room they were yet to see and cringed – I'd have borrowed better ones if I'd known . Such notions were swept away by the sight of a stand of mini gateau, biscuits, and tiny sandwiches, along with a silver pot of tea and two delicate cups and saucers adorned with Scottish thistles.

'Is this all for us?' Jim whispered, 'Is this our dinner?' Moira laughed, 'No silly, it's afternoon tea, dinner will be later,'

'All of that just for us?' said the incredulous Jim.

'Yes and the biscuits!'

'Should we take some back for the others? It seems too much just for us.'

'We don't have to eat it all. Just enjoy it. We'll be back to mince and chicken before long!' Moira said as she took some more.

After two cups of tea and more cake than was good for him, Jim whispered,

'I need the bathroom.'

The wiry lad appeared in an instant, as if he had heard the comment and Jim squirmed uncomfortably.

'Are you ready to go to your room?' asked the lad, who introduced himself as Ben and escorted them up the imposing staircase where they passed paintings of hunting scenes and a large oak grandfather clock which struck five as they neared and made them both jump. Once at the top they turned down a narrow corridor and their escort opened a door and ushered them into their room with all the flourish of a court attendant. The pair stepped in and looked around as Ben asked,

'Is this satisfactory?' and they both just nodded, eyes agog. He proceeded to show them where spare blankets were kept and took them to the nearby bathroom, which would be, 'Entirely for you to use during your stay,' and walked away.

Moira ran to the bed and threw herself on it, bouncing up and down on the biggest bed she had ever seen. The huge headboard was carved oak, the bed spread red tartan, long red drapes surrounded the floor to ceiling windows and were pulled back by golden ropes. The vast room sported Highland paintings and an imposing mahogany writing desk and chair all set on a thick red carpet, with rugs depicting Scottish scenes. Lamps emitted a pale-yellow light that gave the room a glorious golden glow.

'It's perfect,' she whispered.

'I think it's better than perfect. I have never seen anything like it,' said Jim as he walked around the room taking in every detail – storing it all away – never to be forgotten. He felt like a film star, and his new bride was lying flat on the bed and, like all leading men, he knew exactly what to do.

Garments scattered around the room told the story of the last two hours. The couple lay wrapped in each other's arms, glowing from head to toe and gradually roused themselves from the gentle slumber of the satiated,

'We're going to have to go down for dinner,' Moira said, stroking his neck. Jim held her tighter.

'Can't we just lie here for ever?'

Moira snuggled in, gave him a peck on the cheek, then wriggled out of his arms.

'It says dinner is served from seven until eight-thirty, and according to

that clock it's already gone seven.'

'Oh, Ok, if we must. But do I have to wear my suit again?'

'I don't know, but it's the sort of place where it might be necessary, so better err on the side of caution.'

'Whatever does that mean?' Jim asked.

'It means wear your suit,' laughed Moira, who was already gathering up garments and lying them carefully on the high-backed chair in the corner.

'I've left my shoes in the car, can you get them for me when you're ready?' she asked, and wrapped her dressing gown round herself and grabbed the bathroom first.

The couple turned heads as they entered the panelled, candle-lit restaurant. They made such a striking couple. It was difficult not to look. He so tall and immaculate in his suit, she so short even with the offending heels, he so dark and she so fair – a complete contrast. Fellow diners gave little nods as they passed, some smiled, one or two said:

'Good evening.' Others tuttered under their breath and whispered to each other, their comments focused on the negatives of the match; their words fortunately not heard by the couple who were placed at a nearby window with a view over to the Kyle – the land of castles, hills and lochs.

The waiter pulled back Moira's chair, and then with a flourish draped the starched white napkin on her lap, before Jim's was similarly placed as if it were a magician's trick. The menu was of local fare, and they readily accepted the menu of the day.

'I think it's easier that way,' she whispered, before agreeing to take a glass of white wine and Jim a beer. Scallops were followed by a whole fish in a buttery sauce, beans, spinach and little carrots served in little silver dishes so they could help themselves, and neither could resist the elegant meringue pudding adorned with strawberries and cream.

'Better not tell Alex about this,' Moira said, licking her lips. 'I think he would absolutely love it.'

'I'm sure he would, shall we take him some when we leave?' Jim answered, just as the waiter asked if they would like to take coffee and a wee dram next door. They just nodded, unsure as to the proper procedure, and were led into the lounge with all the reverence their recently acquired film star status required.

The arms of the high-backed chairs cocooned them in Ramsey blue tartan, that blended with her outfit. The chair wings were so high and wide that they almost hid them, enabling them to peep at their fellow guests, almost unseen. Some were as smartly dressed as themselves, whereas others looked as if they had only just got back from bracing walks over mountain and moorland, which indeed some had. It was clear that they could relax their dress a little tomorrow. They sipped their drams and drank their coffee, so deep in each other that no one would have dared to interrupt. However someone did, it was the owner, who bent over them in a dignified manner.

'We understand that you only married today and wish to congratulate you both on this, please accept these two drinks, on the house,' as a waiter bent over and offered them two tall flutes of champagne. The pair peered out from their hideaways and raised the glasses to each other as the whole room clapped and sounds of:

'Congratulations,' echoed around the room, drowning out any dissenting tuts or adverse remarks, and for once Moira didn't feel embarrassed at all the attention and just smiled.

Their three days were blissful, they drove to isolated spots, walked for hours over heaths and moorland, sat and watched dolphins in the sea and scrambled down rickety steps to see the caves of Smoo. Packed lunches were eaten on craggy headlands, windswept beaches and beside burns that wended their way to the sea. They revelled in learning more and more about each other, and grew closer day by day.

Moira explained about the deep cultural and historical roots behind tartans and the clans that wore each one, the Highland games, the hunting and shooting traditions of this land, the Loch Ness monster, and how people eloped to Gretna Green to marry.

Some of this sounded strangely weird to Jim who told her of some of the customs of his country and his tribe. They were Christians, but also believed in three gods: Oloron the sky god; Eshu the divine messenger, and Ogone the god of war. She learnt of the importance of the rhythmic music made by drums shaped like an hourglass, which were famous all over Africa. Moira swayed as he beat out a rhythm on his knee, then leaned forward as he continued.

He explained their normal diet: akara: a fritter made from fried beans, amala – blended cassava flour or yam served with a spicy soup called gbegiri, made from ground black eyed peas and Dodo – fried plantains served with salt as a snack or part of a meal.

'Oh, that sounds a bit odd to me. Fried bananas and salt? I don't think I'd like that.' Moira said.

'Wait till you try it, I think that you would like it. It's a bit like your crisps, but without little blue bags of salt. We put our salt on immediately its cooked and only eat them fresh. We love fish of course and very often we dry or salt it so that it keeps longer.'

Moira sat mesmerised as he told her about the folk tales that had been passed down the generations for thousands of years. He described their Eyo festival which traditionally took place to honour the passing of a Lagos tribal leader and to welcome in the new one – the men dressed in long white robes, their heads completely covered with beige coloured veils kept in place by ornate large-brimmed hats.

All of these sounded equally strange to Moira, and they sat comparing these traditions and ways of life, laughing at many but concluding that both were equally strange. It was the difference that made them interesting, just as their own differences attracted them to each other. And, in this way their two cultures began to merge, they had, in the biblical sense, become one, but they had become something more, they were the fusion of two countries, two cultures. A partnership in every way.

So wrapt were they in each other, that time became an irrelevance, but three days only have so many hours and Friday arrived before they were ready for it. They departed – as they had arrived – like honoured guests. Suitcases were carried to their car by Ben, and the receptionist assured them that there was nothing to pay.

'It has all been taken care of,' and she wished them once again, 'a long and happy marriage,' before ushering them into their car, and waving them off as if they were long lost friends departing for their journey home.

They took full advantage of yet another fabulous day, and ambled down to beaches of silver, and sauntered over moorlands, taking in yet more landscapes, before stumbling across a herd of Highland cows, who peered at them from under deep fringes of orange hair, mooing as if to say:

'Don't get too close,' before actually sidling forward to see if there might be a treat for them. They had no fear of people, but Jim was mightily afraid of them. His eyes all but popped out of his head and he turned and ran as rapidly as if a tidal wave was coming for him, leaving

Moira doubled up at the sight of her husband disappearing into the distance.

'Just look at him, you'd think you were lions,' she said to the cattle, who replied with a chorus of moos, before turning their backs and wandering off in the opposite direction. Jim was still shaking when she returned to the car, tears of laughter running down her face and all he could say was:

'They might have killed us, they're wild animals, did you see those horns. What are they?' And it took some time for her to stop laughing, for him to stop shaking, and for her to explain what they were. An incident that would later be recalled by the pair and cause much mirth; one of those memories that could always return the mind to the details of the event; a sort of souvenir that binds people and sets relationships. An incidence they laughed at for the rest of the way home.

Reality met them at the door of number four. The house might be empty, but it was home, the place with a kitchen sink, cooker and washing machine which was speedily stuffed with their laundry and clothing discarded by Alex in the laundry bin. The suitcases were barely empty when Alex darted in and gave his mum a hug, a quick 'Hi' to Jim and was straight upstairs to the Meccano. The honeymoon was over, and the blank canvas of their future lay ahead of them.

Chapter 38

Let us, then, be up and doing
With a heart for any fate,
Still achieving, still pursuing
Learn to labour and to wait.
 A Psalm of Life
 Henry Wordsworth Longfellow

People arrived in a constant stream – like jack-in-a-box at the front door. First it was Iris, then Doreen, then Samuel and then Ade and Yomi, all in a rush to hear of their honeymoon, welcome them home and let them know that there would be no lodgers that night. The men would all stay with Doreen, and Alex would remain with Iris for one further night – Moira and Jim were to be granted a honeymoon extension. Their well-wishers departed as swiftly as they had arrived and left them feeling strangely alone in their home. There was no one sleeping in the lounge tonight, no feeding of others to be done and it made them aware that the future would now be theirs to shape. It would not be moulded, by circumstance, by others, or, as it had sometimes appeared, by an invisible hand, it was theirs to make of as they would.

But for now it would appear that others were still in control. The fridge had been stocked and a casserole waited for them to heat, no cooking to do and a shout of,

'I'm off to Gran's,' as the front door closed, left them totally alone for the first time and for a moment it came across as strangely awkward. It was a mere shudder of a moment, quickly replaced by the delight of each other's company and nothing that the tightest of hugs and the longest of lingering kisses could not dispel.

Their evening was one of tender closeness, not the torrid passion of the last three nights, but one in which they learnt yet more about each other's whims and ways, the quirks that make the person, and they found those both delightful and sources of amusement. The evening concluded with a stroll along Shore Street to watch the late midsummer sun sink slowly into the waters of the loch, turning everywhere red as it disappeared under the increasingly choppy waters, leaving a half light in which to make their way home. It looked as if the sunshine of the last three days was to be a spent force and that clouds were on their way.

They rose early the next morning. Moira set off to the shop and Jim went to check with the others, to catch up on the news. Routines slipped into like old slippers. The honeymoon to be placed into a photograph album, along with the wedding and reception – a fantastic time relegated to the category of recent history – not forgotten – but moved on from.

Angus greeted Moira as if she had been away for months, but there was little time for chat as customers arrived in their droves. There were numerous requests for cheese, ham, eggs, bread and all those other items the never-ending stream of tourists required for their onward journeys. In short they were remarkably busy, and although this should have been her half-day Moira didn't leave until mid-afternoon and was utterly at a loss as to where they were on the catering front. She prayed that it was all under control. Which indeed it was.

Moira insisted that the meal be served at her house, but it was clear that Miss McKay was still in charge. There was a pre-prepared meal waiting, which Jim and Samuel had on the table (now installed in the lounge) in an instant. Ade and Yomi, insisted on clearing up afterwards and wandered off to the kitchen where they could be heard chatting away as they washed all the pots and pans.

'So how did Miss McKay do, did she actually turn up?' Moira asked.

'Turn up? You've got no idea,' laughed Doreen. 'She arrived here the day after the wedding, armed with her wicker basket, apron, cookery book and all manner of gadgets, that were, according to her:

"Essential for mass catering," and proceeded to take over with the precision of a military general, let alone the retired headteacher she is!'

'Was it awful?'

'Well actually, she rather came good,' Iris said.

'In what way?' asked a startled Moira.

'First of all, she looked at the three-day menu we had devised, then listed the ingredients available, and wanted to know why there was no pudding for the men. Lack of money was clearly no valid reason to a woman of her status, so she rushed off, and came back with all the ingredients for a trifle, two fruit pies and cream to put on the top. We later found out that she had wheedled most of these from the McTavish's and some seasonal fruits from the minister's garden. We had to, keep up standards apparently, reported a poker-faced Doreen who couldn't maintain her McKay impression for long and broke into convulsions of laughter.

'She had us running round like school children. Alex and Samuel were on veg prep and she had us whipping and stirring and instructed Ade and Yomi, to go out for a bracing walk to build up an appetite. They left, looking at each other, as if to see if they were still men or had become schoolboys. We all knew who the boss was now!'

'Did she upset them?' Jim asked.

'Actually, she didn't. We were all fairly grateful to let someone else take charge, it meant we didn't need to think. But you should have seen her checking the cutlery that Alex had set. She wanted to know why there weren't any flowers and sent him off to pick some from somewhere – we didn't like to ask where he got them from,' Doreen giggled. 'He came back with a great bunch, which were pushed and pulled, cut and clipped into submission like the rest of us, until they made a centre piece the Women's Institute would have been proud of. Then she was on about napkins, we didn't know what she meant at first, then realised it was serviettes. Again, she wouldn't have it that they were not needed, her precious standards, kept popping up and she sent Alex back out with some cash from her purse telling him:

"White ones, just plain white, nothing fancy you understand." We had to fold them into neat triangles that stood up. I don't know how we managed not to laugh out loud,' continued Doreen who was now on a story telling roll.

'She did go on a bit about showing, foreign types how we do things over here, interjected Iris, and that it was up to all of us to set the standards, or how else could we educate them?

'What, she said that in front of the three of them!?' Moira said looking at Jim in horror. 'Oh Jim, I'm so sorry you had to hear that; she's such a judgemental person, believes that only she knows about standards. What on earth did Ade and Yomi think of that?'

'Oh, they didn't hear, they were on their appetite inducing walk,' laughed Iris. Then Samuel spoke.

'Now ladies, don't worry about this, we have learned in our time here that not everyone approves of our presence, that some consider us to be aliens, people who are a threat to your way of life. But we know that most of you are compassionate and considerate people who have been incredibly good to us. We have good and bad people at home too. Some who think themselves better than others, why should we expect you all to be any different? She can't be all that bad; this trifle is delicious, so I will say, thank you to her, and of course to all of you. Let's be grateful for the help she gave and choose to ignore the rest.'

Moira held Jim's hand firmly between hers, gave him a peck on the cheek, and said:

'What a forgiving man you are Samuel.'

'He most certainly is,' seconded Iris and Doreen, nodding their heads in unison as they all wandered into the kitchen. All debris had disappeared, everything put away and the men were sat happily playing cards. Alex returned to his own bed, Yomi would remain at number four, while Samuel and Ade were to stay with Doreen. Everything was the same as it had been just a matter of four days ago and no one had any idea how long this would last.

Moira had been unable to spend much time with Alex, but managed a catch up with him the next day. School had ended for the summer so she assumed he had played with friends or sat chatting to fishermen at the port or spent yet more hours with his precious Meccano during the time they had been away. But she was wrong and he excitedly told her:

'I went fishing mum. The rod I got at Christmas is great, and... I caught a salmon!' he pronounced as if he had become an angling expert.

'It was a grilse, do you know what that is?' he continued without waiting for an answer. 'It's a young one that had only returned to the sea for one year.' Information that flooded Moira with a sense of foreboding.

'So where did you go?'

'Oh, I went with Uncle Roddy, he had a day spare and called round for me, we had a great time together, I'd forgotten how long it was since I'd seen him.'

'Oh, what a surprise for you,' Moira said, with no outward sign of the thumping heart in her chest. Had Roddy come to his senses? Would all the unpleasantness be behind them? Trepidation coursed through her veins. What if he had spoken out of turn? Was hateful, and she was reluctant to ask more for fearing what the answer might be.

'So, did he catch fish as well?'

'Oh yes, he caught two – one was enormous – Uncle Roddy reckoned it had probably been to sea at least twice,' Alex explained, with a knowledgeable air. 'We took them to his house and Aunty Aila cooked one of them for dinner, it was yummy.'

'Were the girls there?'

'No, on some outing with friends. Do you know we haven't seen them for ages, can we see them again soon?'

'Oh, I'm sure we can,' Moira said, 'We've all been so busy of late there's not been much time for meeting up. Did Uncle Roddy say anything about that?'

'No, just said, it might be some time before we got to go fishing again, matters being as they are. What did he mean by that, do you know?' Alex asked. 'He said something about an interloper, but he expected it to be gone in the near future. I didn't know what he was on about. I think there might be something dangerous in the river and he's got to catch it.'

Moira nodded her head and kept a straight face.

'I expect that's it. I'm pleased you had a good time, but this interloper might be difficult to catch, so we'd better give him plenty of time,' Moira answered, just as Alex rushed out to meet his friends. So nothing had changed. But at least his prejudice hadn't stopped him seeing his nephew, and for that Moira was grateful.

So far Moira had glossed over the problems with her brother, had made it sound like a small matter, but they were married now, and Jim needed to know the truth. It was so hard for her to explain the intensity of her brother's feelings and his appalling actions without upsetting Jim, but she tried, got tongue twisted, mumbled some bits, before taking a grip on herself and getting it all off her chest. He listened, without interruption, nodded sagely at parts, shook his head at others before finally saying:

'Your brother is a troubled man, and we must not let him make us troubled too. He must be frightened to behave in such a way, and we should feel sorry for him. It upsets me of course, but mainly because it upsets you. Your brother should not make his sister cry. He should be your friend, he should be happy when you are happy, and share your sadness when necessary. Until he can find that within him, we must live our lives and show him that we are meant to be together. He'll only change his mind when he's ready, and that could take a long time. Eventually he will surely see the damage he is causing, not only to others, but also to himself.'

The now sobbing Moira nestled further into Jim's arms, and struggled through the sobs to say:

'I'm so pleased I married you. I love you so much.'

'And I love you, more than I can say. We will not let your brother come between us. We are stronger than that.'

'I hope you're right Jim,' Moira said as she dried her eyes, 'but I think he's a problem that won't easily be solved.'

Chapter 39

Should auld acquaintance be forgot,
And never brought to mind?
Should auld acquaintance be forgot,
And auld lang syne
        Auld lang Syne
        Robert Burns

The town had been transformed in their absence. Flags fluttered from buildings – huge strings of them crossed the roads – and notices around the town informed everyone that the bicentenary festivities were to take place this coming Saturday, the second of July. So, while the townspeople polished doorknobs and swept streets, in possibly the best sprucing up in two hundred years, there were three men whose minds were elsewhere. All they could think about was, when, oh when, will we go home? It was as if they had been forgotten – yet again – but chasing phone calls said they had not.

The village hall now displayed not one, but two wall hangings, that showed the history and life of the Loch Broom community. Paintings and artifacts completed the display ready for close scrutiny by residents and visitors alike but Moira stood nearly tall with pride when she saw her contribution taking the most prominent position in the centre of the largest hanging. The brilliant reds of her sky took on a luminous glow under the spotlight and resulted in praise from every visitor.

Bagpipes were heard moaning on the breeze, and young legs practised dances in halls and rooms, in short, the whole village was bustling. A community determined to perfect their day. Even Samuel, Ade and Yomi were joining in, they were applying a last coat of paint to two capstans at the harbour when they saw Angus running down Shore Street his arms waving in the air like a semaphore expert and shouting out something that never reached their ears. As he approached they could hear his words:

'You are going home, you are going home.' Shouted so loudly that they nearly dropped their brushes into the sea, 'Your flights are booked for one weeks' time.' They grabbed each other, laughing, jumping up and down and broke into a song, the likes of which no one local had heard before. They beat out the rhythms on the paint pots and railings; it was uplifting, and when they had finished all the onlookers applauded.

The tourists might have considered it an early introduction to the festivities, and none of the locals told them otherwise. It was a brilliant sound and the crowd applauded loudly, with cries of, more, more. But the audience was to be disappointed – there would be no encore – there was too much discussion to be done, final plans to be made.

They all ate together at number four that Monday night.

'To give Doreen a break,' Moira said, 'and let the men be together, so that they can share their happiness.' The meal might have been basic, but the evening was uplifting. Ivan popped round, to assure them that this time it was for real – they would be going home. No more delays, no more procrastination, just a train and plane and seven days separated them from being reunited with their families.

In their excitement they naturally lapsed into their Yoruba language, their voices getting louder and louder. Jim looked around, it's almost like being back in Nigeria, and it made him feel a little sad. He would not be seeing his mother, brother and sisters, uncles, aunts and cousins and was even beginning to find it difficult to remember their faces. He pushed those thoughts away – his new home was in Scotland now – but he was determined that he would return to his homeland when finances allowed.

In all of this merriment, no one noticed Alex who sat quietly, watching all the animated faces, understanding barely any of the words, but he understood that life would never be exactly the same for him either. These past weeks had imbued his life with excitement, brought strangers to be his friends, and broadened his young mind. He would miss them. Moira caught the reflective gaze on his face and instinctively understood his emotions, and in many ways she felt the same. A well timed:

'Let's get the washing up done,' from Samuel averted any emotional outbursts and Moira wondered if it had been deliberate and decided that it probably was.

The next days passed in flurries of activity on land and at sea. On the Harmony, which had been little used of late, possessions were scattered, and debris littered the decks. Ivan took charge of getting the unloved, unwanted vessel back into some sort of order. He was a proud man and was not about to have anyone say they left a mess. It might be rusty, it might be old, it might be falling apart, but untidy it would not be, not under his watch. He would make the final descent of the gangplank with his head held high, his uniform smart and his record unblemished. The men cared nothing of this, but were keen to stay occupied, to make the days pass as rapidly as possible and they hatched a little plan. Ivan saw them in a huddle in the spruced-up galley, but they were not about to reveal the subject of their conversation and so he left them alone.

In all of this activity, Jim had been summoned to attend an interview in Aberdeen which entailed him catching a bus and train for the first time in his new homeland. Moira offered to drive but he would not hear of it.

'This is for me to do,' was his insistent reply. So, as she served in the shop, he spent time crossing the Highlands of Scotland.

The bus took him slowly past lochs and heather, flat moorland, craggy outcrops and mountains denuded of snow and now obscured by dank mist. He took in the never ending and changing landscapes, until the bus slowed into Inverness, where he would catch the train. The weather improved and now he saw lochs that glistened like glass in moorlands that swept away towards the distant Cairngorm mountains that still sported little caps of white. Then, when the train accelerated, the view blurred into an abstract of browns and greens, blues, purples and greys. Jim contemplated the emotional highs and lows of the last year, and of life changes he could never have dreamt of. His two families separated by thousands of miles and different in every possible way. So deep in recollection did he become, that he had to be roused from his seat by the conductor telling him that his destination had been reached. He had clear instructions as to the route, and easily found his way to the offices of West Star Shipping, said a silent prayer, stood tall and walked in. He was there for such a short time, that the journey seemed out of all proportion, and he made his way back, with fewer thoughts this time, some sleep, and the awe-inspiring scenery to occupy his waking eyes.

Moira became concerned that he might have got lost or missed a connection and kept saying to herself,

'I should have driven him. ... I wish he would hurry up.' By eight o'clock she was even more anxious and was about to ring the station, when in he walked, bright and cheerful saying:

'I'm starving, have you kept me something to eat?' And would utter not one word more until his plate was cleaned of each morsel. He leaned back on his chair, looked her in the eye and announced:

'I start next Monday, I've got a job!' He jumped up grabbed her by the waist, spun her round, kissed her and let his delight fill the room and envelop the startled Alex who walked in to see his mother held aloft, being spun around like a fairground ride, giggling and yelling,

'Put me down, I'm getting dizzy,' which Jim did, only to repeat the performance with Alex, who pleaded to be put down when he could contain his giggling no more.

Jim was to join one of the large trawlers operating out of Aberdeen and would be away for days and sometimes weeks at a time, but Moira had expected this, it was the seafaring way and did not faze her. There was to be a one-trip trial, and that didn't bother Jim. He was experienced, understood boats, and could now speak good English and could think of no reasons why he wouldn't be taken on permanently.

Moira felt as if nothing could go wrong at that moment; life was good. But then her mind would drift to her nieces, to her brother, thoughts that tarnished the silver of the day, and she found it difficult to forgive him.

Saturday, the big day arrived, the village was heaving with people. Tourists had travelled from all around, as if to see a famous pop group, or an international football match, and they crowded the cafes, the pubs and nearly cleared the shop of all stock. Fortunately, they were closing at noon, these were after all their celebrations, and they didn't want to miss them.

Barriers had been erected along Shore Street and people gathered behind them in ones and twos, then groups, until they jammed every available space. At what should have been precisely two o'clock but was actually nearer two fifteen, the sound of bagpipes eerily drifted down Quay Street, where spectators were the first to see the pipe band marching towards them. The band master, resplendent in his full Highland dress, led the procession and was followed by men, boys and girls immaculate in their long white socks, kilts, sporrans, crisp white shirts and black ties, with little black hats firmly resting on their heads. They held their pipes close, enveloped them in one arm to squeeze out the sound that was adored and loathed in equal measure. It mattered not which camp you fell in, it was a sight to see, and tourist cameras clicked away in a frenzy, as if the moment could only be captured through a lens. Following them were the dancers: the men in Highland dress, some of the girls in red, white, and green dresses, others in traditional kilts with velvet waistcoats and white blouses, their feet pointing like ballerinas as they walked.

The crowds cheered them on, and a roar of applause greeted them into Shore street where the pipers stood to one side and the dancing began. Clapping accompanied all the twists and twirls. Pipers and drummers played the melodies for the whirling dancers, before the watching crowds were urged to join in the group dancing that followed. Arms linked, people passing to the left and right of each other, a veritable twisting snake of men, women and children worked its way along the coast road before wending its way back, to the applause of those who considered that their dancing days were behind them or had never actually found them.

As the music subsided, another sound came from the harbour, there was drumming, a flute and singing so loud that no one could believe it was made by just four men. Jim, Samuel, Ade and Yomi walked into the crowds, banging drums made from paint tins and blowing flutes carved from an old chair leg and all wearing colourful shirts over their trousers. They entertained the onlookers, who clapped and swayed to the rhythms. Some of the local pipers joined in and followed the lead of the men. They created harmonies never heard before and possibly never since. Even Miss McKay was seen tapping her right foot and clapping with the rhythms. The McTavish's tried their best to trill along, but were somewhat beaten by the language, so reverted to humming.

Moira and Alex, Angus and Joan, still slightly breathless from all the dancing, clapped along and passed on smiles that progressed from face to face amongst the throng. It was then that Moira glimpsed Aila and the girls across the road and tried to wend her way through the crowds to reach them, only to have them disappear from sight with Roddy at their rear; he turned, looked at her, made not a single gesture of acknowledgment and disappeared. Anger and sorrow make for unpleasant companions, and as the tear slipped down her cheek, the anger within welled up inside. She would have beaten him with sticks and hurt him in any way she could. She now hated him with a passion, and did not like the feeling. It didn't feel right to her, but it was the only emotion that made any sense. How could you continue to love someone who turns their back in such a way?

As the festivities died down, people returned to cars and vans, or bikes and buses, to cafes and pubs that rapidly reopened their doors; the tourist pound was important, and no business was going to let one escape unnecessarily. It was all a bit too much for some who wended their way home as did Moira, Iris and Alex who had more meals to prepare, and they wanted them to be special. The men joined them later, full of joviality and a fair amount of whisky: the crowds had swept them into the Ferry Boat Inn where rounds of drinks had been brought for them, and they had obviously accepted them with some relish. Their high spirits were infectious, and Moira was able to join in and laugh at their antics, she even had a couple of drinks herself and was swiftly back to her normal resilient persona. And so the day ended on a high, with total agreement that, everything had gone well. That it had been fun, and all thoughts moved to Sunday, their last full day together.

The day passed in a blur. The crew dealt with last minute laundry and packed their bags which they piled up on the ship. They sought out acquaintances made at the harbour and around the town and said their goodbyes. Some shook firm hands, others gave hugs but everyone wished them safe journeys home. Their stay had quelled most people's prejudices; they had become part of the community and there were now few who did not wish them well. Hamish had removed three bibles from the mission and had written poetic words in each, along with Proverbs 3:23, 26, which at the point of receipt meant nothing to them at all. Finally they were all together at number four, it was to be celebratory and there would be no division between houses tonight. The last of the union money had been splashed out on venison and Miss McKay turned up with yet another trifle, it was massive and would feed them all several times over.

'You have a long journey ahead of you and will need sustenance, so I've taken the liberty of baking you a Dundee cake,' Miss McKay said, 'I know it's your speciality Moira, and don't take offence, but you've done more than your share to help these men, and they have taught me lessons that I needed to learn, and it is my parting gift to you all.' At which she passed the attractively packaged cake to Samuel, and to all their amazement, shook each of their hands in turn, wished them well and departed in the skin of a changed woman.

Jim had to make an early start, and was gone before many of them were up, but farewells had been said the night before and in some ways he preferred it like this – removed from the final emotions.

So, he wasn't there to see the three men walk down the gangplank of the Harmony for the last time, to see the local photographer record the event, or to see the press asking for comments for their newspapers. He missed the small crowd that waved the men off in the minibus as it disappeared at the end of Shore Street, just as their crew mates had all those weeks before. And, he missed Ivan, their captain, seeing the last of his men disembark. His head held high, as tears of pride and relief washed his face, before disappearing into his handkerchief. His job was done, and he too could now return home to his family, to his friends, to his own country and away from these people who had been so good to them all. He would not forget them.

Chapter 40

You'll travel safely, you'll neither tire nor trip....
Because God will be right there with you;
He'll keep you safe and sound.
>   Proverbs 3;23, 26

Four days had passed since all the men had gone and Ivan had left three days later. Jim was at sea and would not return for at least another week, the house seemed empty and Moira felt lonely. For now, restoring her home to its previous order took all her spare hours; there had been no time for proper cleaning all these weeks, and she found rectifying this as therapeutic as ever. Her mind washed over fond memories of the men as she dusted, of Jim as she hoovered and of a community that had rallied as she ironed. Thoughts of her brother and nieces were painful, so were pushed behind a barrier of mental steel. The forthcoming weekend – devoid of any activity – filled her with a melancholic dread.

During one of these reflective moments her thoughts were disturbed by a ringing sound and it took a moment for her to realise it was the telephone, and only just managed to answer it in time.

'Oh, you are in, I was just going to put it down,' Aila said.

'I was upstairs, deep in thought, so I didn't hear it at first, how are you?' Moira said, regaining her breath.

'I'm fine, but the girls keep asking why you haven't been round, and his lordship doesn't even have the nerve to tell them. I'm never sure what to say either. Up to now I've said it's because of you being tied-up at work, but that won't sound believable anymore.'

'I don't think we should pretend for much longer.' Moira said, 'They should know the truth. But why are we going along with all of this? What right does he have to demand that his daughters can't see their aunt? It's bonkers. We are allowing him to get away with this and it's time we stopped it for once and for all.'

'I know you're right Moira, but I'm the one stuck in the middle here, and I am trying to get him to see reason. I do wonder if he might be seeing things a little differently you know. He's heard people saying how good Jim, and indeed all the men have been, and at first he couldn't understand it, but it's making him think, that's for sure. Let's see what happens during the school holidays – it's only a few more weeks before they go back – and in the meantime, we can carry on being discreet.'

'OK Aila. But Alex keeps asking about going fishing again. It's odd when you think about it, he'll see Alex, but doesn't want us mixing, it's difficult to understand how men's brains work sometimes!'

'I'm with you on that Moira,' Aila chuckled, 'anyway, I didn't ring about any of this. Roddy has a full weekend coming up – another American party here for the fishing, so we could take the opportunity to accidentally meet up somewhere on Sunday – what do you think?'

'What sort of accidentally did you have in mind?' Moira asked.

'Well, I could take the girls to Torridon – the games are on there – and perhaps you could maybe, just by chance of course, take Alex there. How does that sound?'

'That sounds like an excellent plan. Shall we arrive around ten? I think that's when they usually start?' Moira replied cheerfully. 'I think it's best we don't tell any of the children about these plans, then it will be an accidental meeting as far as they are concerned.'

'Fine by me,' Aila said, 'makes us sound like undercover operatives master-minding a rendezvous: quite exciting! It will give the kiddies a real treat. So see you then.'

Moira smiled as she put the phone down, seems like I'm not in full control of my life after all. Good old Aila, she seems to have a sixth sense of when she's needed.

'Better get this work done, Sunday's booked up now,' she said to herself, and hurried back upstairs to finish her chores.

Alex appeared around mealtime. He had been playing out with friends, but his internal stomach clock was never more than a few minutes out, and as usual he was, starving – nothing changed there. He was delighted to be going to the games. The ones at Torridon were small, not like the huge event held each year at Braemar, but the local ones were fun, and you had more chance of joining in.

'Can Granny come too?' he asked, and rushed round to her house as Moira replied,

'Of course if she wants to, just go and ask.'

Iris was pleased to have a day out and to spend time with just her daughter and grandson. She hadn't seen so much of them recently and there had been little opportunity to catch up, or just to watch television together. She sat in the front passenger seat chatting away to Moira and turned her head to include Alex from time to time. The weather was still holding, not as fine as the previous week, but it wasn't raining. The midges were becoming a problem and they had all covered themselves in repellent to ward them off.

'I've lived here all my life,' Iris said, 'but I still can't get used to the pesky creatures. It makes you look forward to October when they'll be gone.'

A nuisance they might be, but midges didn't stop people going to the games. Moira eased the car forward along the congested road, before eventually gaining admittance to car park A, where thankfully the ticket queue wasn't too long.

'Mum, Mum,' Alex shouted, 'look over there, it's Fiona and Flora,' as he dashed off into the crowd.

'What a coincidence.' Iris said.

'Certainly is.' Moira said with a straight face, just as Aila and the girls came over with Alex, gabbling ten to the dozen – his speech so fast that no one had a clue what he was saying.

'Well, this is a surprise,' Aila said, without a trace of irony.

'You've got your work cut out Alex,' laughed Iris 'You've got five ladies to look after.' He turned his back and took refuge between his cousins, who were going to be the only looking after he was going to do.

They watched Caber tossing, hammer throwing, feats of strength – massive, bearded men pulling and pushing all manner of objects. The spectators stood around the roped off arena, 'Oohing,' and 'Ahing,' applauding and sometimes groaning, depending on the successes and failures witnessed. There was Highland dancing and music: much like they had seen the week before. Stalls to visit, produce to try and loads of stuff to tempt children to pester adults to buy, and in their case, mostly unsuccessfully.

Granny treated them all to ice creams and bought a pot of local honey to take home. They sat on bales of straw, licked their ices and watched the best dressed pets competition in one of the smallest arenas. There were lots of dogs: the smart ones with tartan coats, elegant ones with fancy hats and matching jackets, funny ones with pretend dangly ears, and some dressed as if they were characters like Mickey Mouse. There was a pet goat in a top hat and a couple of cats who were decidedly not happy to be taking part and were disqualified and relieved of their burdensome outfits. It was an entertainment enjoyed by most, but Moira disliked seeing animals dressed up, and was glad when it was all over. She much preferred to see the farm animals, which was their next port of call. The youngsters ran off to stroke lambs, calves, kids and piglets, then whispered endearments to them and rushed over to adults shouting, can we have one of those? The adults looked at their offspring with raised eyebrows and continued admiring the livestock and their formidable size. The Highland cattle always drew a crowd, their appeal was universal, and fortunately they were not fazed by all the clicking cameras and the little children pushing hands through railings to stroke them. They were prima donnas and sensed their starring role.

It was a happy day for them all, but it had to end, and with hugs and squeezes all round, they made their separate ways home.

'What a lovely day out,' Iris said.

'Certainly was,' Moira replied

'I can't get over the coincidence of us all arriving at the same time, couldn't have worked better if we'd planned it,' Iris remarked.

'Certainly couldn't.' Moira said with an inscrutable smile. She intended to keep the truth to herself.

Alex entertained them for most of the journey home. He recalled the events of the day, used silly voices and acted the fool, which his mother told him he was particularly good at, and to which his Granny agreed.

Moira's first weekend without her husband had passed better than expected, as did the days and weeks that followed. Jim was given a permanent contract – well as permanent as fishing offered – and was away for long spells. They made the absolute most of their time together and now, with more income, they were able to eat out sometimes, to go to the pub together. In his absence, the Wednesday nights with Doreen were resurrected and Moira was able to spend more time with her mother, especially as the nights started to draw in, and they both welcomed each other's company. There were no quilts to make now, so the knitting came out and winter woollies were made. The evenings became a little colder, wind and rain appeared more regularly, and Alex returned to his Meccano when he could. He had started High School and had additional homework to do, so spent more time in his room. Moira noticed that he was becoming quieter, almost withdrawn, and asked if the work was too onerous. He said that it was OK, but she kept a close eye on him, she didn't want him being put under undue pressure so early on in his new school year. I'll discuss it with his teachers at the parents evening, she thought, pleased that it was only a few weeks away.

Alex remained withdrawn, and this was the first thing she mentioned to his form teacher, Mr Jones, a tall and upright young man, who had only recently settled in Ullapool. He listened intently to her concerns, nodded appropriately, and reassured her that Alex was fine in class. He was a good pupil, diligent and a pleasure to have in the school, a bit quiet possibly, but that was all. His other teachers were equally supportive and suggested that it was probably a part of his growing up – possibly puberty rearing its funny head, they thought. Something Moira had not even considered. Surely her boy was not going to be turning into a man just yet, and the thought made her shudder – it came as a shock.

Alex was watching the television on her return – all his homework done apparently. Moira sat close to the body lying prone on the floor.

'I'm so pleased that you're settling in well at school Alex,' Moira said, 'I was extremely proud of the comments, you must be pleased?' There was no response, he just continued to look blankly at the screen, not like him at all. Moira tapped him on the shoulder.

'What's wrong Alex, you don't look pleased to be told you're doing well. Why?'

'Oh, I'm watching this programme, you're disturbing me.' Alex snapped.

'No need to be so rude though, it's not like you at all. You're sometimes a bit -cheeky, but not rude. You've been brought up better than that,' Moira chastised.

'I'm all right,' he shouted back at her, and immediately burst into tears.

'What on earth's wrong Alex,' Moira asked, as she knelt on the floor at his side and hugged his shoulders. 'You must tell me. It's never good to bottle matters up. You know the saying, a problem shared is a problem halved.'

She held him close and urged him to tell her what was wrong. Eventually the tears abated, and he focused his now bloodshot eyes on his mum's face, and sobbed again.

'Two boys keep ... saying ... horrible stuff to me and I don't like it,'

'What sort of stuff, and who are they?' she demanded as she drew him yet closer, and wiped his tear-drenched face.

'It's two (sob, sob,) boys in the year (sob) above, they keep (sob, sob,) saying I'm (Sob) dirty, that I (sob, sob) smell.' And he broke down into another flood of tears, and was no longer able to communicate. She cuddled him tight, let the sobs and tears wash his hurt away, and eventually he gained a little composure, and Moira was able to ask him some more.

'When is this happening if they aren't in your class?'

'It's at break-time, and sometimes on the way to and from school,' he replied, with a little more composure.

'But why are they saying this, what brought it on, do you know?'

'They say – I'm sorry mum – but they keep saying we've got a black man in the house, and only dirty people do that, and stuff like that.' The tears resumed and Moira's protective mother's instinct kicked into overdrive. She managed to console him, asked for the names of the boys, and gradually calmed him down with the largest hot creamy cocoa ever.

'Oh Alex, why didn't you tell me about all of this? How long has it been going on?'

'Since primary school, but it was OK, I could cope. You had your own things to sort out. I promise Mum, that was all right, you didn't need to know. They just said silly words or tried to pick a fight. They stopped all of that when I started to grow bigger than them. Those boys don't bother me now.'

Soothing words, that belied her anger, finally did the trick and Moira got him to bed. She was relieved to see that the worry and tears must have exhausted him as within thirty minutes he was fast asleep. Not her though, she tossed and turned all night, not knowing the best way to deal with this and thinking:

Should I go to the school first?

No, probably best to see the boys and their parents.

They might be as bad as the boys; they must have got this from home.

Not necessarily, they could have heard it elsewhere.

Oh, I don't know what to do.

Try not to think about it, get some sleep.

It's not as easy as that.

And so it went on all night. By the morning, her brain had spent itself; but miraculously she knew exactly what to do. Alex's spirits had lifted and Moira gave him advice on dealing with bullies:

'You should ignore them Alex, they are troubled children who want to make others as miserable as themselves. Don't worry about it anymore, but if there are ANY problems you must tell me, I'm your mum, and that's what I'm here for – to sort it out.'

'I know mum, I feel much better now I've told you. You won't tell Jim will you? I don't want him to know.'

No, I won't tell him Alex, but you must always remember that skin colour means nothing. Skin is the wrapping paper round the gift of the person inside,' she gave him a little hug and went on.

'Do you remember the Ptarmigan we watched in the winter? How white it was?' he nodded in reply. 'Well, it would have changed back to brown in the summer, but it stayed exactly the same bird. One that would fly in the sky, and swoop down to eat berries, buds and seeds. It was just dressed for the seasons, so as to merge into the environment, just like humans do,' she added. ' Jim has skin to protect himself in the heat of his own country; our pale Scottish skin would not do so well in Nigeria. Those boys are ignorant of the facts, and I intend to rectify that,' she declared.

Alex set off for school, and Moira noted the spring in his step, the smile on his face, and waved him of, as she went to work. Tomorrow was Saturday, her half-day, and it looked as if yet another weekend was filling itself up.

Moira discussed her plans with her mother, who added some sage advice. Iris said that one of the boys was called John Stewart, and that his father had recently left the family home. She wasn't entirely sure why, but had heard rumours that he might have been a bit of a brute, especially after a few drinks. She understood that money was extremely tight for them and best go easy there. As to the other boy, his name meant nothing to either of them, it was Alan, that was all they were told.

Armed with nothing but her love for the boy and man in her life, Moira walked along the street, turned a few corners and found herself knocking on Mrs Stewart's door. No answer. She knocked again, and saw a slight movement in the front room, still no answer, so she knocked again. This time the door was opened, but only slightly, and a timid voice asked.

'Who's that and what do you want?'

'It's Moira from the shop, can I have a quick word please?'

'Is it about my bill?' asked the hesitant voice.

'Oh no, nothing like that. It's Helen isn't it? I just wanted to chat to you and possibly your son if he's home,' Moira took a step forward to glimpse the face from which the words emanated.

'What about?' asked the now more aggressive voice that came from the pale, rather gaunt face of Helen, who opened the door a little, to better see her inquisitor.

'I think it better if I came in, will you let me in?' smiled Moira, as she surreptitiously moved forwards.

'What's it about first? Helen demanded.

'I do think its best if we talk in private, we don't want the neighbours listening in do we?'

'Oh, all right, but not for long,' Helen replied as she let Moira into the kitchen. The house was cold and looked a little neglected, but it was clean Moira noted. John was out apparently, but would be back before tea. Neither was sure what to say and the pair sat in near silence until he came rushing in, threw his shoes on the floor and was sat down in the kitchen before he had even noticed Moira sitting there. He gave her a questioning look.

'Who are you?'

'I'm Alex's mum, you know the one you've been bullying.'

'I so have not,' he retorted with a bullies face.

'Bullying, are you accusing my son of bullying, how dare you?' interjected Helen with a raised voice and a threatening look.

'I've not come here to cause trouble. Just to set matters straight,' Moira assured. 'It would seem that John here, along with his friend Alan, have been calling my son dirty, smelly and other objectionable words because – as they say – there's a black man in our house. On the latter point they are correct, there is indeed a black man, he is my husband – a good man – who would be mortified to hear of what's been going on. I want to assure you John, that no one in my house smells, no one is dirty.' At which he lowered his head, with all sign of the previous arrogance disappearing before her eyes. She continued.

'You seem to misunderstand the differences between peoples, so with your mother's permission, I would like to invite you and Alan to tea next weekend. My husband will be home from work then and you can meet him, ask questions, learn about him and then see if any of us smell.'

'Is this true John, what made you say that?' Helen asked.

'It's what dad says. He says they're all dirty and smelly,' John replied as

he peered at his shoes.

'Oh my goodness, is there no end to the harm that man has caused?' Helen said and looked forlornly at Moira.

'Well, will you come for tea John? Would you come with them Mrs Stewart? I would like that, you would both be most welcome?' Moira entreated.

'Oh, I don't know about that, can't think that's necessary,' Helen said in her previous harsh voice.

'But I want you all to come. I want you to meet my husband Jim, and find out more about him, surely that can't do any harm?'

'I don't understand this. You say my son is horrible to your son, yet you invite us round for tea, why would you do such a thing?' Helen asked. Her miserable face tugged at Moira's heart strings, and she continued.

'Because it's easier this way. I don't want my son upset, and I don't think shouting at you John, or complaining to the school, would improve matters. This could be a better way, one that might work. I don't know who Alan is, but would you be prepared to ask his family if he would join us?'

'Oh, all right then, still seems odd to me,' Helen replied, 'we'll come, meet this husband of yours. I'll bring Alan along, he's my cousin's boy. I'll be giving John here a telling off when you've gone.'

'No please, don't do that Helen,' Moira said, as she turned to John. '
I don't want you to feel uneasy about this John, I want you to try and
clear your mind of prejudice. You know – nasty thoughts about people –
and just have tea with us, and then see if your mind has changed. Will
you do that for me?' and, for a moment, he looked like he might cry,
then gave a rather subdued nod of his head, which was as much as
Moira had expected. They agreed to meet next Sunday afternoon at
three o'clock, and Helen promised to be there.

The next week followed the routine now set down, Alex reported
that nothing had been said to him and was astounded to hear that his
abusers were coming for tea. He was not happy about it. Not happy at
all. He pleaded with his mum to not let them in the house, but she was
adamant, and carefully explained why. Eventually, he sort of understood,
and reluctantly agreed to do as she asked.

Jim returned from his ship on Thursday evening and Moira updated
him with her plans. He sat, mouth slightly open, and for one awful
moment Moira saw tears well up in his eyes. He was clearly mortified.

'This can't be right Moira. I've done no one any harm, yet my
presence causes Alex, the boy I have come to love as my own, real
sadness. I'm not happy about your plan, it seems a strange way to sort
this out, but you know these people better than me, so I will give it a
try.' He shuffled around and continued. 'Perhaps meeting me will make
matters worse?'

'Your presence is the solution, not the problem. Trust me in this.' He
rubbed his chin and looked at her doubtfully – he would have called her
plan quixotic, but he didn't, as yet know that word.

Their punctuality was admirable, Moira had wondered if they would
turn up, but they were all there, even Alan and she ushered them into
the lounge, where she introduced them to Jim, who shook their hands as
if they were persons of real importance.

'So pleased to meet you,' he said, even though that wasn't entirely
true.

They sat like terrified dummies, no sign of the bullies now, and they
gave occasional glances round the room and stared at Jim when they
thought they couldn't be noticed. At first only Moira and Helen spoke –
about day-to-day events – but gradually Moira drew the boys into the
conversation. She asked questions that were easy to answer, then
gradually involved Jim and Alex. Jim was asked to tell the youngsters a
little about Nigeria, how they lived, about their food, what the country
looked like and the wild animals that lived there. At first, they feigned a
level of indifference; they weren't interested in houses and towns that
sounded much like Scotland. Some of the foods, caused a few grimaces

and raised eyebrows, but their interest was gradually aroused, and by the time he came to wild animals they were hooked.

'Are there lions there, wild ones?' John asked.

'Oh yes, not many these days, many have been killed and their habitat destroyed.'

'What about tigers?' Alan asked.

'No, no tigers. But we have leopards, and hippos and rhinoceros, monkeys, and many more,' Jim answered, now rising to the challenge.

'Do you eat monkeys?' John asked.

'I don't, but in some parts of my country and other countries in Africa they do,' Jim replied, with possibly a little too much honesty.

'Ugh, that's disgusting,' the boys said in unison.

'Well you kill animals to eat here, deer, grouse, pheasant, rabbits, and some people even eat squirrels, so were not that different are we?' answered the ever more confident Jim.

And so it went on, dialogue had started and the boys listened to the stories he told so well. His soft voice lulled them into acceptance of the man, and it took Moira quite a time to find a natural break in which to offer them the refreshments that were ready for them in the kitchen.

Armed with plates piled high with food, the boys, including Alex, continued their questioning and barely noticed that Iris had joined them. She chatted to Helen, said how good it was to see her, and before long no one in that room could actually remember why they were all there. It was like a family gathering, with the youngsters hanging around the main man, and the ladies catching up with whatever was the gossip of the day. Alex took his former adversaries to see his Meccano, and at that point the die was set – they were no longer enemies – but equal partners in creating a new model to show off to parents. Her plan had worked and even more successfully than Moira could have dreamed.

When they finally left, all waves, smiles and thank yous, she gave herself a silent pat on the back, fell into the armchair and gave out the largest sigh of relief. She knew there would be other boys, other tormentors, but her son was growing up fast and would be able to deal with them. There would be no more tears.

Chapter 41

Meditating among liars, and retreating sternly into myself
I see that there are really no liars or lies after all,
And that nothing fails its perfect return – And that
What are called lies are perfect returns.
  All is Truth
  Walt Whitman

The eighth of October fell on a Saturday that year. It was Alex's birthday and Moira was keen to surprise him with a special trip, or something more elaborate than he was used to. Jim had started to earn good money, and this made life much easier. Previously unaffordable luxuries were now attainable – but only in moderation – and Moira wanted Alex to reap some of that reward. But she couldn't make up her mind what to do. With only a week to spare Moira consulted Iris, who was somewhat nonchalant about the whole affair.

'Looks like it will have to be the cinema in Inverness,' Moira said to herself on the way home. Her own birthday was only two days before her sons, but she was long past bothering much about that, thirty-eight didn't seem to be something worth celebrating – 'Getting old and not even a nought on the end,' – she said to herself.

Aila, her daughters and Iris had other ideas however, they wanted Moira to have a good birthday and had been secretly working on a plan for some time.

Roddy knew that his family was up to something, they were getting into huddles and shut up when he came near. He was getting tired of being excluded. He acknowledged that his wife couldn't fully forgive his actions of late, and there had been a rift between them. She was civil to him but it wasn't the same, the sharing bond had been broken, and there was only one person who could put that right – but he didn't know how. Over the months he had heard much about this – Jim fellow – as he called him in his head, and it all sounded good, and that irked him. The more he became stuck in his world of prejudice, the less he wanted to hear anything good about any of the men. He wanted them all gone so that he neither had to confront them, nor the issues any more. His sister's marriage had been a devastating blow to him, he couldn't believe she would do such a thing and could find no reason for such a union. It disgusted him. Could not understand it. Did not want to know anything about it.

But time has a habit of blurring harsh edges, of casting different lights on situations, and confusing the memory. Roddy had seen Jim around the town, helping to paint and doing chores for the community. Roddy always walked away, so as not to be seen, and wondered to himself why he should feel that to be necessary. Once he had seen them from a distance, his sister and Jim walking close together along Shore street, and in the fading light, looked like a striking couple. He was tall and straight and she diminutive at his side. Under the red glow of the setting sun, their skins looked similar. That was the first time that he'd even considered his own actions and the possibility that they might have been misjudged.

The girls had been full of the coincidence of seeing Moira, Alex and his mum at Torridon, and he still wasn't sure if it had been the unexpected coincidence that his wife had described. If it had that was fine, but what if they had planned it and had needed to go behind his back? It was then that realisation began to dawn – that his moral high ground was possibly built on quick sand. Should he pull away from it before he was sucked further into a quagmire of hate, and family distress? The acknowledgement was hard come by, but it eased the bitterness that had been burning in his mind and simultaneously presented him with something else. An obstacle that he had no idea how to remove. How could he possibly admit that he might have been wrong? And he had no idea.

He pondered this through the ghillie season whilst he took hunting parties stalking for stags and over the moors for the August grouse season. The weather hadn't been as good as it could have been, but the glorious twelfth always drew in large tweed clad groups to shoot the grouse – their guns cocked on their shoulder as if clothes and accessories maketh the marksman. It was big business and he always needed to be alert. Some visitors arrived for the salmon and watched their agility as they jumped over rocks, determined to reach their spawning grounds, and it was that absolute determination that made Roddy think some more.

If Salmon could swim all those miles from the Atlantic Ocean, find the mouths of the rivers from whence they had previously left, swim against the current, jump up to the highest reaches to spawn and then, for many to die after so doing; surely he could admit to being wrong. But he still did not know how, or even if he should. It was like writing the first word of a novel, making the first mark of a painting – easy in theory, but often hard to do.

Sometimes, in quiet pensive moments, he dwelled on the tragedy of the Herald of Free Enterprise that had slipped into the English channel taking one hundred and ninety-three crew and passengers to their watery deaths, and wondered if any had last minute regrets or words unsaid, or deeds they wished undone. Any seafaring tragedy affected fellow communities especially hard and for some reason had touched Roddy more than most.

Ironically, it was an American party that gave him the first thoughts on how to proceed. Over a fairly liquid lunch they had been discussing world affairs and the collapse of the Soviet Union in particular. This was an unusual topic for hunting parties, who rarely strayed into the world of politics, and this made Roddy listen more intently. They discussed communism, how it never worked, however good in theory. Of the harm it had brought to millions of people, and their admiration of Gorbachev, who had initiated glasnost and perestroika. Essentially admitting that his government and its politicians had got it wrong for all these years. Roddy was not sure what these Russian words meant, but a leader of a country saying they had got it wrong, must have taken some doing and that finally made up his mind. He must be as bold as a world leader, just say, 'I got it wrong,' and move on. If it had worked for this Gorbachev chappy, then possibly it would work for me, he thought.

Roddy tried to discuss all of this with Aila, but was either disturbed by the girls, called into work, or just simply lost his nerve. Time was beginning to run out and finally on the evening of Saturday first October, opportunity and nerve came together. They had the house to themselves until nine o'clock, that gave him two hours, and he took a deep breath, held on tight to the large whisky he had poured and started:

'Aila, I need to talk to you. Will you put your knitting down and listen?'

'I can knit and listen Roddy, that's not a problem, what have you got to say?' Aila snapped.

'This is hard for me, and I want you to hear me out.' Aila stopped knitting and stared right back at him, as he went on.

'I know that I have made life difficult for you and the girls these last months. I don't want our family hurt anymore,' he said with real concern written all over his face, 'I want to make everything right.'

'You most certainly have, you're not wrong there,' she retorted.

'Please try not to interrupt me Aila,' he said in the gentlest tone he could manage. 'I've already told you that this is difficult. I want to say sorry. That I might have got it wrong. That this Jim fellow might not be the heathen I declared him to be, and for the sake of the whole family I want to try and sort it out.'

Aila's knitting fell to the floor, and as she bent forward to retrieve it, she said:

'I'm not sure it's that easy Roddy, words come cheap, you'll have to do more than say sorry to me. What about Fiona and Flora, Moira, Alex, Jim, and your mother? They've all been hurt by your stupidity. Even if you didn't actually like him too much, there was absolutely no need for your idiotic, stubborn, pig-ignorant behaviour. In fact you know nothing about the man, you've never had a conversation with him, nor sat down and had a drink together. You just made up your mind on little more than a whim. What sort of lesson has this been for the girls? Quite frankly, I'm ashamed of you.

'That's a bit harsh don't you think?'

'Harsh, you don't know the meaning of the word. I'd say it was an understatement, you have absolutely no inkling of how much grief you've caused and how difficult it will be to make matters anywhere near right.'

'Will you help me make it right, will you show me how?' Roddy pleaded.

'I don't know if I can, this is entirely up to you. Only you can do it, and you alone. But it might be good to remember that it's your sister's birthday on Thursday and Alex will be twelve two days later. Do you think you could do something before then? Give them a present to remember? Something to make people smile, and stop all this nastiness?'

Aila sank back into her chair, drained by her own vehemence. For a moment, there was total silence, until she asked.

'Will you pour me a whisky Roddy ? and you ought to fill your own glass. It seems to be empty.' They both managed a half-smile.

The girls, on their return, were too full of the party they'd been at, to notice that their parents were sitting drinking whisky together, being sociable like they used to be. Not exactly the same, but certainly not in separate rooms barely speaking.

Roddy was overcome with relief and began to realise how this whole stupid thing had affected him, let alone others. The tension that had permeated his body, was starting to ebb away and he felt better than he had for ages.

Aila just wanted some sort of balance to be restored to their lives. She would have to wait and see how Roddy would deal with the next stage of his metamorphosis.

Moira was washing up in the kitchen the next day when the doorbell rang. Who could it be so early on a Sunday morning? Moira's hands were wet through, so she shouted to Alex to answer the door.

' If it's the Jehovah's tell them I'm out and close the door.' The next thing, Alex was behind her jumping up and down,

'It's Uncle Roddy Mum, he said that he wants you, and he might take me out later, can I go?'

Wet hands were now the least of her worries and she wiped them on the tea-towel and went out into the empty hall and peered into the lounge. Roddy was stood to attention, looking as if he was waiting for a military command. For a moment Moira was struck dumb, but managed a curt,

'What brings you here after all these months?'

'I've come to (cleared his throat) – umm – apologise,'

'Apologise? Anything else?' Moira continued as tersely as before.

'Yes, and to say I am so sorry for my idiocy. That I can now see that I have been a fool and want to make amends – I don't know how – but I want to try. Do you know I've never actually had a conversation with Jim, that's how stupid I've been.'

Moira looked at him in disbelief, unsure as to whether he was truly sorry or not, and so continued abrasively.

'Well, that's good of you, but he's at work and won't be back until Friday, so you'll have to come round then.'

'Oh Moira, I know I've hurt you, but please, please, can we start again, will you please let me try to be a better person?' he pleaded, and to both their amazements he shed a tear, and instinctively, she went to hug him.

'You bloody stupid fool. We're brother and sister, we've always been a close family and what you did was wrong, so wrong. It'll be hard for me to forgive, just like that, the wounds and upset have gone deep. But I'll try, but on one condition – nothing like this must ever happen again. There would be no turning back from that. Jim didn't deserve any of this and neither did I. You have only ever spoken bad words to him. You should feel ashamed?' At which she sank into the armchair looked up at her brother as he said.

'You know what? I do feel ashamed. And a real fool for having let this go on and on. I blinded myself with lies I believed. My thoughts won't change overnight but I've made a start. I can't tell you how relieved I am to finally get this off my chest and to feel a little bit like your brother for the first time in months.'

'Well, we'd better have a cup of coffee then, a sort of celebratory drink, don't you think?' Moira said before standing up to give him a hug and ushering him into the kitchen to join Alex, who had been listening to the conversation at the kitchen door and had already put the kettle on.

It was easy to slip back and conversation came easy. Just like old times. Underneath, they both understood that it would take more than a single cup of coffee to return relationships back to how they had been. But the first step had been taken, they were back on the path of family closeness; further discussion on the matter could wait for another day.

'There's one other thing,' Roddy said. 'Will you come over for Sunday lunch next week? A sort of proper family do. Jim as well of course, and Mum. I'm going to see her next, I'm getting fairly practised at all of this now.'

'Yep, we'll be there.' Alex shouted from the doorway.

Is it all right if I take Alex with me now?' Roddy asked.

'Of course you can,' she replied and turned round to see Alex with his coat on, all ready at the front door.

Moira, settled down on her own. Her emotions were mixed. She was relieved that her connection with her brother had been put back on a firmer footing, but was equally concerned that the tension between Jim and Roddy – when they were finally in the same room – would be too great to overcome. Another restless night left her tired, and it showed. The glow had gone from those lovely eyes, dark shadows took away the luminescence of her skin and Angus couldn't help but comment when she arrived at work. She needed little persuasion to explain the cause, and unburdened herself. Angus listened, then said.

'So, it seems that you are more concerned about the future, than being relieved about resolving past conflict, is that right?'

'Yes, I suppose so,' Moira replied.

'Doesn't that sound like a waste of energy. Your brother wants to resolve matters. Jim will only want what is best for you, so don't worry, take it step by step, let them sort it out. I know them both and they can work through this.'

Angus put his arm around her shoulder and hugged her tight and gave her such a caring smile, that she could only smile back and nod, and her eyes moistened as she looked at him.

'You're a good friend Angus, and perhaps I am worrying unnecessarily, so we'd better get these orders ready!'

Jim noticed on his return that Moira was chirpier than she had been and he soon found out why. He was pleased that harmony had broken out in her family, but for himself he was unsure – surely it would be better if I didn't have much to do with Roddy? But that wasn't possible now. He would have to deal with it in whatever way he could. Sunday would arrive more quickly than he would wish, but in the meantime intended to make the most of every moment with the wife he had not seen for three weeks. First though he had her birthday present to give – a day late – but given with such a flourish. It was small, and she opened it carefully, untying the pretty little bow that held the paper in place. Inside was a small blue box and inside that a ring, with a blue stone,

'To match your eyes,' he said, and took it from the box and placed it on her wedding finger, where it snuggled closely to her gold band. 'It's not big, I couldn't afford more, but you never had an engagement ring, so you can have it now.' She was ecstatic and hugged and kissed him and kept almost constant watch on the ring throughout the evening: like a young girl, who had never worn a precious ring, and feared that it might disappear if unlooked at for too long. She couldn't wait for Sunday and to show it off.

Chapter 42

.....Awed for myself., and pitying my race,
Our common sorrow, like a mighty wave,
Swept all my pride away and trembling I forgave.
>   Forgiveness
>   George William Russell

Alex didn't share the troubled thoughts of his family, he was full of fishing with his uncle and a big family party the next day. It was such a long time since they had all been together, and he now knew why: listening at doors was a much more fruitful way of getting information than asking questions had ever been. Sometimes grown-ups didn't seem to be grown up at all. Why would anyone ever dislike Jim? It was crazy, a question that remained unanswered in his young mind.

It was Jim's turn to have a restless night. Meeting Roddy again was not of his choosing, and he would much prefer for it not to happen at all.

'How do you start a friendship with someone that plainly hates you?' he kept asking himself, and simply could not find the answer. It never crossed his mind that Roddy was in exactly the same mental turmoil as himself, and ironically, they both would have found consolation in that fact if only they had known.

This was a special day, there would be no casual dressing, it was to be only the best for this Sunday lunch which was anticipated with mixed emotions by each participant.

On the estate Aila was fussing around the girls, getting them to set the table before putting on their best dresses. Roddy had clear instructions as to his contributions and he followed them to the letter. He was nervous and didn't want to add to his woes by forgetting to peel potatoes or carrots or load the log basket, and made absolutely sure that his shirt was clean, and his hair was brushed. The former dictator had turned into a malleable puppet overnight and it made his wife grin.

They heard the car coming and such was their apprehension that they stood by the door as if waiting for dignitaries. Aila shooed the girls back to the lounge as Roddy paced backwards and forwards ready to open the door. He swung it open with such forced gusto that he tripped on the huge coir doormat, fell heavily and nearly knocked himself out on the hard tiled floor. Jim helped him up and the ladies quickly had him installed in his comfy high-backed chair by the fire before any greetings could be made. The ice of the moment had been cracked and fortunately Roddy's head had not.

Roddy sat, a little dazed and composed himself.

'A wee dram's needed here,' he said, 'and best give Jim one as well.' The alcohol infused their bodies and relaxed their minds, the first hurdle had been breached more easily than they could have imagined.

Little piles of parcels were waiting for Alex and Moira at the table and Alex had no need of encouragement to open them. There were some sweets from the girls, all his favourites: flying saucers, fruit salads, refreshers, liquorice allsorts and dib dabs. New thick socks from his aunt and best of all new waders from his uncle and he had little difficulty in giving them all a hug as a thank you. Moira had one small package which hid her guilty pleasure – sugared almonds – skilfully wrapped by her nieces, who were thrilled to see the delight on Moira's face. Then, to their surprise Roddy stood up, as if he were master of ceremonies, cleared his throat and announced:

'Ladies and gentlemen, I want to tell you all something.'

'This is home Roddy, not a banquet at the big house, get on with it,' Aila urged.

'Well, it's like this, I have to say sorry.' He looked directly at each of the children in turn and continued. 'It's not an easy thing to do you know, and you youngsters should listen hard.' Aila nudged him in the side.

'For goodness sake Roddy, get on with it will you.'

'There's a man called Gorbachev, he rules the USSR you know, and just recently he told the whole world that he was going to make big changes in his country. That what they had been doing, by making an enemy of the west, was wrong. So, I came to thinking, that if he can say sorry, then so can I. I'll start with Jim.' He looked Jim straight in the eye and with no hesitation declared:

'Jim, from all accounts you are a good man, might look different to us,' Moira, Iris and Aila all shouted in unison,

'Roddy, haven't you done enough damage?'

'Hold on, I'm getting there. But I now know that doesn't matter. Young Alex here reminded me about the ptarmigan yesterday, and he was right to do it. The same bird can look different in winter and summer, but it's still a bird, still feels pain, still eats the same things and still faces the same dangers. Like human beings I suppose.'

Alex, sat a little straighter, looked a little prouder and gave his mum a knowing look.

'Well, before I say too much I just want to say, sorry Jim I was wrong, never gave you a chance, behaved like a fool. You have made my sister happy, my nephew happy and that is all that matters, so will you try and forgive me?'

He held out his arm, extended his hand and Jim took it in a firm handshake and said:

'I have had many problems since I came to your country, but I have learnt to love it and its people, especially Moira here and Alex. I've been too focussed on being both miserable and happy to have been upset by your actions, so I say, yes, I forgive you. It will take time, we need to learn of each other before we can be friends, but I think we can do that, and I need to learn a little more about this Gorbachev man who sounds wise.'

They all laughed, and watched as Roddy handed over an envelope to his sister.

'This is from all of us, for both your birthdays, and for you Jim as well.'

Moira opened the envelope, read the contents, smiled, then passed it to Alex who took no time at all to jump up and shout out,

'We're going to Harris, we're going to Harris, I'm so excited. Look Jim, there's a little cottage, it's ours for a whole week,' Moira gave a little smile and relaxed.

Over a delectable meal, conversation flowed freely, Jim was told about Harris – of its beauty – of Alex's desire to go there. They would be going at half-term, in under two weeks' time. Roddy had even checked that Jim could get leave; he had done a thorough job of organisation and was pleased at how it had gone. It was like Christmas for them all. Back together as they should be. Children retiring to the TV, adults discussing this and that, with Roddy asking easy questions of Jim who was happy to answer. The ladies, who had already heard the answers, discussed family matters and smiled at the men's apparent ease with each other. There was a sense of ease, of calm waters ahead and made them all feel relaxed. But still Moira couldn't help wondering: Will these two men ever really be reconciled?

Chapter 43

The sovereign clouds came clustering.
The conch of loyal conjugation trumped.
The wind of green blooms turning crisped the motley hue.
To clearing opalescent, then the sea and heaven rolled as one
And from the two came fresh transfiguring of freshest blue.

    Sea surface full of clouds
    Wallace Stevens

The cold October weather didn't worry Alex, his bag was packed, and he was off to Harris. He jumped up and down with excitement.

' Oh do hurry up, we mustn't miss the ferry' he urged.

Jim, who had just returned from ten days at sea, would have been happy to spend this week at home, but the enthusiasm that emanated from Alex swept him along on his high tide of happiness and he gladly concurred.

The rising and falling of the waves and the lurching of the boat excited Alex more and more and turned Moira's blue eyes a new shade of green – she sighed with relief when Stornoway came into sight and the ferry began to slow. The rain that was now blowing horizontally, threatened to sweep their car from the ramp directly onto the wild and rugged land that greeted them, but terra firma had never looked so inviting and Moira gave a sigh of gratitude at their safe deliverance.

A ninety-minute drive through mist and rain found them at the tiny white croft house with its grey slate roof that was to be their home for the next week. It stood proud in its isolation overlooking the sea. Smoke was already curling up from its chimney, then merged with the ever-increasing mist and they were all glad to unload the car, and take refuge inside its welcoming interior.

Hand worked rag rugs covered the floor, tartan cushions lolled on seats of tweed, and the walls sported photographs of white beaches, sand dunes, clear blue seas and back drops of rugged mountains and sweeping moors. It was difficult to believe the captions that named each of these wonders as being just outside; they looked more like tropical islands, but for now the fire needed to be stoked, tweed curtains drawn, and the day put away in the anticipation of better weather to come. They rushed to put the kettle on, and had eaten all the biscuits that had been left out for them before the fridge and freezer had been loaded with food from home. Their first night would be one by the fire; hot cocoa, whisky and board games: no television to interrupt them in their snug sanctuary.

Overnight a miracle happened, the wind had blown away the rain to other parts. Calm had been restored. From their cottage they could see the blue sky stretching far out to the horizon, where it merged with the turquoise crystal-clear waters of the sea. Moira smiled at the sight – just like an advert for the Caribbean – and busied herself with breakfast. It was a hurried affair, no one wanted to miss this magnificent morning and before long they were walking along the white sands of Luskentyre beach; inspecting rock pools, chasing each other into the sea, until Alex could resist its lure no longer and stripped down to his trunks, jumped in and out of the waves, and urged the others to do the same. Moira was not to be persuaded – knee high paddling would do for her. Jim managed to get waist deep before declaring it:

'Freezing,' and then stumbled until he was totally submerged and had little choice but to feign delight as Alex chased him hither and thither. Three people had never been as happy as they were that day. Cold eventually stopped their frolics and they wrapped towels round themselves and made a beeline for the cottage and its comforts.

The afternoon was spent walking across open moorland, looking for red deer. Then later they wandered beside the nearby river in search of otters. It was just what Alex had dreamed of, and the adults were swept along with his obvious happiness.

The days were crammed with changing landscapes, and beaches that Jim declared:

'Better than Africa's.'

The weather changed in a moment and waterproofs were pulled on and removed like catwalk models' outfits. There were long walks over hills and moors, that resulted in sightings of red deer that were in rut. Bellowing out to warn other stags from their territory, and frightening Jim nearly as much as his first encounter with the Highland cattle. There were brief sightings of dolphins and porpoises off the coast, and birds too numerous for them to later recall.

Cosy family evenings by the fire, Monopoly, Hungry Hippo and Ayo all the ingredients needed for the close family they had become. Moira would sit and watch the two men in her life laugh and tease each other as they played Ayo and Jim would catch her doing this and give her a little wink – the blink of his eye spoke volumes and conveyed his love direct to her heart.

As Moira watched them together: as close as any father and son, her mind wandered to her brother. Roddy had spent many hours with Alex like this, could he possibly have been jealous of this new relationship. Had he felt pushed out? She pondered for a moment, knowing that she could never be certain either way, yet had an inkling that she might be right.

A boat trip around the coast was to be their final adventure: one they shared with another six passengers, who were mesmerised by their presence and incapable of looking elsewhere. It was something they would have to get used to. Few people in the Highlands, residents and visitors alike had met a mixed-race couple before. They all needed to keep looking – as if it would answer the questions they were probably afraid to ask. The curiosity was forgotten by awesome sightings of porpoise and dolphins that swam near their boat, and were met by the, 'oooos' and 'aahs' of the fascinated onlookers. Round a rocky outcrop there were seals basking in the autumn sun and overhead peregrine falcons and one magnificent golden eagle. Sights that thrilled them all, but especially Alex, who stored it all in the happy box of his mind, ready to be recalled like a film on the television. The captain of the little boat told them stories about the animals, the island, and its people and of an opportunity to watch a rare sight that night.

'Sometimes,' he told them, 'at this time of year, when waters heated by the Gulf Stream reach our coast, the algae can glow and turn the sea blue green. Not solid colour, just here and there, on the crest of waves or in isolated spots.' He recommended that they all went out at dusk, just in case, and as one they all nodded and said that they would.

Before dusk, the three of them wrapped themselves up cosily and sat on the nearby little bench, drink of choice in hand and waited. Moira, sat in the middle with her arm round her son's shoulder and the other locked in Jim's arm, and said that she had something to tell them both before they went home. That she had been waiting for the right moment. It sounded as if it was serious, and they both turned towards her with concern in their eyes and simultaneously asked,

'What is it? Is something wrong?' She laughed.

'No, don't worry, nothing's wrong – in fact exactly the opposite. We've got a new member of our little family joining us in the spring. You're going to be a Father Jim, and Alex, you will have a little brother or sister.' Jim scooped her up as if she were a doll, hugged and kissed her, drew an ecstatic Alex into the bear hug and said:

'Are you sure, are you absolutely sure?'

'Yes, I'm sure.' She beamed.

So ecstatic were they all, that they nearly missed the spectacle they had been waiting for, it was Alex's urgent:

'Look at the sea, look at the sea, it's turning green,' that made them turn, just as the sea came alive. Luminescence sparkled on the edges of waves as they met the beach, then disappeared, then appeared elsewhere, then, as if by some divine intervention the sky started to turn green as well, the northern lights swayed in the sky and mirrored the green edges of the waves where small specks of bright blue twinkled like stars that had fallen from the sky and the beauty of the moment was so great, that a single tear of happiness made its lonely passage down Jim's cheek, overcome as he was by the joy of the news and the splendour of the starry sea.

Acknowledgements

I have often read lengthy acknowledgements and thought, surely that's a bit excessive, but absolutely not. None of this would have been possible without the help and advice from Steven and Audrey to whom I owe a great deal of gratitude.

The writer's journey is a long one and needs many helping hands along the way. There was Gill and Brenda at Frome Writers' Collective that set me off on the literary straight and narrow and showed me the errors of my ways. Felice, Dianne, Bev and Jane who fortnightly shared their thoughts and smoothed my words. I would never have got here without technical support from Adam and Adrian and all sorts of help from daughters Claire and Laura. Then there are those who supported from the very beginning, yes that's you Michele and Nicky who read the first draft and said carry on. Others have encouraged, whilst some joined in supporting me along the way. None of this would have been achieved without the hundreds of cups of teas brought to me by my husband Julian. He carried out the final edit for me, so if you find anything wrong then you know who to blame!